The Magic of Love

Mira was a beautiful Hindu girl. Richard was an official of the British government of India. They were worlds apart, yet they met and fell in love.

This is their story—a compelling novel of two young people whose love cut across the boundaries of hatred, and survived the terrors of war.

"Those who think of Indian writing as flowery and esoteric are in for a surprise. Miss Markandaya's prose is about as floral as Hemingway's . . . she keeps her readers straining at a tight rein." —San Francisco Chronicle

"Some Inner Fury *establishes Kamala Markandaya as one of the major fiction talents that India has produced."*—Santha Rama Rau

Some Inner Fury is a superb successor to the author's highly praised *Nectar in a Sieve,* called by Orville Prescott of the *New York Times* "the finest novel by an Indian I have ever read."

Other SIGNET Novels You'll Enjoy

NECTAR IN A SIEVE *by Kamala Markandaya*
Moving novel of a farmer's wife in India who has the
courage to triumph over disaster. (#P2359—60¢)

A MANY-SPLENDORED THING *by Han Suyin*
A lovely Eurasian woman doctor tells, with honesty and
delicacy, of her love affair with a British newspaperman
in the seething, war-ravaged colony of Hong Kong.
(#T2256—75¢)

THE FEVER TREE *by Richard Mason*
A taut novel of love and espionage in Nepal. By the
author of *The World of Suzie Wong*. (#T2323—75¢)

MOLOKAI *by O. A. Bushnell*
A monumental novel about three people who face
themselves and their separate destinies on a Hawaiian
island of exile. (#Q2478—95¢)

TO OUR READERS: If your dealer does not have the
SIGNET and MENTOR books you want, you may order
them by mail enclosing the list price plus 10¢ a copy
to cover mailing. (New York City residents add 5%
Sales Tax. Other New York State residents add 2%
only). If you would like our free catalog, please request it by postcard. The New American Library, Inc.,
P. O. Box 2310, Grand Central Station, New York, N. Y.,
10017.

Some Inner Fury

KAMALA MARKANDAYA pseud.

SIGNET BOOKS

A SIGNET BOOK

Published by THE NEW AMERICAN LIBRARY

COPYRIGHT © 1956 BY KAMALA MARKANDAYA

Published as a SIGNET BOOK by arrangement with The John Day Company, Inc., who have authorized this softcover edition.

The characters in this book are fictitious, and no reference is intended to any political party, past or present, even where specific names have been used.

SECOND PRINTING

SIGNET TRADEMARK REG. U.S. PAT. OFF. AND FOREIGN COUNTRIES
REGISTERED TRADEMARK—MARCA REGISTRADA
HECHO EN CHICAGO, U.S.A.

SIGNET BOOKS are published by The New American Library, Inc., 1301 Avenue of the Americas, New York, New York 10019.

PRINTED IN THE UNITED STATES OF AMERICA

AUTHOR'S NOTE

*In the struggle for independence in
India nonviolence was the rule.
This book is based on the exception.*

I had not been long in India before I was told that in this country the things that I am in the habit of expecting had no correspondence. A thousand different things which I could expect to be... I might as well... though I didn't expect to see the... ...

Some Indian Words

Gold mohur or Gul mohur	Tree which in its flowering season seems to turn from green to red, so thick and profuse are the flame-colored flowers that it bears.
Bandobust	Elaborate and ceremonious arrangements (for welcome, send-off, etc.).
Veena	Stringed musical instrument.
Presidency town	The main towns of the various Presidencies or provinces into which the territory of India was divided.
Mofussil	The country, as opposed to the towns.
Mofussil towns	Country towns, as opposed to the principal cities.
Khuskhus	Kind of aromatic grass, often woven and bound for use as screens or blinds.

-⟦ CHAPTER ONE ⟧-

I HAD NOT been home for a long time, and so I had forgotten the little silver box lying in my cupboard which no one ever touched. A beautiful thing of filigree, with a raised design of lotus flowers which I knew was there, though I had to feel for it with my fingertips, it was so worn away. I opened it, and inside was the scrap of material I saw torn from Richard's sleeve, from his upper arm where the flesh was like milk, and which I picked from the dust when it was all over. The dust was still there—no reason why it should not be; not reddish hot and swirling madly as on that day, but faded in this sunless air and settled on the cloth in a fine graying powder. I trembled like a coward standing there, wondering if it would, and then the slow pain came seeping up, filling my throat with grief, flowing from throat to temple; I could feel it behind my eyes. I closed the box gently and put it away, waiting for the ebb; a little frightened that I could still be hurt so easily, that time should be so powerless to stanch that flow.

A whole war lies between us, which had hardly begun when we met and is now a thing of the past, a whole struggle whose beginnings we did not see, which used us and wrenched us apart and is now best forgotten. "When this is all over," I said to him—though I could scarcely move my lips, they were so stiff, "when all this is over, we can still be friends."

"Do you think so, darling?" he said gently, and put his arms about me and held me, without passion, compassionately; and he did not have to tell me, nor I to say, that my words were foolish mouthings, fashioned out of despair, empty, and between us meaningless. And yet the first time we met I was so shy, I hardly looked up until someone prodded me and I stumbled forward and garlanded him.

The garland was meant for my brother, who had just come home from England; but naturally guests came first, even if they were English and unexpected, as Richard was. I think he must have found us a little unexpected, too, so many of us gathered there on that narrow station platform: parents, aunts and uncles, friends, all of us carrying garlands in welcome; and beyond, in a beaming semicircle, the servants laden with bunches of plantains and amphorae of rose water; and still beyond, officious peons, green-belted, brass-buckled, hustling aside onlookers and travelers alike that this public platform might be ours alone.

Perhaps my brother had forgotten to tell him there would be this reception, as he had forgotten to tell us he would be arriving with an Englishman, whose presence suddenly made us all self-conscious. Now—straightening his coat under the weight of the flowers, brushing the petals from his clothes—he began presenting his friend, first to my father, then to my mother, then to our several uncles, and then, giving up, to everyone generally.

"We came over on the same boat," he said, forcedly casual. "I insisted on Richard sampling a real curry—the ship's efforts were foul."

The way he spoke, we thought he meant he had invited Richard to lunch, or perhaps dinner.

"Kit very kindly suggested putting me up for a week or two," Richard said, making the position clear, "that is, if . . ."

"Of course, of course," said my father, "we shall be delighted. No trouble, no trouble at all." And somehow he managed to look as if he meant what he said. My mother, less sophisticated, more nearly concerned with the problems of accommodating an Englishman in a Hindu household, could not help showing something of her dismay; our relatives were even more openly disconcerted.

I saw Richard hesitate—he made a small unconscious gesture as of retreat from this awkward position—and somehow, seeing him a stranger amongst us, so different, so alone in this tight-knit family group, made me suddenly ashamed that all we could offer was this meager, uneasy welcome. Echoing my father I said—forgetting not only my timidity, but also my aunts and uncles, "Of course, we shall be delighted."

There was a small disapproving rustle: I knew the

elders were wondering how a well-brought-up young woman like myself could be so forward. I wondered at it myself, but mingled with the surprise was a sense of satisfaction, and I would not have had the words unsaid. Richard did not seem surprised; I do not think he thought of me as a young woman. He thanked me, pleasantly, he smiled at me pleasantly as one does at a child, and with no other awareness.

With the question of Richard's stay settled, we began at last moving toward the cars waiting outside, the peons in front clearing a way for us, my father leading with Kit on one side and Richard on the other, my mother and uncles next, and the rest of us following after.

Kit had become more lively now: perhaps Richard's presence eased for him the strain of reunion after so long an absence. He was relating some story about the customs, then he began recounting an incident of the voyage back.

"We went ashore at Aden—made up a party. But this know-all insisted on going off alone . . . came back with a Hunter he'd bought for ten shillings—beautiful thing, solid, heavy. You should have seen his face when he tried to wind it—there weren't any works inside, just lead!"

He roared. My father joined in the laughter. My mother was smiling too, not so much at his tale, which because of his rapid English and his new accent I do not think she quite followed, but from a general sense of pleasure at having him back, her son, the eldest son and heir.

"Do you not think he looks well?" she whispered to me. "The sea air seems to have done him good." And then, with a pride which on any other occasion she would have suppressed, she said, "He really is a handsome lad—I had almost forgotten."

Somehow her words pierced the shell of my unconcerned youth. I knew for a moment what the separation had meant to her—a brief moment, and then the protective cover was back, smooth and hard and comfortable, and I said, politely, "Indeed he is; he is very like you." But though I gazed at my brother—dark, familiar, with the looks of our common heritage—it was of Richard, who was so different, that I thought.

Outside, the servants were loading the car with the gifts they had unloaded a short hour ago—the fruit, flowers, betel leaves, sugar loaves, and the thick white cups of halved copra—outward array of the heart's welcome which had served their purpose and would soon be heaped in the godowns for bickering division. While they worked, we waited—my mother keeping careful watch to see nothing was left behind—grouped together in the limited shade of an areca palm. It was a hot, dazzling day: beyond the shade, though it was still early, the air rose shimmering from the earth, the midsummer sunlight was nearly white. My brother—in collar and tie and suit, in brown leather shoes and a pork-pie hat—shifted impatiently from foot to foot. Under his arms dark, ugly patches of sweat were spreading.

"Poor Kitsamy," my mother said—she always called him by his proper name, making it sound full and sweet and round, instead of the shorter "Kit" we used, and which he himself preferred, "poor Kitsamy, he feels the heat. He will have to make a lot of—adjustments."

"We all feel the heat," my father said; then to Richard, "We seldom stay in the plains in the summer . . . we go up to the hills, you know . . . much cooler, so much healthier."

"I'm not surprised," said Richard. "It is extraordinarily hot."

But he did not seem to mind. He stood in the open, careless of the shielding palm, bareheaded, with his skin flaming where the sun fell upon it. At last my mother turned from watching the servants and, noticing him there, drew him back into the circle of shade, which common-sense act had not, for some reason, occurred to anyone else.

At last everything was in, who was to go in which car settled, the lesser relatives were already trooping off on foot. My father, who hated driving, climbed in and took the wheel; the displaced chauffeur, who hated walking, clambered onto the running board, winding an arm round the window. My mother sat in front beside my father; Richard, Kit, and I sat in the back. Then, just as we were about to set off, the Brahman priest arrived, bursting importantly through the ranks of onlookers. He was late: we thought he had changed his mind about coming, for priests cannot easily be found to bless the homecomings of those who have crossed the seas. Now we all had to get out for Kit to receive his benediction; and though we were the happier that he should have this auspicious start to a new life, still there was the inconvenience. If Richard had not been there, Kit might have submitted with better grace; now he began muttering, for Richard's benefit, but none too low, about so much fuss and nonsense. His face took on a faint insolent impatience, as if he were above all this sort of thing and amazed that we were not; both my parents, noticing, were at pains to be extra civil to the priest, though I could not help thinking it was not he who had sustained the hurt. Richard himself, outside the play of our feelings, was regarding the proceedings with interest; and suddenly, for one choking instant, I was furious with him, furious with this intruding stranger who came among us, disrupting our harmony, looking upon our religious ceremony with the shameless inquisitive gaze of the tourist. And then I felt his eyes upon me, very steadily upon me, forcing me to meet them; and, looking up at last, knew that he was not, after all, without understanding.

For weeks before the homecoming there had been great activity about the house. The suite of rooms on the first floor overlooking the garden, unused all these years, had been opened up, the dust sheets removed, the floors polished until they were like glass. New-woven blinds of khuskhus grass, water-sprayed, fragrant, hung at the windows, tempering the glare; and in the bathroom a white enamel bath, specially ordered from Bombay and the only one in the house, had been triumphantly installed. Now, because of the bath, this suite had to be given to Richard: Kit, though still vividly bearing the England-returned stamp, could be expected to bathe as we did, standing up; but courtesy demanded that Richard should be given only what he was accustomed to. Accordingly, another set of rooms had to be got ready for my brother, while my mother, with a concealed heartburning which made her snappish, gave instructions for Kitsamy's carefully prepared suite to be made over to Richard. While this was going on, Kit murmured that Richard wanted to see something, and the two of them disappeared in the direction of the town—Kit still in his finery, Richard in shirt-sleeves as he had arrived, but wearing now a dhoti and chappals scandalously borrowed from one of the servants.

"The Englishman has a lot to learn," my father said, "I do not think his countrymen will approve his—unconventionality."

"He will learn fast enough," my mother replied dryly; "teachers will not be lacking. And while it lasts, it is refreshing."

"Nevertheless," my father pursued uneasily, "I would not like it said he was led into strange ways before he could judge for himself . . . the English are somewhat—conservative. He is a newcomer, under our roof. . . ."

"He is doing the leading," I said, "not Kit. And I think it is very sensible of him to dress for the climate—even if he had to borrow servants' clothes."

It was my second pertness of the day; and while they stared at me in surprise, without words, Govind spoke. Govind was a distant relative, and also my adopted brother: he had lost both parents in infancy, and my mother, from caring for him in the weeks following their death, had grown so fond of him that she had eventually adopted him—a course with which his uncles and aunts, with their own numerous children, were happy enough to concur. Govind was silent by nature and by inclination. As a child he had hardly ever cried; as a man it was very seldom that he spoke, and he had never been heard to voice an opinion. Now he said, shortly, "She is right. I agree," and even these few words were for him an effort. I saw the blood darkening his face, and thereafter he sat somberly studying his fingernails.

It was past one when Kit and Richard came into the drawing room where we were assembled waiting for them. This room, which was always used when we had European company and never otherwise, was furnished in the European style: an Axminster carpet covered the marble floor; arranged in a circle round the room, and equidistant from each other, were two sofas and six or seven saddlebag chairs which were as uncomfortable to sit on as they looked. In the middle stood a gate-legged table with a runner across it on which a molded glass vase—usually empty, now crammed with flowers and leaves—was placed. Landscape paintings—heavy, gilt-framed, anonymous—hung on the walls; and in one corner, dubiously ornamenting it, was a bust of Victoria, done in plaster and placed on top of a jardiniere stand. It would have been easier to wait in the room we usually used, which was warmer somehow, more lived in; but there were no chairs there such as an Englishman would expect, only low couches on which he might not find it easy to sit cross-legged as we did. So we sat stiffly in our high-backed chairs with our eyes on the slow-moving, loud-ticking clock, while conversation languished and at last was allowed to die. Then there they were, Kit and Richard, hot, flushed, in good spirits, and the afternoon revived.

"We've been *everywhere*," Kit said, flopping down and fanning himself vigorously. "Richard's mad . . . I shall never go out with him again."

"I hope we haven't kept you waiting," Richard said, "I'm afraid I rather lost count of the time."

"Not at all, my dear boy, not at all," my father reassured him (truthfully, for the servants, in a flurry, had yet to announce that lunch was ready), "but I trust you did not overtax yourself—you look somewhat tired."

"You must be careful," my mother said in her slow English. "It would not do for you to be ill on your first day here."

Richard smiled at her: "I promise you I will be careful . . . after today," he said. And looking up at him—taller than any of us, bursting with health—I could not help thinking, a little scornful, that there was hardly need for such care; then his eyes were on me, half-mocking, half-humoring me as he had my mother, and it was I who had to turn away in confusion.

"I could do with a beer," Kit said suddenly from the depths of the horsehair sofa. "There's nothing I'd like more than a pint of beer—iced. I expect you would too, wouldn't you, Richard?"

But there was no beer in the house; there never was unless European visitors were expected. Now a peon was hastily dispatched—balancing a crate on the handlebars of his bicycle, none too pleased to be out at high noon—to fetch some from the club, which was a good two miles away. The beer, when it came, far from being iced, was hot; there was only one way of cooling it, and Kit made a face when he saw the ice cubes, put in by a lavish hand, jostling below the froth. "Water with a

13

dash," he observed wryly; then, half-humorously, "you see, Richard, the hazards of living in the wilds."

Living in the wilds. It had never occurred to me before that we did; I did not think it now either, but I could see that to Kit, who had lived so long in England, who spoke of London with fond, easy familiarity, it might indeed appear so, that in the glory of this other city, this overpowering capital of another world, our home town might well begin to diminish, to dwindle and recede into unimportance.

"And the joys," countered Richard equably. "What is beer amid so much beauty?" And he too spoke jestingly, with only the barest outlines of truth showing through.

"He means all those flowering trees," Kit said. "You know, gold mohur. They usually affect foreigners that way." But if he had thought to provoke a retort, he was wrong.

Richard flushed a little, but he only said, easily, "Naturally, they affect me—I've never seen giant trees in flower. Copper beeches are about the nearest, at home, but they're not quite so—so startling."

The retort came from Govind, who said—struggling to get the words out as always, "Not only foreigners—they affect the natives also." Somehow—perhaps because he spoke so rarely, and then with such difficulty—there was an intensity about even these simple words which caused an embarrassing silence. Then my mother, composed, serene, admitting no awkwardness, took up the thread of conversation. Gold mohur, yes, they were lovely, especially at this season, and had Richard seen flame-of-the-forest, which many people took to be the same although there were quite distinct differences . . . she explained them, careful, unhurried, making us all relax. Then, at last, lunch was ready.

This first meal of Kit's return was, of course, a feast. A great many delicacies had been prepared and were now arrayed in splendid variety upon the long narrow tables. Silver plate had been brought out, the tall Kashmir tumblers with rims of beaten gold, the rose bowls of jade, the low ebony benches with their edging of carved rosettes which were my special delight. Kit was visibly pleased; he also looked surprised—perhaps after so long he had forgotten what it would be like.

14

"Darling 'Ma," he exclaimed, giving my mother the old favorite diminutive, "what a lovely display!" And he put his arm affectionately about her.

She smiled up at him. "It is nothing," she said, and her eyes, like velvet, repeated: For you, beloved, it is nothing; though if we had been alone she would have added, bridling, "You are not a beggar's son."

"I've been looking forward to this so long," Kit said. "I've missed our food . . . I've only just realized how much." Somehow what he said made me uncomfortable, as if he were admitting something in the mood of the moment for which his reasserted self-sufficiency would later castigate him. But my parents, our uncles, even Govind, looked on approvingly, pleased and gratified: for were not these the proper sentiments of a lad so far from home—doubly admirable in one as Westernized as Kitsamy? And what better than that they should be thus publicly expressed, and in the presence of an Englishman?

"You never said so once in your letters," my father said. "Otherwise . . ."

"What would you have done?" Kit was laughing. "Sent a cook . . . or parcels . . . or mother?"

"Your mother did send lots of parcels," my father said; "nearly all came back."

"Well, the customs, you know," Kit said vaguely, "it's terribly difficult to get anything past them. Ask Richard."

Richard nodded. "Yes. They can be tiresome."

I imagined suspicious customs officers prying open the parcels, probing into the contents, sniffing at the pickles inside, the papadams, the curry and chili powder, being mystified, stamping the parcels, mysteriously, perhaps falsely, "Not Accepted." I did not suspect then that the nonacceptance might have been by Kitsamy, who could not be bothered to clear the parcels or pay the duties on them.

"Well, well," said senior uncle, pressing home the point, "East, West—home's best." Then to Richard, "What say you to that, sir?"

This uncle, when Europeans were present, often spoke curious English.

"Amen," said Richard, which I thought an unusual but very skillful way of parrying a difficult question. It would never have occurred to me; now I marked it and stored it away for possible future use.

Kit was looking slightly irritated. "A trite saying, uncle," he observed, "of greatly varying truth."

There was an edge to his tone which would have given another man pause; but senior uncle, used to deference, indifferent to nuances of feeling, was not to be put off. "Trite but true," he said emphatically. "The longer I live, the more I realize how true it is."

But you've never been away, how can you know?

The thought was there, ready to slip into words, seeking, clamoring for impatient delivery; but Kit held it imprisoned, said nothing, sat quiet, flushed by the effort of silence; and senior uncle, pleased by his triumph, exploiting it, said authoritatively, "There is no place like home. What do you say, Mirabai?" Then, turning to the others, "Let us hear the truth from the mouths of babes and sucklings."

This time it was I who felt irritated: I did not relish being thus referred to, even jocularly, and especially not by senior uncle, who at other times did not hesitate to impress on me that I was a young woman. Besides, I could not think of a reply to please everyone. "Amen" might have done; I would have liked to use this new reply, but it might not sound polite, coming from me, and anyway it had just been used. At last I said lamely, "It is a comfortable place," and somehow this not very brilliant answer seemed to be the right one; it made everyone laugh and thereafter the conversation proceeded on a much lighter note.

No one who could possibly avoid it ever did anything after the midday meal for at least a couple of hours. Now—replete, a little heavy-eyed—everyone began moving off to get their delayed afternoon sleep. Govind had disappeared, my parents were asleep in their bedroom as usual, those relatives still left had been conducted to the guest rooms. Kit, yawning, had taken himself off to his bedroom. Richard, who had protested he never slept—could not sleep—at this hour, was nevertheless slumbering on the horsehair sofa in the drawing room. This room was not meant for sleeping in: the sofa was hard and neither long enough nor wide enough for comfort. There were no blinds at the windows, and the light fell harshly upon him as he slept. I saw with an impulse of pity the sweat glistening at his temples, forming about his mouth, the uncomfortable arch of his body, the fronds of hair fallen across his damp forehead; then he half turned, muttered something, and it came to me I ought not to be here watching a man exposed in sleep with the sentinels of his consciousness withdrawn, and I turned away at last and went upstairs to drowse in my room.

Teatime came, presaged a good half hour before by a banging and a bustling in the pantry. Everyone else was up, washed and changed, tea was ready, but neither Kit nor Richard appeared. "Do not disturb them," my mother said. "They are tired, let them sleep."

Tea was over, the shadows of evening had fallen on the light, twilight came—an amber one today, it had been so hot; the last lingering relative had been speeded on his way, and still—perhaps more exhausted by the long journey, the crowded day, than either had realized—they slept.

"If you do not wake them now, they will be bilious," said my father, and he sent a bearer to rouse them.

"I think they will be that in any case," my mother said, smiling, and she went to give instructions for baths to be prepared. Richard and Kit, when they came in, did indeed both look rather the worse for wear, their faces sluggish with oversleep, eyes puffy, Richard with the creases of the sofa still imprinted on one cheek. I was waiting for them with the jug of freshly made lime squash, sprigged with sage, frosty with ice, tendrils of melting sugar curling up with my vigorous stirring.

"Angel child," Kit said, drinking thirstily, "you've saved my life."

"Mine, too," Richard said, smiling. "You are lucky, Kit—a sister in a million."

I was sixteen: I had been taught a good many pretty speeches, but they never came easily, and now they all failed me. What was more, I felt if I spoke at all I would stammer, and so I kept quiet, holding back even the commonplace politeness of saying they were most kind.

"Name your reward," Kit proceeded magnificently (the lime squash had revived him amazingly), "it shall be yours. A rose for your hair? Or a silken gown? Would you have me take you out? To the ballet—or shall we go dancing?" Then, seeing me staring at him, he said suddenly, gently, "I'm sorry, my pet. Do I sound crazy to you? It must be the sun."

When Kit was gentle like this, you felt there was nothing you would not do for him.

"Oh no, Kit," I said quickly, "I didn't think that at all."

"Charming child," he said quietly, as if he meant it— I think he meant it, and I felt the warm pleasure stirring in me, "where would you like to go?"

"Tonight?"

"Yes, tonight."

"Aren't you tired?"

"Do I look it?"

"Yes," I said frankly.

"Nothing a bath won't cure," he said, standing up. "Well?"

I hesitated. We might go to the cinema, but of the two films showing, I had seen the English one and the other Richard would not understand. Or there was *Shakuntala,* which a touring dramatic company was putting on and which was one of my favorite plays; but again, there was Richard. Or we might go to the club: I thought Richard would like that, I felt sure Kit would, and more than anything I wanted to please him. And when I suggested it, I knew I had been right about Kit from the way he brightened and said, yes, an excellent idea; but I could not be sure about Richard, although he echoed my brother's words, and although even my experienced ear could not detect the accents of duty in his tone.

◄[CHAPTER TWO]►

CLUB-GOING HAD become, for varying reasons, part of the pattern of our lives—of mine, that is, and my parents', for Govind steadfastly refused to accompany us. My father went to the English Club because it provided amenities such as no other place did, because there was a billiard room and a squash court and tennis courts which were infinitely better kept than the ones belonging to the Oriental Club, which a small group of Indians, tired of being blackballed from the English Club, had recently started. Besides, he liked people: and except during the hot weather, you could be sure of a good attendance at the club, whereas at the Oriental—unless you happened to go when the latest appeal for support had spurred a few of the more conscientious members into action—it was sometimes difficult to find even a bridge four.

My mother went to play bridge and to keep my father company. I went because I was taken, and to learn to mix with Europeans. This last was part of my training, for one day—soon—I would marry, a man of my own class who, like my brother, would have been educated abroad, and who would expect his wife to move as freely in European circles as he himself did. But though I knew how important this was, sometimes I could not help sighing and wondering why the lesson had to be learned so hardly.

Tonight, however, I felt would be different. I was escorted: I would not have to watch my parents disappear into the bridge room and then have to sit about, wondering what to do or—even more harassing—what to say. All that would be taken care of by Kit, who was versed in these things, by Richard, who was part of this other world. I could remain happily quiet, listening to their accounts of what-happened-when, to their stories which even I knew to be preposterous, but which made me laugh; and the golden gladness rising in me, I said warmly, "Oh Kit! It's so nice to have you back."

"Is it, poppet?" he said abstractedly; then briskly, "Nice to be back too. . . . It's time we were off, jump in."

There could be no question of my jumping in: I had spent some time in draping my sari just so—but I climbed in quickly, eager to be going.

Kit was driving, though his license had long since expired. Richard sat beside me in front.

"Don't be too late," my father called over the racing engine (Kit could make the quietest car sound noisy), "you mustn't overdo things." He seemed happy enough to see us setting off on our own, though I think he would have preferred to see the chauffeur—whom Kit had sent home—in the driver's seat.

"Remember this is not England," my mother said, "the roads are bad, you must be careful." Though she spoke

19

to Kit, her glance was quietly upon me, making me aware, making me aware twice over, of Richard, who was squashed beside me, and I knew she regretted not merely the chauffeur, but also, deeply, the absence of a chaperon more heedful than Kit.

Saturday nights at the club, even in the off-season, were always fuller than any other. People motored in from the outlying districts—forest officers, junior civil servants serving out their first year in the hinterland, even, sometimes, missionaries who, the rest of the week, buried themselves in villages nobody had ever heard of —and they brought their wives and occasionally a grown-up daughter and stayed overnight at the club. Now, though it was in the middle of May, when all who could had fled the heat, still some twenty people—the majority men, no more than five or six women—had gathered. Most of them were familiar to me from going there week after week, as I was to them, and so nobody looked twice at me. After the first casual glance, they did not look at Richard or Kit either; banished, quickly, the small silence that followed our entry; showed no interest, admitted no curiosity: yet the feel of both was there and awareness of it was a pleasure inside me.

Overhead the fans, full on, were flying silver hoops. They hummed, sending long dry waves of air pounding through the room.

Richard said, "You seem pleased with life—you've been smiling to yourself for the last ten minutes, did you know?"

I hadn't known, was abashed by my transparency, composed my face, then wondered if it reflected how foolish I now felt.

"It's nice being here," I said at last, "I find it—enjoyable."

"Do you come often?"

"Fairly often."

"And you like it?"

Blue eyes on me, direct, questioning. You can't lie before a look like that, and half-truths become lies.

"Not really," I said. "But tonight, yes."

He stared at me. "Why come at all?"

I could not tell him why, could not think of a reply other than that. "I can't tell you," I said, embarrassment fiery within me. Then, to my relief, Kit came back with the third round of drinks, whisky for them, passion fruit for me, and I buried my hot face in the tall squash glass.

"Thought there would be dancing." Kit sounded disgruntled. "There used to be a band here at one time—what's happened to it?"

"It only plays in the season," I said, "I don't think it's ever been otherwise."

"In the 'season'?" Richard looked amused. "What season?"

"When it isn't the off-season——" I began, and broke off, the words sounded so ridiculous.

Richard was laughing. "Clarity," he murmured, "the season is when the off-season isn't, is that it?" And the way he said it, I had to laugh, forgetting my confusion.

"You should see this place in the season," Kit said with a sudden loud guffaw. "It scintillates!" He and Richard began chuckling, their chuckles growing more and more loud and helpless. People were looking up.

"Let's go in the bar," I suggested; there was seldom anyone there because there were no ceiling fans, only one small revolving table fan. We left our table, carrying our glasses, and pushed through the swing doors into the bar, but no sooner had we grouped ourselves round the counter than Mrs. Miller came in. She was a woman of about thirty-five who never went to the hills because her husband had only a junior post and could not afford to send her, and the lines on her face showed the ravages both of a harsh climate and of a discontented spirit. I knew her only slightly, but now she greeted me as if we were very good friends.

"Hello, Mira! So nice to see you. How are you?"

"I am very well," I returned, "how are you?"

"You look well," she said, "extraordinarily well."

There was a silence: I wondered why it was I could never keep a conversation going.

"Well," she said, "aren't you going to introduce me to your friends? Or do you want to keep them all to yourself?"

When she said that, I knew with a sudden flare of possessiveness that this was exactly what I did want to do; but I said sheepishly, "Of course. This is my brother, Kitsamy. And this is——"

21

With consternation I realized now I did not know Richard's surname. In that moment I hated the Englishwoman for showing me up before Richard: what would he think of me, so wanting in courtesy that I had to be reminded about introductions? And now I did not even know his name. . . . I writhed, hating her, hating myself and, most of all, hating Richard, who had seen this sorry display.

". . . Richard Marlowe," Kit was saying. "We were at Oxford together."

They were shaking hands. Another man came up; then another woman with her husband; there was a lot of handshaking. Another round of drinks, passion fruit for me. Everyone vastly friendly. Richard the center; looking even here, among his own countrymen, so different, with the colors of a gentler climate fresh upon him which in these others had begun to crack and fade.

Warm in here, someone suggested. Let's move out. We moved out, sat round a table directly below a fan. The evening, which had bubbled with laughter, which had been shot with splendor, was now just another Saturday-at-the-club.

-◖ CHAPTER THREE ◗-

AFTER THAT NIGHT Richard was invited out a lot; nearly every day bearers would arrive with notes for him, salaam, and wait for his reply—we grew used to seeing two or three each day gossiping in the shade of the mango tree. Sometimes, too, there were joint invitations for the two of them, but these were less frequent. Both Richard and Kit seemed to find this amusing, but before long Richard, who had to write the replies, grew, I think, a little weary of his popularity, though he never said so. It was of course only natural that the small English community should ask Richard out: what seemed strange was that he should never want to go. He seemed perfectly content to stay where he was, doing things he said he had always wanted to do, some of which my parents, at least, considered rather odd.

I do not know whether he was comfortable with us or not: we did our best, and he said he was, but it was not always easy, especially for my mother. The house itself was equipped to cope with both Europeans and Indians: there were two dining rooms, two kitchens, even two sets of servants, the one lot knowing Indian cookery and service, the other, trained by European memsahibs, knowing how to deal with such abominations as meat and capable of waiting at table. The European side of things was, however—could only be—a façade, meant for guests, for an evening, or a meal. With Richard as it were behind it, it could not last: and if it had crumbled sooner, we should all have been happier. It was Kit who insisted on using the "proper" dining room. For the first day, with all the extra fare, the festive atmosphere, the other was fair enough: now we must be civilized, especially since Richard was here. Then my mother insisted that since he *was* here, we must feed him on what he was used to, not thrust Indian food on him which he, she said, would eat through politeness. She was not prepared, however, to have fresh meat brought in daily, and for four days Richard was given corned beef out of a tin. When the corned beef was finished, she consulted him about his taste in tinned meat, of which, she said to him, you of course know more than I do. She came away from this conversation persuaded that meat was not indispensable, and thereafter Richard was allowed to eat what we did, which was simpler all round.

Then Kit started complaining about that toothless old woman Dodamma—she's everywhere, you can't help bumping into her, *must* she be so evident? And what he meant was that he found her, perhaps vicariously, unlovely and embarrassing as she went about—as a widow should—with shorn head and wearing no blouse under her sari, as you sometimes saw when the cloth slipped from her shoulders. But there was nothing to be done about Dodamma, who lived in the house, was a poor relative and a member of the household, and entitled to be accepted as such. Kit expected her somehow to lose herself, and indeed the whole of the first day she was not to be seen anywhere: but, of course, she could hardly keep this up. Govind, unexpectedly vocal, aligned himself with Dodamma: why should she, his own kith-and-kin, put herself out for this Englishman? As a matter of fact, Dodamma was no more closely related to him than she was to the rest of us, but he made it sound so. His words stung Kit, already a little ashamed of his outburst: and a quarrel was only saved by Dodamma, an inveterate eavesdropper, who said what a scandal for two fine young men to fall out over a worthless old creature like herself. She really did sound shocked, but this only made Kit feel worse, and he flung out of the room in a black fury.

If Richard was aware of these cross-currents, he gave no sign: perhaps we concealed our conflict, perhaps he hid his awareness. Mostly I was thankful for his serenity, as one ever is for peace amid petulance: but sometimes it irritated me to see him walk among us untroubled and untouched, and I would wonder suspiciously if indeed insensibility lay beneath that calm. Curiously enough, when we were alone together I never had these doubting thoughts: they only came with the fretfulness of others.

It was largely because of Kit that we were so often alone together, for he, fresh from an English spring, had wilted with the heat; was seldom active until the cool of evening; repeated, and kept, his promise never to go out again with Richard—at least until the sun had lost its savageness. Take the child, he would say, sipping buttermilk, forehead flushed, spotted with prickly heat. She knows her way about, she'll show you much more than I ever could—you won't find a better guide. And while I tried not to show my pleasure, my mother would strive not to betray her misgivings, hiding them that she might not thwart her son or risk his light, piercing scorn, his "Darling, why *ever* not?" And so, unopposing, she let us go, hoping none of our relatives would come upon us alone together, knowing they would see us as she herself did, man and woman, bearing each within them the spark which waited only the hour, the opportunity—a look, or a touch—to burst into flame; and knowing too they would not withhold their censure, against which she had no defense.

But Richard, outside these complexities, simply accepted Kit's evaluation: I was a child, Kit's sister and, as he had said, a good guide. I was content enough: for three years, since leaving childhood, I had not known the sweetness of walking alone. If I went to the temple, my mother accompanied me; it was no longer permissible to meander through the bazaars—I must go by car;

or if I insisted on walking, an ayah or a peon trailed behind me, reluctant ball-and-chain, mumbling complaints if I went too far or too fast.

Now there was Richard, but his presence was company, not an intrusion. There was nothing he did not want to see, the day was not long enough for all he wanted to do: tireless himself, he almost—almost—tired me out.

"One would think you had only a month to live," I said to him one day, sitting down breathless on a step cut in the face of the rock we were climbing.

"You may be right," he replied, standing, surveying me, "who knows?"

"Why," I stammered, "is there—are you . . ."

"Of course I'm not," he said. "Don't be silly—do I look as if I were dying?" And he yanked me up, saying time was getting short.

"No," I said, climbing obediently before him, "but what did you mean?" And I stopped for his answer.

"Oh well," he said, prodding me on, "chains of office, you know—in a month's time I may not be able to roam as I do now."

When he said that, I knew what he meant, too well. I did not want to think of "in a month's time": happiness enough to be here today, here and now, high above the earth, the humming town, where you could hear the whisper of the hot soft breeze and look down upon treetops, see about you the grain and glitter of the rock in the sunlight.

At the top, the cave we had come to see; and at its mouth, intruding, a figure in a turban, with the metal tab of office, exacting dues, leechlike; but when we had shaken him off, the magic returned.

Inside, black and blinding, with the chill, dank smell about us of unlifting darkness, of earth and rock and rotting mold—very smell of universe—we stayed for a while in silence before moving forward, feeling for the tapers grouped along the ledges; and when these were lit, the cave flowered slowly, revealing surface after surface of carvings in the stone. Here someone—more than one, unknown—had worked with patience, passionately, giving lavishly, leaving in this rich pattern of form and design testimony of beauty experienced and loved.

We came out subdued, blinking in the strong light,

tranquil in the continuing silence; and then the official leech was upon us with his packet of yellow-edged postcards, his collection of plaster casts of the carvings inside—ugly imitations with their outlines blurred, and the seams of the mold which clapped them into figures running clumsily down each side. Pretty dolls, he said. Buy one, bring you luck; and when he saw we wouldn't, changed his voice and whined, poor man he, living on what he sold, no one comes here. At last Richard, helpless, bought one from the man and gave it to me to carry, and when we had gone a hundred steps, he took it from me again and sent it hurtling down the rock face, which I would not have done—but was glad he had—for it was the cast of a goddess; and now the silence shivered and fled.

"I suppose it's true," he said, "not many people come?"

"Very few know," I said. "Then there's the climb. It puts most people off, especially in the summer."

"Any other country," he said, "would have lifts or railways or something."

I nodded, agreeing. "It is a pity, we have nothing."

"Would you have it crowded then?" he asked, curious. "More guides, more people filing in, and a rupee for a candle?"

"No, not that," I said, unsure, groping for expression, "only it seems a pity to keep it for the few . . . there is so much to see."

He said nothing to that; we went on descending in a sober silence until at last we reached level ground, and looking up from here, standing on the white, dusty path, the rock stretched away into towering remoteness, and the trees were once more ordinary.

Although Kit was seldom around during the day, he and Richard would go off together in the late afternoon to play squash or tennis at the club. Exercise is so important, Kit would say, stiff from his midday sleep, hair rumpled, face puffy, and go yawning upstairs to bathe; in a quarter of an hour he would be down again, cool and spruce and fresh, very handsome in his white tennis clothes; and my parents would be there, approving, to see the two of them drive off. But this did not last—not even the week.

"Too much like hard work," Kit said, "it's not good to tear round in a climate like this."

"But you must do something," said my father anxiously. He also was a great believer in exercise, and would never lightly forego his daily five-mile walk.

"Of course," Kit agreed, and promised to think of something not quite so energetic.

The next day my father presented him with a set of dumbbells, which might do, he suggested, until such time as he was able to locate a rowing machine, which he was hoping to do shortly. Except for this, I do not think Kit would have bothered his head further about exercise; now, galvanized, he announced his intention of swimming every day.

"Where will you swim?" my mother asked. "The rivers are dry."

"The swimming pool . . ."

". . . is closed in the hot weather," my mother said gently. "Do you not remember?"

"Oh, we'll find somewhere," Kit said. "Come on, Richard—Mira . . ." Eager, enthusiasm rising, he ran upstairs, came back with his swimming trunks, a pair for Richard, towels, threw them in the back of the car. My mother said no more; she knew we would find no water.

We cruised along the banks of the river, following the curves and twists of its course; then we parked the car among the casuarinas that bordered it and we walked on the river bed, on and on for furlongs that felt like miles through dry white yielding sand, the silver river sand shaped in ripples and waves as the cool-weather water had left it. But still there was no water, until at last we turned from the plunging beach to walk among the trees, upon the thick-piled casuarina needles plump and springy as a well-filled quilt; and here, surprisingly, where the trees grew close and the shade was greenest, we came upon a pool of clear still water which had somehow resisted the summer.

"What did I say!" Kit exclaimed, jubilant. "Nothing is impossible if one sets one's mind to it. Trouble in this country is no one makes the effort!"

Already he had disappeared to change, appeared a second later in his swimming trunks, dived into the pool and came up again, shaking the water from his eyes and hallooing to Richard to join him. I had not thought to find water, and having nothing to change into, sat watching on the bank; and as I watched, saw very lively swimmers, a colony of young green snakes whose peace we had disturbed; but they were small and green and harmless, and I said nothing, not wishing to alarm Richard, who was new to the country. It was Kit who saw them, and he came out at once, shuddering, not frightened but disgusted, for he had always had a loathing for anything which was, or looked, slimy. Richard followed; what he thought I do not know, but we never went back to that pool.

Kit, refusing to accept setback, desire redoubled with his brief taste of pleasure, proposed the following day that we should run down to the coast. "Just over an hour's run," he said. "We'll picnic there, what do you say?" Richard was delighted. I was delighted. Even Govind, who had so far steadily declined to accompany us anywhere, preferring his own company, seemed to tremble on the verge of Yes, though finally he said No. I flew, excited, to tell my mother: and she, at the end of my breathless exposition, said I was not to go.

"Why not?" I asked; and I cried to myself, *Why ever not!* while the wings of my anticipation began slowly to fold.

"Modesty graces a woman," she replied. "It is not right for a young woman to go among young men."

To go among them touched by the alchemy of water, transformed by it; hair become a skull cap, garments a gleaming sheath.

"He's my brother," I said.

"And the other?"

"I *said* I would go," I cried. "What shall I say now?"

"You will have to say you cannot swim."

"But I can!" I said furiously. "I swim very well!"

Anger blew open the gates of defiance; but while they swung wildly, before I could advance, my mother said —and her voice was low and loving, "Dearest, go if you must," and the wind died and in the lull I heard the gates shut.

"What shall I say?" I repeated, in the calm.

"It is not so difficult," she said, half smiling at me. "Only that you cannot swim today. They will understand."

And so I did not go. Richard and Kit went that day, and again once more, and on the third day, having developed large raw patches of sunburn, they both lost interest in sea bathing. Kit thereupon gave up all idea of exercise. One can but try, he would say, pointing to his red scaly forehead, laughing at himself; and he would shrug philosophically and resolve to wait on the weather.

Richard had no thought for exercise: he liked walking for its own sake, and I went with him and he seemed to like my company; or there was something he wanted to see—a festival, or a fair—and I took him and was glad to do it. We wandered through the bazaar, its narrow, crooked lanes, and Richard bought cheap, useless things for the pleasure of haggling and to try out on amazed shopkeepers the few words I taught him. We went to see the birth of the new year, joining the bright procession that wound round the town, and, when it was dark, sent rockets streaming into the night sky to illuminate the event. We spent long hours sitting on the steps of the tank in the center of the town, where beggars came to wash their rags and milkmen their buffaloes, where women stared and giggled in the middle of their idle gossip until they grew used to Richard, and their children pelted the water with stones; and the skimming pebble, or a jar being filled, was enough to set the water rocking, making new, tender patterns of the waterwort and lilies that floated on its surface.

One day, suddenly, Richard asked me about my education; and when I had come up out of my absorption, I answered him, In a month's time. But already the month—the full shining moon of this month—was no more; and though I lagged, the days sped by and the moon waned; and when it was a crescent, it was time for Richard to leave.

He had come for a fortnight, and—Kit pressing him to stay on, and my parents sincerely endorsing the invitation (for I think they had come to like him, and not only for Kit's sake)—he stayed for another. At the end of it he thanked my parents, then Kit, and, when we were alone—for he had not lived among us for nothing —he kissed me lightly and asked, Did I dislike him less?

"Dislike you less?" I repeated, amazed. "Whatever do you mean?"

"Less than you did at first," he prompted.

I stared at him: had I, then, been so obvious? Obvious to others, obtuse myself?

"You were—prickly," he said, half accusing, keeping his eyes on me, and I could not deny it, I could not lie.

"Only at first," I said at last, "in the very beginning."

"A poor beginning," he said, "a happier continuation." And somehow—although it was only a word—I felt absurdly glad that he had not said "end."

We went, the four of us, to see him off. No bandobust this time, Kit said, laughing, slapping him on the back: You must come again soon. And Richard nodded and smiled, and even this to me was a warm small comfort.

-⟦ CHAPTER FOUR ⟧-

UNTIL KIT'S RETURN I do not recall that there were ever many letters for us—excepting my father, and his were mostly to do with business, with lands and litigation and unco-operative tenants—neither for my mother, who was wholly absorbed in her family, nor for Govind, who was an orphan, nor for Dodamma, who was a widow, and certainly not for me, for who was there to write? Kit, from England, wrote erratically: a dozen blue-winged envelopes one month, then a long stretch of silence, followed by vehement cablegrams; and all his epistles were addressed to all of us (because as he said it was silly to write the same thing five times over) and everyone read them, or had them read. On the rare occasions when there was a letter for one of us, it was a matter of honor that the recipient alone should open it; my father, especially, insisted on this, and had even been heard to rebuke Dodamma (who did not subscribe to these foolish new-fangled views) for opening a letter of Govind's. On the other hand, it was also not honorable for whoever got a letter not to open it before the others, say who it was from, and quote from it—extensively.

The code held, the mild censorship worked very well, until Kit came home; but he simply ignored it. For now letters came in shoals, and they were mostly for him; and he, thumbing through them, chuckling over one or

30

two, making no comment, would carry them away to re-read in his own room. Moreover, he said nothing further about them: and who knew, who could say, where they came from, and whether from men, or—fearful thought —from women, those fair, unscrupulous sirens of the West who spread the silken nets of their beauty to en-snare the innocent?

My mother asked no questions. When Richard was gone, she had Kit's things moved into the rooms that were originally meant for him, minutely watching while the servants packed and carried, herself seeing to his books and papers which they, being illiterate, might not treat with the appropriate care. At the end of all this she came down, flushed with the exertion but looking much more tranquil than she had of late; and Kit, from the depths of an armchair, glancing up from the book he was reading, said softly, mocking, "No barmaids, after all," knowing somehow that this—a liaison with a bar-maid—symbolized for her, and to many like her, the dangers of the West—its brazen ways, its painted wom-en, its easy morality, the glitter which could reach across the seas to claim a man. And my mother, with height-ened flush, but quickly recovering her composure, said, "I did not visualize barmaids for my son."

What had she visualized? What did I? I cannot re-member, save that she was very different to my imagin-ings. I came upon her unwittingly, for Kit himself had asked me for some fresh blotting paper, and as I eased the used sheet from its leather corners, I saw her photo-graph below. Her face was young and soft; she had a tender mouth and fair hair that fell to her shoulders like a shining curtain of silk. I felt almost as if I had come upon her unawares—there was something about her, de-fenseless—she looked as people sometimes do when they think they are alone; and I wanted to cover her quickly, the feeling was so strong. But I could not de-cide whether I should put the old blotting paper back and say nothing, or whether I should let Kit know I had seen the photograph, and while I hesitated, I heard him come in.

"I did not mean to pry," I said, "I'm sorry."

"No need to be," he replied, and he came over to the desk and stood gazing down at the picture; and after a

31

little he said, "She is beautiful—do you not think so? So very beautiful."

I nodded, not looking at him, and there was another silence, and at last I said, "Who is she, Kit? Do you know her?"

"Who is Sylvia?" he said gently. "Oh, just a girl . . . I used to know her."

I went away, leaving him alone; he was so withdrawn, he did not look up; I do not think he heard me go. Afterwards, I always thought of her as Sylvia, the silken-haired girl my brother had known.

I do not know whether it was the undiminished size of Kit's mail, or the approaching marriage season, or the desire to see him safely wed before he left to take up his appointment, which influenced my mother. At any rate she now began what she herself called "looking to the future." She made frequent trips to see our several relatives, and our several relatives—women, for men do not concern themselves with the tedious preliminaries—came to see her. There were long conversations with Dodamma, and the old lady, bright of eye, a new vigor in her, went purposefully to and fro on her various missions.

The sequel to all this was that, toward the end of the month, my mother began to get nearly as many letters as Kit, most of which came in large envelopes with stiffened sides to protect the photographs and copy horoscopes inside, so that the postman was no longer able to slip them into the letterbox nailed to the gates and had to trudge all the way up the drive. My father philosophically tipped the man: it was the only indication he gave that he was aware of what went on.

Kit noticed nothing: the whispers, the visiting, Dodamma's new importance, the sly looks of the servants, might not have existed for all he cared, or perhaps he did not care and that was the explanation of it. I think he missed Richard, for there was no one else to share and enlarge his memories: the flow of reminiscence, so lively when the two of them were together, gradually died, and now there were no more stories of what-happened-when.

It is the heat, my mother said more than once; and certainly he was suffering from its effects. The prickly

32

heat had spread, his limbs were covered with the irritating rash which he would not stop scratching; then, when the land was at its hottest, the angry red spots erupted into boils. Thereafter, cautious, he would sit moodily in his room, dabbing ammonia on his arms and legs and quarreling with whoever took him his meal or was sent to coax him down for it.

Between us I think we tried Dodamma sorely, for Kit was indifferent, and I, somehow, could not even make a show of participating with pleasure in this exciting matter of choosing a bride for him.

"It is not normal," she said to me disapprovingly. "It is not natural that a girl of your age should take so little interest! Why, do you not know marriage is the second milestone in life?"

How could she ask? She had told me so often enough before.

"Yes," I said, "I know."

"Show some enthusiasm then," she exhorted. "Think of your brother—be glad for his sake."

It was of him that I thought, and I could not be glad.

"If that is the best you can do," Dodamma said, glancing at me sourly, "you had better stop thinking. You look as if there were a death in the house, no less. What is wrong with you?"

"I do not know," I said wearily, tired of listening to her, wishing she would go away and leave me alone; but she did not: she never did, being one of those people who never sense others' thoughts.

"You are feeling the heat," she pursued. "Every year you go to the hills—as if you had been born and raised in Iceland. I warned your father against it, but who listens to an old woman?"

Everybody had to and did, in fact; but I could not say this.

"No wonder you cannot stand the climate," she said. "Now I suppose you are hankering to be up in the hills!"

I did not contradict her: but though I liked the hills for their cool and quiet, it was the plains that I loved. Especially now, in the hot flush of summer, when the land blazed with a color and a beauty such as there was at no other season. And each year it was for the plains that I hankered, to see the cassia and gold mohur in their splendor, and wait for the cactus to bear, all at the same time, each plant its one bloom of the year, so that suddenly, overnight, the dark green hedges that crisscrossed the country were crimson-bright with flower, and for a whole week the land was full of this new brilliance.

At last she had finished; her voice became a low rumble in which the words were lost. Perhaps she was not conscious of it, this thin sound that kept on long after it had ceased to be speech, as the old often are not conscious of the betrayals of the body. I wandered out, away from the house, to sit beneath the mango trees; and leaned my back against the rough bark and breathed the scent of the ripening fruit; but was not at peace. Near by, too hot to move, a chameleon lay still, throat alone pulsating, a faded green like the fallen leaves upon which it rested. Idly, I pelted it with gravel, watching while it moved a few lethargic yards and settled now upon a patch of bare ground and took to itself the hues of the earth; and pelted it again, forcing it to move from background to background for my amusement, that I might see it change its color, until at last wearily it dragged itself out into the burning sunlight, and now I saw it was hurt, not merely drugged with the heat as I had supposed, and I turned away sickened; but now, hating myself, the impulse grew to torment it further, was so strong I could barely resist it, might not have done if Govind had not come upon me.

"What possesses you!" he said harshly. "I have been watching you—I could scarcely believe what I saw."

I looked at him, too miserable to speak, and perhaps he sensed my bewilderment, for he did not compel an answer, but sat down beside me in silence, which was often his way; and after some time I heard him say quietly, "We not always understand what we do." And he took my wrists and drew my hands away from my face.

"I do not know what came over me," I said. "I must be——"

"You must learn to take things—less hardly," he said. "The lesson must be learned if you are not to wear yourself out."

So easily said. As if the human heart could be turned by the will into stone, unfeeling, unbreakable, resisting whatever forces might assail it.

"You miss your Richard," he said. "Why deny it?—

we are alone. You worry about your brother. They cripple you now, these feelings, but in a few months' time —do you not see?—they will be as nothing. You will hardly be able to remember what it was like."

Impossible to believe, though he spoke with certainty: for others are always sure, but oneself one never can be.

"Will you miss me too?" he asked. "I shall be leaving here soon. Did you know?"

"Leaving?" I echoed, jolted out of my abstraction, dismayed. "Why? When?"

"Soon," he replied. "I've been offered a job. . . . I propose taking it."

"But I thought—my father said—you were to enter his business?"

"I have no wish to work for your father," he said, "I have no wish to be a clerk."

"It would not be only that," I said, "that would only be a beginning."

He looked at me, somber-faced, and looked away and said shortly, "Possibly. Still, I have decided otherwise."

"When will you go?"

"At the end of this year, after I leave college."

Now, myself forgotten, I was full of questions: What was this job and how had he got it? Where would he live? Would he be alone? But he said little more, for already he was back among the silences which were a part of his nature, and which he had abandoned only for a while, seeing how it was with me. After a little I was quiet too; he had come here, had sought me out, because of his care for me: I knew it, but there was nothing I could say, no way I could tell him of my feeling; for, sometimes, there are no words that will do.

CHAPTER FIVE

THE MARRIAGE MONTH of June went by, and Kit had yet to choose his bride. My mother, some time since, had presented him with a short list of eminently suitable young girls—modern, college-educated girls, accomplished in music and painting, of good family, whose horoscopes were in accord with his; well endowed, besides, with looks and dowry. But, said Kit, it was far too hot to think, let alone about this sort of thing! So my mother waited, and the monsoon came and the winds tore at the trees, and the grass and shrubs were flattened; then they picked themselves up and were spruce and green and glistening; and in the calm when the earth was fresh and the air was clear, she went to see him again. But this time he said it was barbaric to marry a girl with a dowry, he was against the dowry system—all decent people were—and was he to marry a woman for her money? He repeated this, many times, and at length my mother said coldly, with acid in her voice, The dowry is not for your benefit, it is for the girl's self-respect, that she may not have to beg from you for her keep. You may be sure, she said, the money will be in her name, and the jewels will be upon her body.

Kit was silenced; and the weeks went by and my mother approached him again and he cried, I *cannot!* How can I marry a girl I have not even seen? Sleep with her, call her my wife? I cannot. But he did not say, I *will* not, and my mother was gentle with him, knowing he was used to the freedoms of the West and would never be weaned from its ways with violence.

Only choose, she said to him. The girl shall come here, to our house. I do not ask you to marry a stranger.

And if I do not . . . ?

There is no compulsion, my mother said. There are many girls.

And so Premala came to stay with us, bringing her mother with her who, having also an England-returned son, readily understood the need for this strange new pattern of courtship, deplorable no doubt, but what the times demanded. She and my mother, mutually sympathetic, in deepest accord, were even able, though it took the two of them to do it, to quell Dodamma, who thought the whole proceeding shameless and dangerous and did not hesitate to say so; and when at the end of the week Premala's mother left, it was with regret on both sides, and the fullest confidence in a happy outcome.

Premala knew, of course, the object of her coming, knew that her stay with us would be a long one—for

36

there was to be no haste in the matter—and what it was hoped the culmination might be: but no woman, after all, goes lightly to her marriage, there are always shadows before. Premala, besides, had never left her home, had never before been alone, and so for her it was doubly difficult. Now, standing beside her in the porch while our mothers exchanged farewells, I felt her trembling, and looking up saw that her face was wet. I knew then what it must be like for her: her loneliness touched me and flowed into me, my throat felt tight with pity. She is too young, I thought, forgetting she was older than I. To me she seemed a child: and this feeling was always to remain, for, like a child, she had no defenses.

This time there was not, of course, the upheaval there had been with Richard's coming: for Premala was after all of our caste, and though her home was a two-day journey away, still our ways were not very different from hers. But Kit's were: and though she tried desperately, she plainly found it difficult to adapt herself to him.

"Come on, Prem," he would shout, "time for tennis!" —for the cool weather had revived him, and his ardor for exercise; and he would come running down the stairs, twirling his racket, and the two of them would drive off. At sundown they would return, Kit none too good-humored, Premala looking mortified, for she was no good at the game and heartily disliked playing. It would have been far better had she said so: but she did not—she persisted, perhaps having been warned that a woman must be companion as well as wife to her husband.

"You know, you *could* be quite good," Kit said to her one day, "only your sari does seem to get in the way. It must be awfully difficult to dash about in it."

Premala nodded, glad enough that he should find excuses for her, and Kit went on, "You ought to try wearing shorts, like Mira. She used to be quite hopeless before she did."

"I've always worn them," I said before I could stop myself, "I'm still quite hopeless."

"Well anyway," he said, "I'm sure it would make a difference to you, Prem. Really, I do. You've got some excellent shots, only you're not quite quick enough."

37

The next day—I was not surprised, for she would have done anything for him—Premala came to borrow my shorts; put them on, blushing; blushed again furiously when Kit looked at her bare legs, for she had never worn anything but a sari. But this modesty, which is supposed to grace a woman, found little favor in Kit's eyes. "Really Prem!" he exclaimed, between amusement and irritation. "You seem to think you aren't decently dressed! It'll be much easier playing in those," he added, "you'll see."

I do not know whether she saw, or if her tennis improved: but gradually their outings grew fewer and fewer. Perhaps what she gained in freedom of movement was more than lost by her self-consciousness.

Her other ordeal was going to the club: for, like me, she never knew what to do or to say. Even less, in fact, for I had been many times before, and she not at all, for even with the utmost care it is not possible, in India, to match gradations of behavior, and Premala's family was less Westernized than ours.

Watching her—embarrassed, hands nervous in her lap, smiling her stiff, set smile when others laughed, otherwise sitting silent with taut face and eyes lowered —I felt my own stature grow. My confidence feeding on her lack, it seemed to me now that I could almost claim to be sophisticated; and perhaps by comparison, I was.

If Kit had known what it was like for Premala, I do not think he would have taken her. But how could he? He liked people, he enjoyed going out, he had never been shy—or if he had he had long since forgotten its torments. Moreover, people liked him, for he was gay and good-looking and did things well; besides, he knew England, which was the next best thing to being English; had only recently left there; and somehow any connection with England, however small, reflected credit on you and inclined people, at least at the club, in your favor. So they clustered round him, asked him to join in this or that, bore him away to the men's bar or the billiard room, begged him to repeat this story and that; and Kit, laughing, responding, from the summit of his popularity had little time to be aware of the bleak slopes below.

Premala made no complaint: she thought it right that she should be by his side, and whenever he asked her— sometimes two or three times a week—she said she was happy to go. But she was young still, unfledged, unskilled in the craft of concealment which does not come until one has been hurt many times, and by some is never learned. She could bring out the words, but she could not control her voice; the blood in her face, the look in her eyes, these were her betrayers, they gave her away in despite of herself.

My parents, if they saw the signs, said nothing: to them it was wholly proper that Premala should wait upon their son's pleasure. But it was a little different for Govind. Even so, he spoke obliquely. "It is not a vital matter," he said, watching her remorselessly, "this of moving among the English."

"Not vital," she agreed. "It can be important."

"To you?"

She did not answer, and he repeated, "Is it to you?"

"Yes," she said, "it is to me."

But even now he would not let her be. "It is foolish to force oneself," he said. "One cannot——"

"One can try," she answered quietly. "I would make a poor wife if I did not."

He looked at her for a moment in silence; then at last he said quietly, "No man could have a better."

By the time she had been with us a month, there was no one who did not speak of Premala with affection, for she was gentle and unassuming, and had tender, pleasing ways. Dodamma, vocal where others were perforce discreet, said she would make a fine wife for Kitsamy. "She is at the right age too," she announced with satisfaction, and her eyes were knowing and almost bold, "in her first bloom, supple and soft to delight a man."

My mother nodded. "Seventeen is the right age," she said, half to herself. "Perhaps she seems a little young to him, but the difference in years will be nothing, later on. She will not have to worry—they will grow old together."

By the end of that month everyone knew, and was delighted, that Premala would marry my brother. Even my mother, though naturally no girl could be quite good enough for Kit, seemed satisfied; and when at last she suggested, tentatively, that October might be a good month for the wedding, he agreed at once.

"You are quite sure," she said, anxious, searching his face, "you would not do it just to please me?"

"I would do anything to please you," he replied light-ly, "but I am quite sure."

"No doubts?"

"No, darling. None."

Still she lingered, and placed her fingertips upon his face as the blind sometimes touch the face of a loved one, as if to draw the truth from there, and asked once more for reassurance. "The girl pleases you?—you think your mother has chosen well?"

"You have chosen well," he said. "I am very fond of Premala."

I knew he was fond of Premala—we all were. Since her coming, he had lost his old moodiness, which was a relief to everyone; the fits of peevishness, of solitary brooding, grew fewer and fewer: he seemed to have re-covered something of the zest there had been when Rich-ard was with us. And away from the club he seemed happy enough in her company: he liked talking to her, for she listened well, he was proud of her accomplish-ments, and delighted in her beauty. What else? What feeling, more than all this, for the girl he would call his wife? I watched him closely, but I could not tell, for he had locked the coffers of his thought and stood vigilant beside them.

-❨ CHAPTER SIX ❩-

THOUGH THE WEDDING was still some two months off, preparations had already begun, for there was much to do. Premala's mother would have been glad to help—she said so, in a series of letters; but, she wrote with some asperity, her young sons were at school, and her husband said nothing must interfere with their school-ing, so that she could not bring them with her; also, he refused to permit her to leave them in his care a second time; men were so difficult, and her hands were tied. Accordingly my mother took over—and was not reluctant to do so—the duties which normally fall to the bride's mother. Each day she awaited the jewelers' arrival—by no means certain, for good jewelers, being few, are way-ward men, not easily enticed; and when they came she and Premala would pore over their catalogues together, or watch while the precious stones were set in wax that the patterns might be studied, or argue the merits of a rose-cut over a table-cut diamond. Together they went out paying calls on our relatives—a courtesy not lightly to be overlooked, and to be carried out with care and scruple, for they determine what good will the couple later receives.

And of course there was the shopping: for bangles, for saris, for sandals; for silver and brass, for soaps and scents. Soon news spread that there was to be a wedding, and hawkers came with their wares, which they laid out on the verandas, and were content to sit beside them, unfretted, patient, for hour after hour: itinerant vendors, like tramps, have all the time in the world. Sometimes their vigil would be rewarded: my mother, or Premala, would buy a length of pongee from a smiling, willing Chinese, or a silk sari from the merchant from Benares, or select a few colored bangles from the brittle glittering heaps on the floor.

All this left my mother with little time for running the house; and Premala and Dodamma being equally absorbed, much of it was left to me, so that I too found myself unwontedly busy. Each morning I had to watch while the cows were milked to make sure the milk wasn't watered; then I had to see to the boiling first of the milk for breakfast, and then of the drinking water for the day—both these being tasks that could not be entrusted to the servants. Next, food had to be measured out: gram for the cows, oil cakes for the goat, oats for the horses, and rice and wheat for us. All fruit and vegetables must be washed in permanganate—these were my father's standing instructions; and marketing for them must always be done by oneself—these, my mother's. The activity that had preceded Kit's arrival, so impressive at the time, seemed now a mere nothing: looked at from here, it was almost a period of calm.

"In another year we shall go through all this again," Govind said to me gloomily. I gaped at him, and he said, grinning now, "Seventeen is the right age—did you not hear? Soon it will be your turn."

"Yours before mine," I retorted, "you are older."

"And you are a woman," he said.

"I have no time to gossip with you," I said tartly, "I

41

have enough on my hands," and I flounced out of the room.

Outside, there was Dodamma.

"Dear child, I hardly see you these days," she said kindly. "Are you busy?"

"Yes," I said, swallowing my sarcasm; besides, if I said No, she might find me something to do.

"You look the better for it," she said, "now that you don't spend all your hours dreaming."

"How do you know I don't?" I asked.

"You have no time," she replied, rubbing her hands with satisfaction.

"It would be best," observed my mother, puckering her brow, "if you stayed away from college for a while. There is a lot to do. Perhaps you had better see your principal about it."

In other circumstances I would have fallen in with her suggestion, for I neither liked nor disliked college— I just went. Now it was different. "Why should I?" I said. "It is not *my* wedding."

"I thought it might be easier for you," said my mother calmly. "Besides, it would be rather nice to have you at home."

"If I stayed at home," I said, "how should I pass the examinations?"

There was a pause. Would that matter so much? my mother asked.

To me, it would, I answered her. Only we didn't actually say these things, but neatly exchanged our thoughts.

"You seem to have changed," my mother said at last, slowly. "Since—Kitsamy came."

And though she said Kit, she meant Richard; and I realized, surprised, that there was something of truth in what she said, for I do not remember having crossed her before: only, to me his arrival was something purely extraneous—a date to look back on and say, *from then.* But she chose to discern in it a cause.

The days advanced, and the place seemed fuller than ever. Indoors, painters and plasterers were busy, for it had been decided to redecorate the main rooms. Outside, the gardener and watchman had long since given up the attempt to keep children outside the compound, for there was no distinguishing workmen's children, who were allowed in, from village urchins, who were not. During the summer, when the mangoes were ripening, they had been kept at bay by the Gurkha chowkidar, specially engaged each year to guard the fruit. A broad, squat man this, slit-eyed, who struck terror in their breasts—for this is what he was paid to do—with his strange, outlandish gruntings, the short curved kukri he carried strapped to his side or sometimes unstrapped with menace. Now they swarmed unchecked into the garden, or perched upon the compound walls, chirruping like birds. No fruit to be had, of course, not even for the brave or the cunning; but there were always leftovers from the kitchen now that there were so many more people to be fed, when for anyone to go short would be a humiliation, a failure of hospitality on our part.

So they waited, watchful even while they played, brown, wily urchins with the warped bodies of perpetual hunger and the bright uncomplaining eyes of children who somehow contrive to ignore it.

It was the presence of these children which led to discord in our house, marring the bustling, happy prenuptial atmosphere.

The daily fight for scraps had distressed Premala—perhaps she had not seen starvation so close before. Parents, wealth, servants, house and car and compound wall—all these combine to keep poverty comfortably distant; the stricken cannot approach. Superficially you may be aware of it: its accusing visage may even disturb the surface of your mind, like images that drift across the face of your dreams, and yet comprehension does not come, there is no realization.

Premala knew only simplicity, being without any sophistication of any kind. She suggested the children be fed.

This is a suggestion so troublesome it is seldom made: for if they are fed today, what of tomorrow and the next day? Then there is ever after. And if these few today, how many tomorrow? A hundred? Legion? There is no end. These questions, being unanswerable, are not asked. But sometimes this code, by which all respectable people abide, is broken by people of innocence or troublemakers; and when this happens, everyone is rendered savage, because all those regions of willful paralysis, decently covered and forgotten before, now lie quivering and smarting in the open.

My parents not being there, senior uncle took it upon himself to reply.

"A preposterous suggestion," he pronounced it, frowning, and he turned away as if there was nothing more to be said.

"They would eat you out of house and home!" exclaimed Dodamma. "Have you lost your senses, girl? As well feed a tribe of monkeys."

"Or a swarm of locusts," said senior uncle, unable to resist this comeback.

In all things Premala had shown herself to be docile and obliging: but, as is sometimes the case with such people, these qualities were due not to timidity but to the graces of her nature. No longer pliant, refusing to bow to the elders, she said, with reproof in her voice, "These are not monkeys or locusts; they are children."

There was a shocked, insulted silence. Then Kit said, irritably, "Really, Prem, you must try not to be so emotional! There are limits to sentimentality."

"It is neither emotional nor sentimental to call children children," said Premala, refusing to withdraw.

"You must keep a sense of proportion about these things," said Kit, and his voice was that of a man who is trying to be reasonable. "Once you started, where would you stop?"

Govind had listened so far in silence. Now he said—addressing himself to Premala, sneering, "Why start at all? To exact gratitude for these crumbs from your table? Or to become known for your charity?"

I do not know in what black blaze these words were forged: I could scarcely believe they came from him, for perhaps of us all, Govind had been gentlest with her, seeming to realize more than anyone else how easily she bruised.

Yet it was he who had spoken.

For a moment Premala stared at him, bewildered; then slowly the sense of what he had said came to her: she passed her hand slowly over her eyes as a child does, and her face seemed to wither. At last her resistance yielded, and she said no more.

The silence that followed was raw and hateful, ugly, unquiet, waiting to be filled with harshness. Then Kit

44

cried furiously, "Do you know who you are speaking to? To my wife! Premala is to be my wife, do you understand?"

"Perfectly," Govind spoke coldly, holding his tones level, and his very restraint was a goad.

"You will speak to her with respect in the future," Kit's voice was mounting. "Remember who she is and——"

He stopped, for even his passion could not eject those cruel final words. The two men confronted each other: Kit, bright with anger, its banners vivid and flaring in his cheeks; Govind, dark and smoldering, the blood slowly ebbing from his face and leaving it the color of ashes.

"I do not forget," he said at last, steadily, "neither who she is, nor who I am."

I did not wish to hear any more . . . already, too much had been said. The same thought was with everyone; and now a general babble began. Voices were raised, Dodamma's loud and shrill, senior uncle's loud and reproving, reaching at last my mother, who sat with a jeweler on the outer veranda; and she came running in, her face sagging when she saw the two angered men. But it was not to Kit she went, or to Govind, but to Premala; and put her arms about the trembling girl and held her, and spilled her wrath equally upon the two men.

I went to Govind afterwards; and found him at last where, unbounded on one side, the garden tumbled into wilderness. Here the umbrella trees grew, and thornbushes, and the grass was tall and coarse; and tangling it, and twined about the bushes and clasping the boles of the trees were all manner of creepers, swollen and fleshed with rain, and exuberant now in the surging growth that follows the monsoon.

He did not look up when I came, or say anything, but shifted slightly to make room for me on the log on which he was sitting. It had been there a long time, this log: taking to itself through the year the garb of each season, so that it lay unnoticed, and nobody came to split it into firewood, or hack it into something else. Now it was cool and wet and smelled freshly of rain, and moss had mantled it richly. I sat down on it, beside Govind, and slipped my sandals off and laid my feet upon those velvet sides; and the silence between us was kindly, and about us it crooned, full of the whir of wings and of the wind among the grasses.

How long were we there? How can one say? It seemed to me a moment, a full, rounded moment, no more: but now I heard my name being called, and guessed from the tone the calling had gone on for some time, and rose hurriedly to answer the summons. And then at last Govind said, in a wondering way, and almost to himself, "I must love her, to want to hurt her so much."

I stared at him, and he glanced up quickly and said, with a small, queer smile, "Have I given you something more to worry about?"

"Why, no," I said, "what makes you think——"

"The way you look," he said. "Dearest, do you want to haunt me too?"

I turned away, and he fell into step beside me, and as we neared the house he said—and this time he spoke lightly, "You mustn't let me hurt you, because I love you too, you know."

But when you have spoken from the heart, you cannot call back the truth so easily—neither by repetition, nor exaggeration, nor mockery, and least of all by recantation: what follows has a way of emphasizing with its own falseness the truth that went before.

-[CHAPTER SEVEN]-

DESPITE THE FACT that preparations had started early, nothing was finally ready until the very night before the wedding.

With less than a week in hand, Premala's jewels were yet to be finished, the sari she would wear was still being embroidered, the crockery that had been ordered was held up somewhere en route, and no more than one small sack of rice had so far been delivered and the cooks were threatening to leave. It is almost a tradition of Hindu weddings that there should be this last-minute rush: people are not happy if the fury slackens before the climax. So now they scurried about, hot and harassed, snapping at one another, endlessly active; and the jewelers worked till midnight, and extra garland weavers were engaged, and my mother had no time for meals, and my father locked himself in his room and was never seen. And of course, on the day, everything was ready.

Ask whom you like, my mother had said to Kit. Only, I must know how many are coming. So he made out a list, and for the first few weeks dutifully ticked off acceptances on it; but this zeal did not last, and when the day came round, no one—least of all Kit himself—knew how many people to expect.

"Your guess is as good as mine," Kit told my mother, laughing; then, contritely, "darling, I *am* sorry."

There was something about Kit—you could never be really angry with him: he disarmed you in spite of yourself. So now my mother, who had come determined to scold him, found herself smiling, though she was in fact quite put out.

Knowing him, however, what everyone did suspect was that Kit's friends would be drawn from circles of some catholocity, and in the event this proved to be so.

For the actual ceremony, of course, only Hindus were present, and these, mostly relatives of both sides; but afterwards, at the two receptions, there were Moslems, and Parsis, and a lot of English people too, of both sexes.

"We were at Oxford together," Kit would say, or "We came out on the same boat," or "We met at a party in London." These were the main bases of his friendships, though he had also made many friends since returning home. Inevitably, the majority of them were what our relatives, with a hint of censure, labeled "ultramodern" —young men in Western clothes with English accents who flaunted their unorthodoxy and (rather fewer) self-possessed girls with shingled hair and advanced views which they were not afraid to air. And of them all it was Roshan—in a chiffon sari colored like a rainbow, and slippers with rhinestone heels, and a mouth as bright and vivid as a geranium petal—who was easily the most striking.

It was a quality she never relinquished: for I was to see her, not many years later, in the cheapest of homespun saris, with her hair more brown than black with dust, and again in prison, without a trace of make-up and her skin beginning to show the effects of coarse

47

soap and lack of sunlight; and always, wherever she was and in whatever company, Roshan was the one who arrested attention.

"This is Roshan Merchant." Kit introduced her casually. "We used to know each other in London. She used to write poetry then. I don't know what she does now—something outrageous, I expect."

"I used to call myself a poet," Roshan said cheerfully. "No one else did, so I had to give up. I'm a columnist now."

"A columnist?" Kit sounded amused. "Does anyone read your column?"

"No," Roshan conceded, "but they will!"

My mother, I could see, did not know what to make of her: she was "ultramodern," but not aggressively so; "forward," without being conscious of it, so that it did not irritate. But what was a "columnist"? Also, Kit's introduction had left us without a clue to her status: was she married or single? She was long past the marrying age—at least twenty-eight. But then, where was her husband?

My mother determined to settle this important point at once.

"You must find it difficult," she said politely, "to travel alone?"

"Oh no," said Roshan, "I'm quite used to it."

"Do you always," my mother pursued, "travel alone?"

"It all depends," said Roshan, smiling, "whether I'm feeling sociable or not."

My mother tried once more. "Do you support yourself," she asked directly, "by your work?"

Roshan looked at her with candid eyes. "I haven't thought about it before," she confessed. "I own the paper I work for, but I'm blessed if I know if it supports me. You see, I haven't the faintest notion how to read a balance sheet."

Roshan had been invited to stay with us for a few days; now I showed her up to her room, and when we were alone together, she said with a chuckle, "I didn't help your mother much, did I?"

"No," I said, and I could not help smiling.

"My husband and I have parted company," Roshan said, "I didn't want to shock her—it would have, wouldn't it?"

48

"Yes," I said honestly.

"I shall have to try and be discreet then," she said, "only, I'm not very good at it."

She was not: for though very few people could get the better of her, she was too honest and too lazy to keep up the constant deception; and before long she admitted she had a husband.

"We haven't lived together for years," she said. "We used to squabble like anything when we did, but now—funny thing—we're the best of friends."

My mother thought this levity, and it did not appeal to her; and her disapproval changing to dislike, she was never more than formal and distantly polite to Roshan. But I liked her—there was something about her that was turbulent and unafraid which you sensed beneath the light, sparkling surface she presented; and I admired her because she stood alone and thought nothing of it. I know Premala liked her too—if Roshan had stayed longer they might have become very good friends; and even Govind unbent so far as to say she was pleasing.

With the older generation, however, she found no favor. Perhaps they sensed that she would never hesitate to challenge them, or anyone else, or allow prudence to point the way; and saw that where she went, others would follow. And the more they were uneasy, wondering into what strange paths she might lead us, and the more they tried to keep us from her, the more we flocked to her side.

For myself, I shall always be grateful to Roshan. She gave me the chance to go, and I took it; and though I left my home, with its peaceful, ordered living, its tender setting in the countryside, its mellow sights and sounds, its myriad scents, from syringa buds at dawn to queen of the night at dusk—though I left all this that I loved to live in a city that was arid and brown, still it was a fair exchange: for—more precious than any of these—I discovered at last the gateway to the freedoms of the mind, and gazed entranced upon that vista of endless extensions of which the spirit is capable.

Kit had no great liking for the elaborate ritual of marriage. If he had had his way, the whole thing would have been a brisk one-day affair, or—even more preferable—a half-hour ceremony at the local civil registry.

Both sides, however, united against him in this, and he had to give way, for massed opinion is a weighty thing, not easy to withstand. If the matter had been of greater consequence, he might have made the effort; as it was, he submitted to the lengthy ceremonial with such grace as he could summon. Yet though he tried, the best he could achieve was a contemptuous tolerance, tinged with a faint mocking hostility, for the varied endless formalities of a wedding: for the attendants who fussed about him, and relatives who lectured and advised him, and priests who prayed over him and made him listen to their earnest counsel and took no thought of his rising impatience.

It must have been difficult for Premala, too—to sit there day after day for a week, the center of attention, with the eyes of the crowd upon her, young bride-to-be, virgin on the threshold of knowledge; eyes that were sometimes covert and speculative, and sometimes open and appraising, and mostly full of bright, slavering anticipation.

But she was gentle and docile, and if she found the proceedings trying, she kept it to herself; besides, she knew what satisfaction it gave our families to see the wedding conducted in this slow, traditional manner, and it was not in her to stand in the way of their pleasure.

Whatever she may have thought of the attendant formalities, however, with the actual religious ceremonies she was deeply in accord. Several times I saw her praying, eyes closed, forgetful of the crowd, with that expression of desperate entreaty that you sometimes see on the face of a small, pleading child.

On the last day, just before Kit clasped the thali about her neck that would make her his wife, she turned away from him and covered her face with her hands and bent her head and lost herself—unmindful of the waiting priest, the watching people—in the depth of her prayer; and emerged from it with her face pale and clear and serene; and turned to Kit and bared her throat for the necklace he held, and smiled at him as if he were the only one there.

Then the marriage music, stilled all those minutes, began again. People began streaming forward to congratulate the young couple, and to bless them. Tremulous, side by side, the mothers stood watching, with

50

that tear-stained happiness which overcomes women when they see their children married; while the two fathers stood near by, also side by side, in the cautious affability of men who, never having set eyes on each other a week before, now suddenly find themselves related.

Everyone, even outsiders, was visibly delighted with the marriage: no ulterior motive for it could be found, not even by the most assiduous seeker. They were evenly matched, point by point, even to their looks. And when a marriage is thus visibly in balance, there are few who are not pleased.

—¶[CHAPTER EIGHT]¶—

AT THE END of that year Kit left to take up his appointment, leaving Premala with us until such time as he was posted to a better district. She had wanted to go with him, had pleaded with him to let her; but Kit was firm: he would not take his wife to such a place as he was going to—back-of-beyond, he called it, though it was only slightly smaller than the town we lived in. The conditions of living there were not, he said, such as she was accustomed to; he could not ask any woman to put up with them, least of all his wife. So he went off alone, leaving a flat, colorless emptiness in our midst; and our living was quieter, and the house seemed to darken a little without the candles of his presence to illumine it; and time went by, and the fugitive light and laughter came creeping back again, and we were as before.

Kit had not been gone long when Govind approached my parents for permission to leave. His doing so was in fact no more than a courtesy, for he was twenty-one —his coming-of-age celebration that year had been postponed because of the wedding—as my mother realized, though she attempted to dissuade him.

"There is no need," she said to him, "to jump at the first job you are offered. Why not wait? You are young, there is plenty of time."

"The job may not wait," he said. "What then?"

"There will be others," she said. "There may well be better ones offered you, later on."

"This is not just *a* job, or just any job," he answered carefully. "It is what I want to do, and the opportunity may not come my way again."

My mother was quiet for a while, then she said gently, "Do you think we would not see to it that you were properly placed? Do you think we would be happy if you were not?"

"No," he said slowly, "I do not think that. Only, your ideas are not mine, and what you may wish for me I may not wish for myself."

My mother gazed at him in bewilderment, and shook her head sadly, the way women do who feel their children have advanced beyond their understanding; and she said no more.

Afterwards Govind went to my father; and my father, knowing no man can decide for another, said so: but upon being pressed for his advice, suggested tentatively that it might be better to wait. "In another six months you will take your degree," he said. "It is not without its uses."

That was as much as he would say: but Govind knew, as we all knew, that my father never spoke with a cautious eye to his own ease of living and a cautious thought to secure his own peace of mind, but always without a care for himself; and so Govind said he would think about it again.

A week went by, and we saw nothing of him; and though we were used to his abrupt disappearances—often for three or four days at a stretch, during which time none knew where he went or what he did—still he had not been so long absent before. My mother wondered where he would find shelter, as if the whole country were a wilderness, and worried about whether he was getting proper meals, and sent servants out scouting for him. They—having pleasantly idled the day away in the next village—returned at nightfall with little other than accounts of their weary searching, livened occasionally by tales of his having passed through this town or that, or of his having been seen in a cross-country bus, or flashing past in a northbound train.

At the end of the second week he returned, somber, forbidding, and announced that he had decided not to leave until he had taken his degree the following year—that and no more, no word why he had gone or where he had been; and his manner was such that no one dared to ask.

His decision pleased both my parents, if for differing reasons: my mother, because she would not have found it easy to have two sons—she never thought of Govind as other than a son—leave home within so short a time of each other. Kit's going had left the house echoing with loneliness: she had no desire to set the echoes resounding again now that they were falling into silence. And it pleased my father because he believed it was best for Govind, for neither the moment, nor expedience, nor present advantage, nor even his solicitude for another, could ever touch his integrity.

Looking back now, I wonder that they did not see, either of them, the danger in which they were placing Govind—a danger which he would have fled but that they called him back; a danger of which the very fates seemed aware, since they had, in rare commiseration, sent him this job to take him from it. But perhaps they did not see it because they were people of honor: and in the minds of such people, dishonorable thoughts do not easily insinuate themselves.

And the fates, once flouted, grew thereafter malicious: and when we would have gone our several ways—Govind and Premala and Kit, Roshan and Richard and I—they flung their trammels wide and caught us all and drew us in together until none of us could break away, not one. There was no escape from those triple-meshed nets.

-=[CHAPTER NINE]=-

THE NEXT SIX months passed quietly by. Kit, his arrival and departure, Richard's stay with us, the descent upon us of our relatives and Premala's, above all the wedding, had sent the days racing past, leaving us breathless in their wake: now at last we were in step with time.

The new year began, and it was my seventeenth birthday. My father, who always gave you what you wanted, never mind what people thought, had bought me a bicycle. ("Now what does she want with *that*," said my mother. "Have we not got cars?" "I don't know," said my father, "I couldn't think of anything else.") From my mother there was a gold sovereign, to be strung on the readily convertible necklace which already held sixteen other coins. Dodamma gave me cooking vessels to add to the collection I would take with me to my husband's house; and from Kit, some three weeks late, came a sari, a splendid thing of tissue shot with iridescence like a pigeon's neck. I drew it from its wrapping of mull, and as I did so, a small flat box fell from its folds at my feet. I picked it up and opened it, and inside was a carving of that same goddess whose image in plaster Richard had sent hurtling down the rock face; but this time loving hands had fashioned her, out of the palest ivory, and set her upon a pedestal of gold, and I would have liked to place her in my room where I could look at her; but I was not sure whether it would be wise to show anyone my gift—what if I were made to send it back because it came from a man? And so, regretfully, I put her back in her box, and carried the box into my bedroom, and locked it away in my cupboard, and hid myself for the rest of the day in case anyone should see reflected in my face the rich glow of pleasure within me.

That new year went by; then it was the Telugu new year, then the Tamil, for in India the year has many birthdays. The cool-weather spring of slow, mild growth, of delicate budding and burgeoning, was over; and now the winds blew hot, and the plants gave up their sap, and the soil was parched and dry; and under the white May sun the hot-weather trees were massing their buds, ready to burst into red-and-blue flame.

At the beginning of that month we went as usual to the hills: my parents, Premala, Govind, myself, some half a dozen servants, the cats, the dog, and the yellow-crested cockatoo. Dodamma stayed behind, as usual: she would not melt in the heat, she said, she was not made of sugar. She said this every year. The annual trek to the hills irked her, partly because she believed we should stand up to the climate, partly because she saw it as a custom started by Europeans which there was no reason at all for us to copy. In fact, it was just as well that she did elect to stay behind, for there were the larger animals to cater for, which we could not take with us.

The monsoon came early to the hills that year, and we fled before the driving winds, the night-long creak of the blue-gum trees. When we returned to the plains, it was still in the height of summer. No rain had fallen, though the sky was swollen with cloud: and the air was close and sullen, and the earth was shriveled and brown. Then, late in June, the monsoon broke. Brown gave way to green and green deepened to emerald, and once more it was spring—that second wild spring of tumultuous growth that comes with the rains.

In the following month Govind sat for his finals and passed, and left almost at once to take up his job. What it was, no one knew. When questioned, he grew vague. Questioned further, he told my mother it was community work, and beyond that he would not specify. My mother, unquiet, appealed to my father, but all she got from him was that a man must do what he must, and that no man is accountable to any but himself, and other such sagacities which were no help to her at all.

"Tell me only," my mother said to Govind, anxious-eyed, "will what you earn be commensurate with your qualifications . . . your upbringing?"

"For what I do, there will be fair return," he said.

"But is the pay good?" she persisted.

"I shall not grow fat on it," he said, with one of his small rare smiles, "but it will be sufficient."

Before we could even accept the fact of his going, he was gone—and a day sooner than he had led us to expect, so that the formal send-off planned for him fizzled out. In a way I missed him even more than I missed Kit, whose absences in England I was used to, and whom from childhood I had known only at intervals. But Govind had been with us all my life; he had come to us a year before I was born, and had never left home except briefly.

Govind had not been gone a week when Kit arrived, unexpectedly, one morning.

"A pleasant surprise," said my mother, embracing him; then, reproachfully, "why didn't you let us know? —you young people never tell us anything." And there was chagrin in her voice too, for the send-off she had arranged for Govind he had ruined by his abrupt departure; now here was Kitsamy turning up when nothing at all had been done to welcome him home.

"I did let you know," said Kit glumly, who had walked from the station. "I telegraphed."

The telegram arrived the following day, by which time he had left, for he had only come on a day's leave to collect Premala.

"I've been transferred," he told her, naming the town. "I think you'll like it—it's a reasonable sort of a place. Nice house too—I haven't seen it, but the chap who's just moved out wrote me."

"Is it a permanent posting?" Premala, smiling, sat down at his feet.

"Good gracious, no!" said Kit. "No such thing in the civil service. But we ought to be there a couple of years at least. It'll be *marvelous*," he added, "I can hardly wait to get there."

I had not before heard him speak with warmth of any place in India: his enthusiasms and his loves had been all for the West. Perhaps back-of-beyond made any large town seem wonderful.

"When shall I join you there?" Premala asked, leaning her head against his knee. "Will it be soon?"

"In thirty-six hours, unless the train breaks down," replied Kit, grinning. "I've booked a coupé for us on tonight's express."

"Kit!" Premala exclaimed, dismayed, sitting bolt upright. "How can I! The packing, the——"

". . . won't get done if you sit here," Kit interrupted her.

"Really, Kitsamy!" my mother expostulated. "It is very inconsiderate of you. How can the poor child get everything packed and ready in such a short time?"

"What are servants for?" Kit demanded.

"You know quite well," said my mother coldly, "perfectly well, that it would be disastrous to entrust everything to servants."

"Oh, I don't know," said Kit. "They wouldn't get things done the beautiful way you do, darling, but then, can anyone?"

Even so, my mother was not altogether mollified. "I suppose we shall have to do the best we can," she said, sighing, "but I do wish you had let us know earlier."

"I didn't know myself," said Kit earnestly, and though

we none of us believed him, we all pretended we did, for not to have done so would have made us feel brutal. Kit had this curious power of always managing somehow to reverse the guilt.

"Well, I suppose I'd better go," said Kit casually, "otherwise I shall only get blamed for being in the way"; and he walked off, whistling, calling out over his shoulder that we were not to work too hard.

But you can hardly pack, with the intention of setting up home for the first time, without a certain amount of hard work—even with servants; and by the time we sat down to dinner that night, we were a thought silent. Kit and my father, however, were in good form. Between them lay a conscious sympathy, that camaraderie that establishes itself between men who, seeing their women-folk drooping from fatigue, tacitly agree that women are foolish creatures, who slave because they like slaving— it is their nature.

Kit had a whole host of new stories; and my father, between rich chuckles of appreciative laughter, was full of questions about the transfer, the new posting, and what it was going to be like: which Kit, bubbling with eagerness, was happy enough to answer. Listening to them, we gradually forgot our weariness, and what had started as a silent meal threatened to become an uproarious one.

I cannot think of that evening even now, without a piercing sadness. It was the last time we were all to be together, as a family, in happiness, yet we did not know it. We sat there in amity, warmed by laughter, carefree in a way we were never to be again, and saw no shadow, heard no whisper, to warn us it was the last time. And if we had, what then? We should still have gone our way, moving in orbits we ourselves created, and could not help creating, because we were what we were. For myself, if I had to choose anew, in full knowledge of what was to come, I still would not wish my course deflected, for though there was pain and sorrow and hatred, there was also love: and the experience of it was too sweet, too surpassing sweet, for me ever to want to choose differently.

Nine o'clock came all too quickly. Kit went up to his room which still held many of his things. He was there so long my father began to fidget in case he missed the train, which was due to leave at half past ten, though nothing would have delighted him more than to have Kit stay a little longer. At a quarter to ten Kit came down. He had washed and changed into a white shark-skin jacket, and looked formal and somehow aloof. Gone was the light, gay mood which had made the evening sparkle; he was very quiet now, and seemed of a sudden to have retreated into himself. On an impulse I went up to him.

"Kit!"

"Yes?"

"Oh, nothing," I said, feeling a little awkward, "it's been nice seeing you, that's all."

"Funny child," he said gently, "it's been nice seeing you, too. You must come and stay with us soon."

"Really?"

"Yes, of course, really."

From the porch came my father's voice, calling anxiously. "Kitsamy! Hurry up, it's past ten, you'll miss the train!"

Kit turned to go, and I said hurriedly, "It was nice of you to—to send me Richard's present with yours—so carefully, I mean. No one saw it."

"Darling," he said warmly, "do you think I am blind *and* stupid?" and he kissed me and went out to join the others who were waiting, in a flurry, outside.

Although she had been with us a comparatively short time, in the days following I found it was Premala whose absence I noticed most, for of the three of them it was she who was most often in evidence at home. During the months he had been with us, Kit was rarely in: he was always going off to meet someone or play something, or to the club; and Govind, preferring his own silences to others' chatter, seldom sought you out for your company. Premala was different: quiet, home-loving, with no great liking to be always out and doing, but without those contemplative expansions of the mind which keep people content in their own company. And so she would come to help with the housework, following my mother as she went about the house, or sit chatting with Dodamma, or play for us on the veena in the evening. When I came home from college, she would come to meet me,

58

or sit with me in my room reciting verses from the Gita, most of which she knew by heart.

And now? What would she do in this Presidency town Kit, with such glee, had taken her to? In the lonely, large house he had described? She had taken her veena: but Kit, though he was proud of her accomplishments, had no liking for Indian music. She had her Gita: but the Hindi we had learned at school Kit had long since forgotten in his sojourn at Oxford.

I asked myself why I should imagine my father's house alone compounded of such bliss, and no other. Might it not very well be that she would be far happier with Kit than she had been with us?—and in reply told myself I was a fool. I called myself, in Govind's words, a born worrier, with nothing better to do than to imagine calamity. I tried and tried not to think about Premala. But it was no good, there were reminders of her everywhere: a piece of embroidery she had begun for my mother and left unfinished; her easel, standing on the veranda, which had been overlooked in the flurry Kit had loosed upon us; books, for which there had been no room left in the bulging cases; a box full of tangled tinsel and cotton thread she had been sorting for Dodamma. Listless, I wandered through her room into Kit's, which adjoined. Here, too, there was confusion, for my mother seemed reluctant to begin the work of tidying up, nor would she allow anyone else to do it either without her supervision. The wing that had been made over to Kit and Premala had been closed as they left it: flower petals lay withered on the floor, the water in the vases was green and slimy, even the blinds had not been rolled, and the light came through watered and dim. The ash trays were full: Kit must have smoked several packets of cigarettes in the short time he had been here, there were any number of stubs. The wastepaper basket, overfull, had toppled over on its side, spraying torn scraps of paper around it in a semicircle. Automatically I bent to right it, and as I did so saw, half hidden by the wastepaper, the photograph of the girl with hair like silk my brother had known. It had been torn right across, once only, and thrust savagely down so that it was wedged against the sides of the basket. I don't know why I did it, but I took up the pieces and smoothed out the creases as best I could and laid the

59

halves together on Kit's table, and out of the still-crumpled photograph she gazed up at me, young and clear-eyed as I was always to remember her.

Then at last—feeling as if I were tearing the wings from a butterfly—I tore the photograph into shreds and set a match to the pieces.

If it had not been for the departure in close succession of Kit, Premala, and Govind, negotiations for my marriage would certainly have begun; but I think my mother could not face the thought of my leaving as well, and so—despite several reminders from Dodamma as to my advancing years—she did nothing to further matters. She approached no one, would not permit Dodamma to do so either, and even neglected the inquiries that came from the mothers of marriageable sons. Her listlessness lifting a little one day, she told me it was not fair to me. "I ought to find you a husband," she said. "It must be very lonely for you."

"No indeed," I said as earnestly as I could, "I am perfectly happy."

Maybe my words carried conviction, for she said, turning away, "Well . . . perhaps waiting won't do you any harm—you are not so very old after all."

"She will be sorry later," said Dodamma, glowering, pitching her voice so that my mother could not help overhearing, though she addressed herself to me. "Mark my words, she will regret it."

Perhaps my mother did, for when at last she got round to thinking seriously of my betrothal, it was too late. I had left home by then—as it turned out, for good; had discovered that the refusal to acquiesce is not, after the first time, as formidable as it appears; and had dwelt with temerity upon paths I might take other than the one marked out for me; and so, in more ways than one, there was no going back.

CHAPTER TEN

PREMALA AND KIT had left us in July; in the following month I got a letter from him repeating the invitation to stay with them.

"Richard is spending the weekend with us," he wrote. "He wanted to know if you were coming too. He suggested you should, and threatens to shoot me if I forget to ask you, or even if I ask you and you don't come. Angel child"—Kit could be very extravagant—"save my life! Say you will come!"

I wanted to, very much. I said so, to my mother. What about your college? she wanted to know. I could not help feeling a little abashed, but I said earnestly, "A week won't matter . . . I can work as well away as at home."

"A week plus three days traveling," she said.

"Ten days then," I said, trying not to sound impatient. "I can easily make it up, I'm not an idiot."

"Very well," she said, smiling, "if your father agrees."

This was a pure formality, as we both knew. I thanked her, and was turning away when she said, frowning, "I hope Kitsamy is not forgetting his manners . . . has he asked you for only a week?" and she held out her hand for the letter.

There was nothing I could do, except give it to her. She read it through, making no comment, while I waited fearfully for her to rescind permission to go. Waited, wondered. Oh Kit, did you not tell me you were not blind and stupid? Could you not see this would happen? Or did you imagine it could not? But all my mother said, handing the letter back to me, was that of course I must take a bearer with me, and she thought it would have to be Das, who was used to traveling; and that if I was going, I might as well stay for a fortnight. With both these suggestions I was willing enough to concur.

I was to leave on Wednesday night, which meant I would arrive on Friday morning.

On Wednesday morning Das did not show up for work, and at noon his wife came to say he had been suddenly taken ill. No, nothing serious . . . a bilious attack; but he was not fit to travel.

"Poor old Das," I said, cheerful and callous, "I shall have to take someone else, that's all."

" 'Someone else,' " said my mother, "won't do. Das is an old and experienced servant. I certainly would not allow you to go without him. Nor would your father."

That was that: for when my father's name was invoked, the matter was at an end.

Consequently I arrived on the Monday morning, just missing Richard, who had left the previous night.

"Such a pleasant man," said Premala, who had come to meet the train, "you'd never think he'd been in India as long as he has—a year, isn't it? . . . He asked me to tell you how sorry he was to have missed you—he said he had been looking forward to seeing you again."

Somewhere amid the ashes of depression pleasure began to glow. He was sorry he had missed me; he had been looking forward to meeting me again. Words which anyone might say to anyone, warned my wary suspicious self, instantly raising its guard against possible hurt; a formality, a courtesy, a manner of speaking, no more; but my other self, warm, impetuous, unafraid, cried that these words for me meant more, much more. And I, the arbiter, placing the truth halfway between, found, even so, that the glow was not doused.

"Anyway, it's lovely seeing you again," Premala said, tucking her arm in mine. "Come on, let's go."

Das had gone ahead. We followed, picking our way slowly between the crouched figures of intending travelers, who squatted patiently waiting for their trains, their boxes and bundles spread about them, past the prone forms of those habitual users of station platforms who, at this early hour, were still slumbering.

By the time we got out of the station, Das had somehow spotted the car, although he had never seen it before, and my cases had been stowed in the trunk.

"Your mother has such excellent servants," Premala said. "They always seem to know what to do."

"Das is certainly well trained," I agreed, and this self-same excellence, on which I had reflected so sourly before, I now found tolerable in the cheer of the moment.

The porters had already been paid, but they saw we were women, and young, and so they lingered hopefully. The presence of Das held them back, but the moment he climbed into the car they were upon us, noisy, importunate, such heavy cases, so little money, young memsahibs with kind generous faces, do not be hard on us, remember our families.

And then, as ill luck would have it, the car refused to start.

For a full minute, with admirable persistence, the chauffeur kept his foot on the starter. He then got out of the car and opened the hood. But men who drive your car for you in India do so in a trustful simplicity: they do not know how it works, they have never pretended to you that they did, and so when it breaks down they set off in a kind of blameless virtue for the nearest "mechanico." So now the chauffeur, having demonstrated his willingness to try, closed the hood, informed us there was nothing he could do, and went off to fetch help.

There is nothing like a stranded car, of course, for drawing a crowd; and throngs of cheerful idlers sauntered up to join the beggars who already surrounded us, and who, seeing we could not escape, were pressing their demands with increasing vigor.

The hubbub was at its height, the chauffeur had not yet returned, we had been stranded about an hour, when we saw a taxi drawing up alongside, and from it, with a face like thunder, and before it had even stopped, sprang Kit.

An Indian mob knows exactly when to disperse: this knowledge is almost an instinct, evolved through generations of browbeaten and uncertain existence. Now, in seconds, the crowd about us melted, and Kit stalked up to the car. "What happened?"

"The engine stalled," I said, obviously.

He walked round and began tinkering with the engine, and—perhaps because he loved cars—when he pressed the starter, it purred into life.

"I *knew* it wasn't the car's fault," he said triumphantly, and his face cleared a little. "I *said* it must be that idiot driver. Driver! He couldn't push a pram!"

"Perhaps we ought to wait for him," I said. "He's gone to fetch a mechanic."

"Let him walk," said Kit, letting in the clutch. "Do him good. Bloody incompetent ass."

It was a lovely soft morning: the sun newly risen, mild and warm, the air still flecked with darkness, falling cool and fleecy on our skins.

As we drove along, Kit seemed to recover his good humor: he began first to hum and then to sing, and then, interrupting himself, he suggested a drive before going home.

"A spin before breakfast," he called cheerfully. "Do

63

you good. Smell the air, it's like wine! I've never known such a wonderful day!"

Premala, responding to his mood, looked at me smiling: How could he? He never, except under duress, and then loudly protesting, woke early: and for those who lie abed there is no wine left in the air, the morning is soon stale.

We had been going for about an hour when Premala said, hesitantly, "Perhaps we ought to turn back, Kit. Roshan will be wondering what's happened to us all."

"Not if I know her," said Kit, chuckling. "She won't even notice we're not there!"

"Roshan!" I said, surprised. "Is she staying with you?"

"Oh yes," said Premala, "I forgot to tell you in all the—I forgot to tell you."

"But she *lives* here," I said. "She's got a house, she told me so herself!"

"I know," said Premala helplessly. "She's a little crazy. Her house isn't half a mile from ours, but she said the change would do her good and could she stay. Of course I said Yes. She's wonderful company," she added, "I've never met anyone quite like her."

Neither of us had: for the comparative freedom which was hers by birth had been augmented during her education abroad to a degree greater than most other women of her class enjoyed; and on her return home what it still lacked of full measure she had appropriated for herself without vaunt or notion of defiance. It was with this same ruthless simplicity, as I was to discover, that she always looked at things, so that walls fell, and veils lifted, and somehow when you were with her she lent you her vision, and you saw things as they were.

When at last we reached the house, she was sitting on the top step leading up to the veranda, a cup of coffee in one hand, a newspaper in the other, a second newspaper, shaped like a coolie hat, protecting her head from the sun.

"I expect you thought we were lost!" said Premala, running up the steps to her. "I'm so sorry! Kit—we decided to have a run first, it was such a nice morning."

"I haven't really done any thinking yet," Roshan confessed. "I've only just got up."

It was now nearly nine.

"I've been up since six," said Kit, smugly. "Glorious morning. You don't know what you've missed, Roshan! Tell her, Prem!"

But Premala was too polite to do any such thing, and Roshan said, lazily, "It wouldn't do any good if you did. The morning isn't made that would get me up to look at it. You forget, I'm an ex-poet."

"If you don't hurry," said Kit, "you'll be an ex-whatever-you-call-yourself."

"Columnist," said Roshan cheerfully, not attempting to move. "I choose my times, and I call my soul my own, too. *I'm* not a civil servant."

Kit grinned. "Come and have some breakfast," he said. "Civil servants keep a good table, even if they do nothing else."

"No one disputes that," agreed Roshan. "I'll be with you in a minute. I want to see the end of this."

"This" was the unloading, which she was surveying with a thoughtful eye: and I found myself saying, defensively, "It's not all mine. A lot of what's there is for Kit, and Premala left many of her things behind, too."

"It did seem an extraordinary amount for one person," said Roshan, laughing. "I wondered how you managed."

"We're not all fools," said Kit, leading the way in, "we don't all travel on the buffers."

"On the buffers" has many meanings. It might mean traveling without a ticket; or third-class; or like a pilgrim who, unable to get on the crowded festival special, hangs on as best he can outside. But somehow I could not imagine Roshan doing any of these things: why should she? She was not poor, or a peasant, and I could not visualize her as a pilgrim either. One of Kit's phrases, I thought, following them in; an exaggeration, perhaps, of some occasion when she had forgotten to buy a ticket, and I thought no more of the matter. But I was wrong.

CHAPTER ELEVEN

AT HOME, OUR house had had a dual character, being furnished in both the Indian and what we believed the European style; and we lived in the part that was Indian, and thought little of the other.

Kit's house was different: the furnishing had been left in the hands of a European firm, and there was nothing that was Indian about it. There were Wilton carpets on the floor, wing chairs and a cocktail cabinet in the drawing room, chintzes in the bedrooms, the sideboard held English bone china, and of the Pahari miniatures Premala had collected and the Kashan rugs she had been given, there was no sign.

"Everything's been beautifully done," Premala said, showing me round; then, hesitantly, "I wouldn't want anything changed you know, only . . . it would be—useful—to have another dining room. . . . You know what one's parents are—they prefer their own ways, especially in this; they wouldn't mind other things so much. . . ."

"Oh, they won't mind," I said, uncomfortably, for I had thought the same thing. "Besides, they aren't likely to come for some time, are they? Perhaps you might suggest it to Kit later on."

"He thinks it a bit of a waste," Premala said, "you know, having a whole room set apart; and it would mean a separate kitchen too. . . . I agree with him," she added. "It's not as if we have many—orthodox—friends; and it's not as if we're at home either, with relatives to think of."

"No," I said, glad to agree with her. "It simplifies housekeeping too, not having two sets as it were."

"Oh, the housekeeping's nothing," Premala said, "we've got rather good servants. Mrs. Halliday—she's a friend of Kit's—sent us her own butler, and the cook's been trained in the Burdett household—they're friends of Kit's too. I'm very lucky, the house almost runs itself."

In a way I think she was a little awed by these well-trained servants, perhaps because she felt they were more used to English ways than she herself was. I never saw her giving them instructions, and she seemed content to accept whatever they did; and, certainly, the house ran well enough without any effort on her part. All this left her with a great deal of time on her hands: and although I knew they went out most evenings, or had people in, I could not help wondering what she did with herself all day. But, of course, I could not ask.

If Premala had more time than she knew what to do with, it was just the opposite with Roshan—not that she would ever admit it.

"I own my time—I'm not its slave," she would say, sitting on the veranda steps in the sunshine as usual, mocking, lazy, watching while Kit set off for the office. Or else, slowly sipping coffee, "Time's pretty elastic, why rush to snap it?"

Yet there were days when she was up and away before any of us had even come down to breakfast. Often she did not come in for lunch, or scamped it when she did, and there were evenings when we did not see her until long past dinner.

"She really works much too hard," Premala said. "It can't be good for her."

"Good gracious, she doesn't *work*," said Kit, "she just fools about!"

"Oh Kit!" Premala remonstrated. "How could you? Sometimes the poor girl looks quite tired out."

"Goodness knows why," Kit replied. "I don't believe she does anything at all." And he called loudly, "Roshan! Come and tell us what you do, we're curious to know!"

Roshan sauntered up, smiling. "Come and see for yourself," she offered, "what better way of finding out?"

Kit shook his head—he had, he said, more important things to do; and Premala did not seem keen on accepting the invitation either. But I could not restrain my curiosity, for in my experience women of our class, whether Indian or English, especially married women, did not work, and the exception intrigued me and I said quickly, before she could change her mind, "I'd like to. Very much."

"Come when you like," Roshan said, looking amused. "You'll probably find it exceedingly dull."

But I was not to be put off, and I said, doggedly, "When? Tomorrow?"

Roshan nodded, a little to my surprise, and so it was settled.

I cannot say why it was that from the very beginning I should have felt attracted to the work Roshan was doing, especially as I hardly knew what it was.

"We just write," Roshan said when I questioned her. "What about? Oh, anything! So long as it's interesting—or we think it's interesting!"

This appealed to me, though it still did not mean much; but the following day I went with her again and spent an instructive morning and afternoon watching other people work. That night I took home a pile of back numbers of the magazine, and it was with a triumphant feeling of knowing what it was all about that I spent the third day alone (Roshan had had to go off somewhere) in the office. When on the fourth day I asked if I might accompany her again, she said, laughing, "This thing's growing on you! If you're not careful, you'll become a permanent fixture!"

"I wish I could," I said.

There was a silence. Roshan's eyes were on me, questioning, quizzical; she shrugged slightly. "You can, if you want to."

I made no reply. The whole of the following week I spent at the office, envying the others who worked there, wishing I could be one of them. In a way I felt I already was, for now when I went in, no one took any notice of me. The sense of strangeness, of being a woman among so many men, had lasted briefly and gone, annulled in the cheerful, impersonal atmosphere; and I found myself not merely taking part, but included in a life which, if utterly new, I also found utterly pleasant.

The days sped by, too quickly. "I shall hate leaving," I said to Roshan. "It has been so—so nice."

"Stay on," she replied.

"How can I?" I said. "I would never be allowed to. I must go back."

"Say you have sprained your ankle," she said. "It sounds feeble, but it'll probably do."

I stared at her: such a simple device, but behind it the breathless labor of barefaced lying. How could I?

"It will give you time to think," she said.

I thought over what she had said, and put a bandage round my ankle, and in the morning Kit sent the telegram for me.

A week, a fortnight, a letter from home: was I better now, well enough to travel? It was time I returned.

Now, at last, it had to be done: and when I had written the letter and posted it, though I felt as washed out and as empty as one does after a long bout of fever, there was also a queer relief, which passes almost for peace, of having done something, for good or ill, beyond retraction.

It was soon after I had decided to stay on that Roshan suggested I should share her house with her. She was moving back that week, and proposed that I should leave at the same time.

"If we're to work together, we may as well live together," she said. "It's more sensible."

It was a tempting enough proposal, for though both Kit and Premala had insisted on my staying with them, and though I knew my being there would not inconvenience them—the house was too large, well staffed and well run for that—it was seldom now that I found myself at ease with Premala.

It was not that she minded my working—I do not think she held any strong views on this either way; but in the time she had lived with us, she had grown very fond of my parents, especially of my mother, and it saddened her to think of the anxiety and distress I was causing them. Besides, she could not understand why anyone should choose to leave home; and if she had asked me, I could not have told her, for I did not know myself. However, she did not ask; she said nothing; and her silence was a whetstone to the knives of my guilt. And so I would have liked to go with Roshan, who was as free as the wind and no man's warder, but this I could not do.

"I agreed to stay with Kit," I said at last. "My parents—my mother—think it . . . seemly . . . that I should do so."

She looked at me, I thought with scorn; but she only said, quietly, "Yes, of course . . . I quite understand their wanting you to stay with your brother."

But though my parents spoke of my brother, and
69

Roshan left it at that, it was not of him that they thought but of Premala, for Kit was too far outside the code of our caste and society to be more than its indifferent custodian, or to be more than a perfunctory guardian to me.

⊰[CHAPTER TWELVE]⊱

IT DID NOT take long for me to modify my first unquestioning acceptance of Roshan's casual "one writes about what interests one," or to lose—never to recapture again—the feeling I had exulted in, at the end of the first triumphant week, that I "knew all about it." Certainly, Roshan did write about what interested her, her articles ranging widely from tracing English influences in Persian poetry to the advancement of such political ideas as appealed to her. So, I suppose, did the editor. But for the rest of us there was rather less choice. I did not mind: indeed, had I just been told to write I would hardly have known where to start, and it was something of a help to be told to do this or that, or to go here or there.

The fact that what I wrote was not always read, that it was cut, criticized, reworded, often omitted altogether, did not particularly worry me: I liked writing, it kept me busy, and the pleasure of achieving print was sufficient recompense for these, as it seemed to me incidental, rebuffs. Curiously, too, the slight shift in emphasis, the looking-on at functions, instead of participating in them, made the difference, for me, between ennui and interest. At home, too, there had been weddings; flower shows; amateur theatricals with socialite casts; exhibitions of pottery fired in the nearby ceramic kilns, or of handicrafts from the local women's clubs and institutes. I went to these because I was taken, or expected to go, and the expressions of felicitation or admiration, cast in polite molds long since decreed standard, required little in the way either of variation or of observation, and choked whatever interest there might otherwise have been. Now I went as an observer: and it was almost as if I had a new pair of eyes, for I began to perceive, beneath surfaces glazed by familiarity, colors and values that had never been apparent before. Moreover, the power, handed to me so lightly, of being able to cast my own molds, of finding my own expression for feelings which had hardly been evoked till now, was one which, not having exercised before, I found exhilarating to a perhaps disproportionate degree.

"What you really find so pleasant," said Chari, whose full name was Venkatacharya, "what you really like so much is being given a free hand to criticize."

Chari was one of the younger members of the staff. When I started, he had more or less taken me under his wing—not because he particularly wanted to, but in the way such things happen in an office. After the first self-sufficient week I had turned to him for help, assuming from his youthful looks (wrongly) that he could not be either senior or important. Later, undeceived, but familiarity being what it is, and rather than confess my ignorance to others, I kept on going to him; and before long I had acquired a protector, and he had on his hands a ward—a relationship reinforced by the mild consternation which greeted any departure from this routine. But most of the time Chari did not seem to mind; or if he did, he hid his impatience.

Now I began wondering whether he was right: if in fact it was writing that I liked, or the scope it gave me of being critical. But: "You can look up all the back numbers," I said. "You won't find a single issue in which I have criticized anyone or anything."

"Because the offensive bits were taken out," he said, "not from any charity on your part."

"You can compare them with the originals," I offered. "They're much longer, but they say the same things." Which was substantially true: whatever cuts your reports suffered, if they were used at all, they said what you meant—there was seldom any distortion.

Chari said, "Well, if you didn't actually criticize, you came pretty close to it."

"When?"

"When you said the orchids looked like ice-age blooms."

"They did. The hothouse heating failed. I said so."

"And when the prizes couldn't be found."

"They couldn't. It was chaotic."

"There was no need to say so."

71

"When things are," I said, "I'll say so. When they aren't, I'll say that too."

"You've learned to talk," he said. "You talk more than anyone I know. If you hadn't been so dumb when you started," he added, "I'd never have encouraged you. Now you'd argue the whole day if anyone let you. Like a fishwife."

The sudden shift in ground left me a little breathless: moreover, it struck me there was something of truth in his words, and I fell silent. Even so—and to my own surprise—I found that what he said pleased me, rather than the opposite: and such dismay as I felt over the deterioration in the standards of decorous speech and manner of my upbringing I found oddly counterbalanced by the delight that any man should address me with such complete, if uncomplimentary, frankness.

Chari had other uses, apart from making salutary disclosures to me about myself. His father was an editor, and although he often claimed he would die rather than work for that old fogy with his one-track mind, still he had profited from the relationship; and having been reared in an atmosphere of journalism, he knew a good deal about it. Quicker than anyone, and more merciless, he would pounce on any lazy reporting, or gaucherie or inaccuracy, and give it an airing which sent you, red and white and smarting, to correct the fault, and determined never to risk such a drubbing again. Moreover, he seemed to know instinctively where a story lay, and possessed a generosity which allowed him to share his belief with you, so that you knew which meetings to go to, and which you could safely avoid—a quality of his which later on, when I graduated to political reporting, was to stand me in good stead.

For the moment, however, my writing was confined to what everybody, except myself, regarded as trivia; and even knowing what other people thought was not enough to disrupt my serenity.

"I wonder you don't get bored," Chari said to me one day, "going to all those fatuous functions."

I made no reply. Snipping and pasting, I went on making up my page.

"I suppose you're used to it," he continued, putting as much offense as he could into the simple words. "It would bore me stiff."

I had to reply then. "I don't know how you can say so," I said, "when you believe nothing is intrinsically boring."

This was indeed his favorite dictum, and having it quoted back at him silenced him for a moment. Then: "Of course nothing is," he said, "if one has the right sort of mind. I was putting myself in your place."

I do not suppose this conversation influenced me, either to develop the right sort of mind, or to begin feeling bored with what I was doing. But gradually, and perhaps inevitably, I began to be conscious of a slight restlessness, and to be aware of wider and more inviting, if far distant, fields.

CHAPTER THIRTEEN

IN SEPTEMBER OF that year the war in Europe began, and before long India was somehow involved in it.

I do not think anyone quite knew what to expect next; and the weeks that followed were hushed and uneasy, full of shadows and fears and a sense of the tragic fury gathering across the seas. But time went by, and the atmosphere lightened; it had to, in a way—no one could have borne much longer that overpowering oppressiveness. Then followed a brief flurry, during which peacetime soldiers were hustled into considerations of war; and the maidan which children had thought of as their playground was given over to their parades; and the bogy of rationing was dangled before civilians without really frightening them; and Englishmen spoke of joining the Army, and the Englishwomen, of driving ambulances; and Indians were quiet, aware of that other storm impending in the country.

The flurry was over, settled now into more serious patterns, the war was nine months old, when—without telegram or letter, unannounced, with the same abruptness with which he had come and gone before—Govind walked in on us one evening.

It was late, nearly ten. Kit was at the club; Premala and I had dined and were sitting on the veranda as we usually did on nights when the moon was full.

For a moment we did not recognize the figure standing on the graveled drive looking up at us: then Premala rose quickly, exclaimed a little as her sari caught in the cane of the chair, jerked the garment free, and flew down the steps to meet him.

"Govind! It's you! My dear, how nice to see you!"

Her voice was rich with pleasure, warm, eager, with a note in it that had not been there for a long time.

I did not hear what he said to her: he had taken both her hands in his, was looking at her as if he could not take his eyes away; as they came up the steps, he still held her hand in his. I do not think he had even seen me, or if he had, he had forgotten, for as I rose to meet him he started a little in surprise, then he disengaged himself, and put his arm around me.

"Mira—grown up," he said gently. "You don't know how good it is to see you."

"And you," I said. "It has been a long time, since you left."

"Too long," said Premala. "We have missed you. Come in, let me look at you."

She took his arm and we went in, Govind smiling at the warmth and welcome in her voice, Premala with a sort of shining happiness about her, her eyes very soft and bright.

In the drawing room there was only one light burning, a low shaded lamp that left the room half glowing, half gray: but even in that light it was easy to see how much, in less than a year, Govind had changed. Always, before, I had known him grave, somber, dark-browed, lacking that quick, careless gaiety that lightens the faces of young men: all this was still there, but now—dismaying, disquieting, impossible to evade—there was a hardness about him, a harsh implacability, that had never been there before. I looked at him, sunken-eyed, the lines on his face firm and deeply etched, and looked away not wanting to believe, not wanting to believe anything save that he was as he had been before.

Premala was gazing at him as if she, too, could not believe; her eyes were on his face, searching, anxious; and at last she said, troubled, "Govind . . . is there anything the matter? Anything wrong?"

"Wrong?" he repeated. "No, there's nothing wrong. Why?"

"You look different," she said, turning away. "I wondered——"

"We all change, with time," said Govind, "why should you wonder?"

"In less than a year? Is that time enough?"

"It depends on the passing," he said, watching her. "Do you need to ask?"

She dropped her eyes; did not answer for a little; then quietly: "Do you find me changed?"

"Yes."

"Which is hardly a compliment," said Premala, essaying inconsequence, failing, realizing failure, and falling once more into silence.

I looked at her as she sat, hands crossed in her lap, head bent, a sheen on it like a black pearl's, eyes down, lashes in half-moons on her cheeks, hiding, almost, the shadows beneath; and I knew then that he was right: only I, living with her every day and day after day, had failed to note the signs.

This time it was Govind who broke the silence, and he spoke lightly.

"Let us not talk of change," he said. "That is pastime and preoccupation for the middle-aged, not for us. We are young."

Premala looked up and smiled: not disputing his words but not agreeing, knowing, what we all three knew, that we were young in nothing, save our years.

"We will talk of you," she said. "But first . . . I was almost forgetting . . ."

She went quickly from the room, to come back in a few moments carrying a tray on which were set out small cups filled with curd, and fruit and nuts and sliced copra, the traditional hospitality of an Indian household. Only betel leaves were missing, for these must be fresh and bought daily, and it was so seldom now anyone came to the house who might expect such traditional courtesy that Premala had long since given up ordering any.

"Now," she said, placing the tray before him and curling up on the settee, "tell me where you have been all this time . . . what you have been doing."

"Working," he replied, "what else should a man do?"

"Overworking," she said, her eyes on his thin, gaunt face, on the lines too deeply scored on it. "Other men find time to relax, to play. They even marry, and have children."

Was it cruelty that prompted her? I could not believe it. What then? Innocence? Or an instinct to drag into the open the unacknowledged, so that it might perish there? I do not know; and perhaps she herself would not have been able to answer.

"I have not the desire to marry," Govind said at last, "I have other things to think of."

"Yet there is nothing more important."

"So my mother tells me everlastingly," he said with deliberate lightness. "And Dodamma. Now you. I am almost beginning to believe it myself."

"Your mother!" Premala exclaimed, sitting up. "Have you seen her recently? Have you been home?"

"Yes," he said, smiling at her eagerness. "Quite recently."

"How is she? And your father? How is Dodamma?"

"As vigorous as ever," he said dryly, "more talkative. And my mother is—a little quieter, and my father lives rather more in the clouds than he used to, or perhaps he is allowed to more often now. Everything is much the same, you see, even though we are no longer there."

He was smiling at her, gently mocking; but she did not seem to mind. Eager, happy, she smiled back at him, Govind, link with a life she loved and understood, part of a home which had become hers too. And he responded as he had always done, speaking as no one but she could make him, rapidly and without restraint. Question and answer, more questions, flow of words, all the trivia which is so important, the very heart of our feeling. Yes, 'Ma still looked the same, she had taken up painting again, now that she had more time . . . and there were more animals, more cats, more dogs, and an outdoor aviary had been built to take the birds. Half the house was closed now, which was sensible . . . the garden was looking lovely. . . .

In the months I had been away I had thought often enough of my home: but always warily, within the sanctuary of my own mind, moving softly so that there was no hurt. But to hear it spoken of by another, openly, so that there was no retreat . . . I got up, restless, and went and stood at the window. At home, on a night like this, you could smell the wild jessamine, all the way from the very end of the garden, which was the only place my mother, for fear of snakes, would allow those thick luxuriant creepers to grow. And, mingled with it, the scents of the fruiting trees, in bloom now—custard-apple and pomegranate, and sapodilla, and of the papayas my father had planted which all turned out to be male so that we never had any fruit, but he never had the heart to cut them down because of their fragrant flowers. The scent of sandalwood too, from the trees which some official busybody had long ago ordered my father to chop down because sandalwood was a government monopoly . . . and we had all turned out, fierce and defiant, to confront him, poor man; and he had gone, and the trees still flourished.

I turned away at last, aching. All this I had known, it was my home, part of my life: I had left it of my own choice, and had no wish to rescind the decision. Yet there were times when I looked at myself in wonder: was it really I, moving, working, living in this city to which I did not belong? This jagged city of strife and stridency, of littered streets and endless pavements and air that smelt of dust? It seemed, almost was, too difficult to believe.

In the distance I heard the sound of a car, and roused. There followed a furious honking, perhaps at some luckless carter, asleep at this hour, to get his bullock cart out of the way. More honking, while a sleepy watchman jogged off down the drive to open the main gates leading to the grounds, always barred at night. Then the car's headlights swept round the drive, touching with lightning brilliance the crotons and palms in pots that lined it; there was a final surge of gravel as the car pulled into the portico and stopped.

Already, though Kit was not yet in the room, the atmosphere was changing; shifting, dissolving, surrendering its glow, taking on neutrality as if preparing for something alien to be introduced into it. Yet why? Kit was no stranger: the background we knew was his too, he was as much a part of it as we were. Govind had fallen silent. Premala said, unnecessarily, "It's Kit," and she went out of the room to meet him.

"I've a surprise for you," I heard her say, "you'll never guess, Kit."

"I won't try then." He sounded good-humored. "But

whatever it is, it's a pleasant one: you look quite excited, Prem."

"Yes"—Premala could not withhold the news any more—"it's Govind!"

They had been coming up the steps: now abruptly the footsteps stopped. I heard Kit say, carefully, "Govind? Really?"

"Yes, really. Didn't telephone or anything, he just came. Mira and I were quite startled——"

Premala was still speaking, quickly, a little nervously as they came into the room. Govind rose as they came in, the two men stood looking at each other for a second, then Kit said smoothly, "Govind, my dear chap. Nice to see you. You should have come to see us before."

"He's only just arrived," Premala began; then, realizing he had not said so, she turned to him. "Govind! You've not been here long, have you? *Have* you?"

"Two or three months," he answered her, "with breaks, not continuously."

"And this is the first time——"

"There has not been the opportunity," he said, curtly, with a finality which put an end to further questioning.

Kit had walked over to the table where, on a salver, glasses and bottles were lined up; now he turned enquiringly. "Govind? Have you taken up this pernicious habit yet?"

"No. I cannot afford to drink."

"You don't mind if I do?"

"Not at all. Why should I?"

"I merely asked. This country breeds critics, as you know." Then abruptly: "I hear you have been home. I had a letter from my mother."

"Yes. It was a short visit."

"So I gathered." Glass in hand, Kit came over to the settee and sat down. "My mother said—complained—that you stayed only a day."

"I was not on holiday," Govind spoke carefully. "I was breaking my journey, no more, as I explained to your mother."

Your mother. All this time he had been content to call her "my mother." Why not? She had brought him up from early childhood, he had known no other. Yet now, stiff, formal, correct, it was "your mother." Why?

78

Why? What quality was there in Kit that could affect him so? What black power lay between these two men, who were my brothers, that could turn them into strangers?

"My mother thinks you are trying to do too much," Kit was staring at his glass. "She thinks you ought to have a rest. Perhaps she is right."

"Perhaps." Govind shrugged. For a moment his eyes rested on Kit, taking in his dark, gleaming hair, the well-cut dinner jacket he wore, his well-kept hands; then he said, coldly, "I do not think she realizes I have to— work. And keep on working. I cannot stop now."

The easy, friendly warmth of the evening, frightened, had fled. In her corner Premala sat silent, her fingers pulling at the silk fringe of her sari; there were strands of floss on the settee, on the green pile carpet. There was nothing she could say, there was nothing I could say: we could only wait, in a silence that had begun to shriek.

Then at last Kit spoke. "Naturally I have heard," he said, slowly, "something of your activities."

Govind looked up. "Naturally," he agreed, "as magistrate of this district it would be surprising if you had not."

It is, of course, easier to come to terms with the known than the unknown, and I think in the days that followed both of us, Premala and I, realized this to the uttermost. Of our imaginings we hesitated to speak, each fearing to outstrip the other, and neither Kit nor Govind had told us anything further. Govind had gone into the night as he had come, abrupt, locked in silence, refusing even to leave his address. Kit was equally incommunicative. There is a tradition, perhaps not only in India, that women should not be worried, that the best way to ensure this is to keep them as far as possible in ignorance: and so now Kit insisted blandly that there was nothing to tell.

"But what did he *mean*," Premala persisted, "that you should know, as district magistrate?"

Kit spread his hands. "My dear girl, how should I know? I have never understood Govind. I never shall."

"You said you had heard," she insisted, "something of his activities."

"As district magistrate I hear a great many things," he returned. "It is part of my duty to listen. Do you expect me to remember and retail all that comes to my ears?"

After that there was no more to be said: certain domains belong to men alone, and Indian women learn early not to encroach. Kit knew he would not have to remind Premala a second time.

It was from Roshan that I learned the truth. She saw that I was worried—my face had not yet learned to keep its secrets; asked me what was wrong. Nothing, I said. She did not press me further, having a masculine way with her of never probing, of being able to drop a subject completely—however curious she might be—when she saw discussion of it was unwelcome, or the time for it unripe.

A few weeks later I told her.

"He's a member of the Independence Party," she said. "I am too, in a sort of a way."

"I didn't know you knew him," I said.

"We met, briefly, at Kit's wedding," she reminded me. "I didn't realize he was your brother."

"My adopted brother," I explained, "only I never think of him that way. . . . Is he—what does he do?"

"Organizes civil disobedience to government," she said, "only he goes further."

I think in that moment I first knew the meaning of fear. I could feel its slow black coils unwinding, felt the sudden hollowness of my body as all else retreated before that creeping darkness.

How much further? I said, and realized there had been no sound, and licked my lips and said again, "How much further?"

Roshan looked at me with pity. "A lot further," she said. "I do not think there are any lengths to which he would not go. Do you not know your own brother?"

I knew. Indeed I knew. Only I had hoped I was wrong.

-[CHAPTER FOURTEEN]-

IT WAS SHORTLY after this that Roshan went to prison for the first time.

She had been campaigning for some months to try to get third-class travel conditions improved. Each week she wrote an article describing some intolerable journey or other (all of which she had undertaken: I do not think she wrote even once of anything at second hand); of traveling a whole day on a slow train on a blistering day with no provision for water; of traveling on the footboards because the carriage would hold no more, or jammed in with a hundred people in a carriage meant for half that number.

Nothing happened. None of us, except Roshan, had expected anything to happen, and she alone was intensely and genuinely surprised by the result. However, she did not give up: arguing that the railways were guilty of cheating their passengers, she concluded (and published her conclusions) that it was in order for passengers to defraud the railways. Thereafter she gave up writing for a while and went off to organize passenger revolt, offering herself as leader.

Again, we did not think it would come to anything. People who travel, after all, wish to arrive; the idea of acrimony and arrest en route is not attractive. This, precisely, was what Roshan offered, and yet, before long, she had a following. Several times I went with her—at first out of curiosity, later because I could not help myself—watching while she harangued people on station platforms. It always came as a surprise to see—not how quickly she drew crowds, for I had got used to this quality in her—but how soon men and women were ready to follow where she led—not merely hotheaded youths with time on their hands, but ordinary sober (and mostly illiterate) people to whom the thought of flouting authority must have been terrifying, and to whom the sight of Roshan—fair-skinned, elegant, in vivid, lovely clothes and patently not one of them, whatever she might proclaim—could hardly have been reassuring. But they crowded round her to listen while

81

she disposed of their scruples one by one, and when she had finished, they would have gone with her wherever she went. This faith in her remained unshaken even when numbers of them were arrested while Roshan herself went free, and batches of travelers being hustled away under escort still turned to look at her with trusting eyes.

I think this injustice infuriated Roshan more than anything else, and day after day she undertook long provocative journeys in the hope of forcing the authorities to act. However, when you step out of your class and environment and embroil yourself in affairs which are clearly not your concern, no one is quite sure what, in the absence of precedent, to do. Moreover, if your father owns half the mills in the area and your husband is a member, reputedly influential, of government, there is even more embarrassment. The authorities preferred to turn a blind eye.

In final exasperation Roshan wrote a scurrilous article in personal terms about the management of the railway company, was sued by them, went to court, lost her case, was fined, refused to pay the fine, and went off, exulting, to prison.

I went to visit her there. The jail superintendent, a tall, frosty Scot, interviewed me first. Was I, he wanted to know, associated with the prisoner? Had I indulged in similar unprincipled activities? I was employed by her, I said, but no, I had not written any exceptionable article, or any part of any such article, which had been published. Also, I had never willfully traveled without a ticket. He was glad to hear it, he said, losing some of the disapproval with which he had been regarding me; the country could do without one more addition to its troublemakers.

"Roshan is not a troublemaker," I said, stung. "Or if she is, she has been forced into that position."

For a moment he surveyed me in silence, then he said icily, "Well, you may be sure she is not behind bars for keeping the peace."

"If she did break the peace——" I found myself saying, though the thought was there that I ought not to argue with this man, who might so easily refuse to let me see her——"if she did, she had good reason for doing so."

"No doubt," he said. "Most people can think up very good reasons for what they do."

"You don't know her," I said, "She——"

"On the contrary," he interrupted, "I know her exceedingly well. I've known her since she was born, and I knew her father long before that. We're very old friends."

I did not know what to say: so long as I thought of him as a jailor, argument came without difficulty; but seeing him now in this other role somehow dried that easy flow of words.

He did not look away, he kept his eyes on me remorselessly, almost as if he relished my confusion; but he only said quietly, "Naturally her father is——concerned that she should be here. So am I."

"I think he is," Roshan agreed when I repeated the conversation to her. And she added, with detached sympathy, "It must be difficult for him. I know my father badgers him, but what can he do? What could I have done either? I don't *enjoy* being an embarrassment to other people, I just don't shirk it either."

She may not have enjoyed it, but on the other hand it did not actively worry her; nor did the fact of her imprisonment.

I glanced at the bare square cell they had put her in, and in which—because of her father, I suppose—I had been allowed to see her alone, noting the gray stone floor, the hideous makeshift furniture, the small joyless window, the handleless door; and when I looked up at those steep converging walls, though I tried not to, I could feel a dry slow suffocation insidiously beginning; and I could not help wondering at, and envying a little, her imperturbability.

"I hope you're not too uncomfortable," I said at last, guardedly, and then honestly, "it must be very unpleasant."

"It is," she agreed. "Still, it's an experience."

She was one of those people who reckon almost no price too high to pay for it.

As I was about to leave, the wardress came with a message: the superintendent wanted to see me.

"This is no place for young people," he said peremptorily as I went in, "I hope we shall not have any fool-

83

ishness from you—I do not wish to see you where your colleague is."

"I hope you never will," I said, too chill and depressed to even attempt a spirited reply.

He glanced at me, and then his blue eyes suddenly lightened and he said, "It isn't all that bad you know . . . besides, people get used to it."

I did not agree with him—I was too young to realize he was right, that one does, indeed, get used to anything; but I nodded, grateful for his kindness, and mumbled my thanks and went out into the sunlight, and at the sight of the sky and air and all that space about me, felt my throat tighten once more in gratefulness.

Three months later Roshan was released. Had there, she wanted to know, been any improvements? There had, in fact, been some mild minor ones, but hardly such as would satisfy her; and so she proposed to publish what she called "some more home-truths."

It was Mohun, the editor, who dissuaded her. He was a tall spare man with a face the color and shape of an old violin, who had spent twenty of his forty-five years working under an Englishman who had forgotten the decencies of England amid the authoritarianism of Empire; and from this employment he had emerged with the wings of his self-respect permanently crippled. It was Roshan who had taken him from it; perhaps no one but she could have done so, and perhaps no one but Mohun knew what it cost him—a married man with children—to make the break: to turn from the security of a steady job on a government publication to the hazards of reporting for, later editing, an avowedly experimental magazine founded by as unpredictable a person as Roshan.

However, the combination had worked: she provided the fire, and he set up the safeguards, and the venture had at last reached the stage where its own circulation, and not Roshan's money, kept it going. Between them lay a steady regard, based on mutual liking and respect, and strengthened by a feeling in common for the magazine, which they had together nursed as it were from inception.

In the mood she was in, Roshan would hardly have listened to anyone else.

"One cannot rush matters," he said quietly. "Above all things, in this country, one needs patience."

"I like to see things happen in my lifetime," Roshan rejoined. "Do you think I care what comes after?"

"And do you think I do?" he retorted. "I also am only concerned with the present."

She stared at him, and he shrugged and said, "If people give trouble, they are locked up, but they survive . . . I would not like to say the same of a paper that was banned."

So long the feeling in the room had been divided, uncertain, wavering: now suddenly coalescing, it swung violently in favor of the editor, against Roshan, against any rashness which might lead to disaster. And at once Roshan gave way, for it was almost instinctive with her to know what people were thinking and to respond automatically to their reactions.

Roshan had not been out a week, and was still looking round for what she called "something worth while to create about," when Govind approached her—I think for the first time.

I had not seen him for four or five months—not since the night he had come to see Premala—and in that time I had thought of him always as he had been, discounting the evidence of those few brief hours. Now as I looked at him again—not twenty-three yet, but with the knowledge of twice as many years imprinted on his face—I knew the change was real, not a trick of moonlight or lamplight as my hopeful heart had made me believe; and the memory of him I had clutched so long slipped from my grasp and fell.

"We want your help," he said to her bluntly. "We need all the help we can get from people like you."

Roshan looked up. " 'We'? Who is 'we'?"

"Myself and my associates."

"And who are your associates?"

"Those who interest themselves in freedom," he said slowly, "as I think you know."

Roshan did not reply at once—she seemed to be studying her fingernails; then at last she said, equally slowly, "Everybody is interested in freedom . . . only, we do not all agree on the means to the end, as I think you know too."

He nodded. "Differences of opinion are not bars to service," he said to her. "We need people who can organize, and lead . . . not everyone has the gift. We need people who are not afraid of prison."

She was silent for a long time. On her table stood a small plaster model of a dam—a scale model, constructed with beauty and precision to the last detail, which some friend of hers had given her; she picked it up, handling it gently, lost in thought. Govind waited —silence was still his familiar, though the days of his inarticulacy were gone—showing no signs of restiveness. At last Roshan said, half to herself, "There is no power in violence . . . only destruction."

He made no reply, and she put down the model she had been holding and turned to him. "You see," she said, looking at him steadily, "I am not really interested in destruction."

Govind's gaze did not falter. "The one follows the other," he said. "First things first." But he attempted no further argument, accepting, for the time being, her decision.

After this, though I myself did not see him again for some time, I heard he came frequently to the office to visit her, or went to see her at her house. I was not surprised—he had all the patience that men bring to the stalking of a prize worth the capture. Nor did I find myself unduly anxious. Perhaps I might have worried more if I had been less fully occupied: but I was absorbed in work which took me out into the country a good deal. Also, I had met Richard again.

-◄[CHAPTER FIFTEEN]►-

MOHUN, THE EDITOR, often had what seemed to the rest of us strange ideas. However, they were so often proved right that we had learned to respect them: besides, one does not, after all, argue with one's editor, however approachable he is, however informal the atmosphere.

"More people are peasants than anything else," he said one day. "We ought to write about them."

"They can't read," some hardy objected.

"Others can," said Mohun shortly.

Another time he said, addressing us as if we were a class of schoolchildren, "The peasant is the backbone of this country. Never forget, he is extremely important." And then one day, to me, out of the blue, "There's a peasant resettlement scheme being started—I understand Her Excellency's the leading spirit . . . go down and see what you can make of it."

Why me? I knew nothing about peasants. Moreover, if they were as important as he said, why not send someone of equal stature to write about them, instead of the juniormost on his staff?

"Because you belong to the country," he said, "though you have strayed into a town. Besides," he added, "you're getting restless. A change won't do any harm."

I was used enough to having my thoughts read, it happened so often, but now I felt the blood mounting in my cheeks and turned to leave the room.

He called me back. "Why are you touchy about it?" he demanded. "We can't help what we are."

"I'm not," was all I could find to say.

To my relief he changed the subject. "This thing'll get more publicity than rural affairs generally do," he said. "But I don't want you to go to Government House and come back with a handout . . . I want you to go and see for yourself."

"All right," I said.

"On second thoughts, perhaps you'd better collect the handouts," he said. "Then you'll know what not to say."

"All right," I said again.

So I went to Government House, reluctant, a little resentful, because not only did I not know anything about peasants, but I was not especially anxious to learn either: but I am glad I went, for if I had not gone, I might never have met Richard, because I seldom went to parties and he, as one of the Governor's aides, never, he said, seemed to do anything else.

He rose, smiling, to greet me as I was ushered in. You would never have guessed, from that smile, that he was merely being polite, that he had had to be polite like this a hundred times before; but when he saw it was me it became different somehow—warm, real; the way it was now you could see what a paper thing it had been before; and one by one the tapers of pleasure began to glow within me.

"Mira! What are you doing here?" The same warmth in his voice, his voice the same as I remembered it.

"I don't know," I said, "what are you doing here?"

"You've changed," he said, "you'd never have dared to ask questions in the old days."

"I used to be full of questions," I protested.

"Not straight off," he said.

"It's three years, since," I said, "nearly three years."

Nearly three years. Was it? Could it be? Curiously, it seemed much more than that, and yet much less: an infinity to the day I had gone to welcome my brother with garlands and had given them instead to Richard. Yet it might have been yesterday—so clear-cut the memory, so crystal clear—that this same man had kissed me, lightly, and hoped for a happier continuation.

For the second time that day I felt the unruly blood come hot and panting to my cheeks, and I turned hastily and went and stood by the open window. Outside, a mali was watering the flower beds: the battered tins he carried flashed silver in the sunlight, the water flowed silver. His body, bare except for a loincloth, was almost the color of bronze against the baize green of the lawns. These lawns were the pride of the Government House: better than any in the residential areas, better than any in any of the clubs—almost as green, the English said, as the grass that grew in England. And surging over them, wave after wave of color, the cannas in their brilliant beds, vermilion and yellow and red.

"It must be lovely to work here," I said when my face felt cool.

He came and stood beside me. "The gardens are beautiful," he agreed.

The room we were in was beautiful too: large, high-ceilinged, with gilded cornices and a cool mosaic floor, the double doors with carved panels, the hangings of heavy brocade, richly patterned. In the middle of the room, under the fan, a mahogany table, inset with red morocco leather with a blind-tooled edging of arabesques, on this an ornamental brass inkstand and quills in the empty inkpot.

Richard sat on one side of this table, in khaki, wearing the scarlet aide-de-camp's armband. I sat on the other. We talked about grants and administration.

His hands were on the table, I saw how brown they had become; the hairs that lay on them had golden tips.

We talked about wells, and paddy fields.

How does one know when a man looks at you—when his eyes are on your hair, on the curve of your lips, on the lines of your body? I cannot say; but suddenly the knowledge is there and somewhere within you the tumult begins, you do not know how or where, and you find yourself responding, your whole self responds and it is none of your doing.

At last I rose to go. I did not want to: but that part of the mind which is not the heart insisted, coldly, that I should.

"Don't go—" he said abruptly, "unless you're in a hurry?"

"I must get to the village," I said, "I've been warned not to come back with a handout, or anything in lieu. I've been told to see for myself."

"You're too late to do that," he said cheerfully, "it's a good two hours away and no proper road yet. You shouldn't have sat here gossiping so long."

"You did most of the talking," I said.

"Because you know so little," he replied.

"I'm not a peasant," I said, "how should I know about villages?"

"Am I?" he asked.

"There are still hundreds of things I could show you," I said, annoyed, "which you know nothing of."

"You must," he said.

There were so many replies I could have made to this that I could not think of a single one: moreover, I was not sure whether to be pleased, or to keep on being annoyed.

He said, "I'm going to the village tomorrow. Would you like to come with me?"

Yes! I wanted to say, but a part of me, neither mind nor heart but a tortuousness whose existence within me I had not suspected, would not allow me to. I hesitated, I tried to be offhand. "I don't know . . ." I began.

"Please come," he said.

Somehow then I felt it would be all right to say Yes; and, also, it had become impossible to say No.

In India there is no fog. If you rise before the sun, on

89

a November morning—which is the best of the cool-weather months—there is a mist, filmy and beautiful like a woman's veil, and sometimes it is a pale, soft grey like fledgling down, or faintly purple, and you know it is going to be a cold day; and sometimes it is not grey but gold, even before the sun has risen, and then you may be sure it will be a hot day, as hot as the season can make it. But some mornings the air has many colors —as many colors as the lining of a shell—and these mornings are the most beautiful of all, and there is no way of telling what the day will be like, and because of this it is the more enchanted.

I rose early, that morning. Richard would not be calling for me until nine, but I woke at dawn and could not sleep again, so I dressed and went out, and when I saw what it was like, I was glad I had.

Kit and Premala were still asleep. None of the servants had stirred, except for Arikamma, the indoor sweeper, who was expected to finish her work before the others began and was bullied if she didn't; and she smiled when she saw me, a little surprised, but full of friendliness—the intimate friendliness that wells up between two people who find themselves alone awake in a world asleep.

"You are up early," she said, straightening up, one hand supporting the small of her back.

"Yes. It was too pleasant to stay in bed."

"It is the best time of day," she said simply, though I suppose she must have been used to it, and she smiled and went on with her work, stooping, sweeping in wide regular arcs, somehow accumulating, from the speckless floor, a small pile of dust and fluff.

I left her and went into the garden. Dew still lay on the ground, caught and sparkling in the overnight cobwebs, silvering the palm fronds; the gravel looked like wet shingle.

By seven it was all gone, and I went in, suddenly hungry: but breakfast was never before eight, however hungry you might be, and I had to wait, with little patience, while the servants looked at me, I thought, with equal impatience. . . . Then at last it was ready, eggs and toast, marmalade, coffee, which was the kind of breakfast Kit had got used to, and now Premala and I had got used to it as well.

Premala did not come down that morning—she had not been well for three or four days and had asked for a tray to be sent up. Kit seldom appeared before nine. I breakfasted alone, and had nearly finished when—unexpectedly early—I heard the sound of a car and gulped down my coffee and went out.

"I'm early," Richard said, getting out of the car as I came up. "I hoped you'd be ready. I was prepared to wait if you weren't."

I tried to think of something bold to say, but then I saw he was waiting for me to, and so I did not.

"I've been ready for hours," I said, climbing in. "I've been up since five."

"Whatever for?" he asked.

"It seemed such a nice day," I said lamely, feeling a little foolish.

"That's why I'm early too," he said, and somehow when he said that there was suddenly a new feeling between us, full of warmth and understanding.

The area in which we lived was always known as the residential area, though far more people lived outside than in it. It was also quite extensive for the comparatively few people who resided there. A half hour's driving, and we were still moving past whitewashed bungalows—large, airy, standing in spacious grounds, surrounded by well-tended gardens with neat clipped hedges and flowers in beds forming prim, precise patterns. There were no actual boundaries to this area, of course, but you could tell easily enough when you were no longer in it, because there were no houses or gardens like these anywhere else.

People like us lived in the residential area. Everyone else crowded into the city proper: and here the streets were narrow and the houses jostled each other, and there were no gardens and there was no order or pattern, only a great spreading untidiness.

And on the fringes of this untidiness, soiled and ragged and stained like a bandage that has been on too long, was the poorest district of all, where people no one else knew anything about lived: and here there were no houses at all, only hovels or shacks, built or fallen out of the perpendicular, tumbledown, inhabited, and here and there a lean-to stall selling beedis or sweet-

91

meats with flies clustered black and thick upon them like sunflower seeds, and everywhere mangy pi-dogs, scratching and bleeding in the dust.

I was glad when the last straggling hovel was past, and the city lay behind us. The road had narrowed now, there were deep ruts in it; you could see it winding away in front of you for miles, the country was so flat, but behind you could not see anything for dust—the swirling clouds of dust like paprika powder that the wheels of the car flung up on either side.

We stopped at the first village we came to, set in the pattern all villages are: a well, a paddy field, a clump of palms, a cluster of huts. It did not look as if anything was going on here—certainly not resettlement—it was too calm and peaceful for that.

"I thought you might be tired," Richard said.

I was dusty, but not tired. The day had turned out cool.

"Well anyhow," he said, "it's pleasant here. Don't you think it is pleasant here?"

I nodded, and we sat in the car in the shade of the trees, in front of us the limpid green of young paddy, while naked brown children came to look at us and the car, not clamorous but intensely curious, and with all the time in the world to stare.

We had not, but still we lingered, until at last Richard said, "I'm thirsty. Have you brought anything?"

"No," I said, "have you?"

He laughed. "Darling," he said, "am I a woman, to think of these things?"

So I climbed out of the car, and sent one of the children to bring tender coconut, and we drank the milk and I thought, It is full of sweetness. The world is full of sweetness.

It was, consequently, long after noon when at last we arrived. A great many people had gone there before us, who must have set off early and traveled without stopping; they looked heated and a little tired, as if they had been here some time and as if that time had not passed any too smoothly. There was a good deal of discussion going on, as there always is when plans which have been passed on paper reach the stage where they are being translated into reality. Also, it is no easy matter to construct, as it were overnight, a complete village: for villages cannot be rushed into life like towns. Theirs is a slower flowering, slower, and milder, beside a river or a grove, hut by hut, a thatching here, perhaps another tomorrow, a reaping and a sowing in the season, year by year, while a rhythm is established.

And yet, because of men, the attempt must sometimes be made.

The villagers, the first batch to be resettled, were standing in a group by themselves apart from the various officials. They were quite silent, even the women were silent, they looked a little dazed; and suddenly, watching them, I knew what it must be like for them, knew how it must feel to lose the land in which you have put down your roots. Dispossessed. That was the word used to describe these people; only, they had never possessed anything—certainly not the land by which they lived; although, because there is no other way of living, they had dared to imagine they had.

"Things need to—mellow a bit," Richard said, "before they look any good."

"Yes."

"In a month it will be quite different," he said; "I have seen it happen—twice before."

He had seen it happen twice before, who had not been three years in the country. For me it would be the first time, and I had come reluctantly.

"They are almost like weeds," he said, "they strike root so quickly."

But first, there must be the land.

I said, "I hear Her Excellency's gifted the land."

He looked at me queerly. "Does it matter," he said, "who gifted it?"

To those most concerned, no. To everyone else?

"Well," he said, ruthless, "does it?"

What could I say? In other countries, in other times, perhaps not: but here in India, in the middle of war and civil war . . . ?

I was silent and he sat quietly, "Has it infected you too—all this 'your people' and 'my people'?"

I thought, and I said No. I thought I spoke the truth. I thought there was no region of my mind I could not enter if I tried. I did not know—I was too young—that no man knows himself.

So far only a few huts had been completed—not by

93

the villagers who were to live in them, but by labor brought from the town. Several tents, however, had been erected—I suppose for the officials—looking curiously bleached and out of place on the red-brown soil—the largest of which seemed to be a sort of temporary headquarters for the various organizers.

A number of people were inside, both European and Indian, most of them standing—there were no chairs—but a few Indians squatting self-consciously on the ground.

In the middle, on a square deal table, a model of the village, mounted on hardboard, had been placed. It was crudely built, and painted in bright watery colors as if from a child's box of paints. Except that they were flagged, you would not have known what the various small buildings were: but the flags were explicit enough. "Dairy," one said; another, "Clinic"; a third proclaimed a school. There was something about these triangles of pasteboard—so forthright and bold, untouched by any doubts, so fearless in their claims—that moved me, making me wish that nothing would happen to belie those words.

"Richard——" I said, and stopped.

"Yes?"

"I hope nothing goes wrong . . ." I said. "I mean, I hope the money doesn't run out."

We had left the hut and were walking toward the car; now he stopped and surveyed me.

"Why?" he said. "Do you care?"

"Yes," I said.

He grinned. "Yesterday," he said, "you were not so concerned."

"How do you know I wasn't?" I said.

"Well," he asked, "were you?"

I said nothing and continued walking toward the car. He did not speak either until we had moved off. Then he said, "You aren't the only one—most people haven't any imagination either."

I made no reply. I sat huffily, looking out of my window.

"Darling," he said, "you look so lovely like that. Or any way. Did you know?"

The words fell sweetly on the ear. The heart did not

pause to question their truth. Pleasure came welling up and flowed and overflowed, a golden flood.

We were approaching the first village we had come to that morning—the palms were stiff black fans against the darkening skyline—when we stopped. I knew why we had stopped, I did not have to ask, but I asked all the same, and had not finished the sentence when I felt his mouth on mine, felt my body reaching up, straining toward him; but as we touched he drew away abruptly, and put me away from him and kissed me so that the flames died.

When I was calm again, he said, "You've grown. My God, how you've grown. In only three years."

But I had not been a child when we met, only he had thought so. And three years is a long time, to feel like this about a man.

⫷ CHAPTER SIXTEEN ⫸

To A LARGE extent life in a Presidency town was no different to that in the mofussil; the pattern was basically the same, though the colors were richer, the designs more elaborate. You went to the office from ten till five, played squash or golf, depending on your age, later; then there were drinks, and afterwards you dined with someone, or someone dined with you, or you went to whichever club you belonged to for bridge or billiards, or more drinks at the bar. On Saturdays the clubs held a dance, and fairy lights were strung among the trees in the garden. On Sunday mornings you joined a crowd in someone else's house for drinks and tiffin, or else you had a crowd in your own. If you were a woman, you arranged to meet other women three or four mornings a week to play mah-jongg, and another two or three mornings to roll, as part of your war effort, bandages for the Red Cross. And then there were the Government House balls—one when the hot weather began and the season ended, another when the hot weather ended and people came trekking back from the hills, and the third when the Birthday Honours Lists came out. Not to be seen at least at one of these balls was enough to consign you to that social limbo where no one recognized your existence any more, and no further invitations came your way. So three times each year there was some anxiety and some tension and some heartburning, and much journeying to and from the lodge at the gates to the Government House where the Visitors' Book was kept, and a great deal of maneuvering which only barely managed to stay polite, and the atmosphere did not relax again until, thank goodness, the gilt-edged card arrived.

For those who knew its codes and customs—many, and unwritten, and not only sparingly communicated to uninitiates but often incommunicable—for them it was an agreeable enough life. For those who did not, there was no place: and, if they still presumed to enter, no pity. Govind was not and had never been a part of it. To him it was the product of a culture which was not his own—the culture of an aloof and alien race twisted in the process of transplantation from its homeland, and so divorced from the people of the country as to be no longer real. For those who participated in it he had a savage, harsh contempt. But Kit did not merely participate in it: he was a part of it; his feelings for the West was no cheap flirtation, to be enjoyed so long, no longer, to be put aside thereafter and forgotten, or at best remembered with a faint nostalgia. It went deeper: it was understanding, and love.

It was Roshan who came nearest to him in liking and sympathy for the ways of the West; but she belonged to the East too. Born in one world, educated in another, she entered both and moved in both with ease and nonchalance. It was a dual citizenship which few people had, which a few may have spurned, but many more envied, and which she herself simply took for granted. And curiously enough, both worlds were glad to welcome her in their midst. After she came out of prison, both the jail superintendent and the wardress came to see how she was getting on, and counting both as friends, she treated the one as she did the other. She visited her father's mills regularly, and the spinners and weavers spoke to her as if she were one of themselves. She went to dances wearing red lacquered slippers and saris as bright as butterfly's wings and not only Indians but Englishmen as well were eager to partner her. The mark of the West, which she wore so lightly, did not brand

96

her even in Govind's eyes: and his were stern and jealous eyes which had never softened lightly, or easily, and, of late, hardly at all.

And Premala? I cannot think of her even now—in the quiescence wrought by the passing of a decade—without flinching, without wanting to shy away from the memory of her, her quiet, pained bewilderment, her hurt, lost face. A lovely face, tenderly molded, which never lost its tenderness because she could never learn to be tough, but which gave up, one by one, the lights and colors of happiness.

If she had not loved Kit so much, she would not have tried so hard to please him: and the very earnestness of her endeavor, the awkward conciliatory concentration with which she strove to do the right thing, would have driven many a man more patient than Kit to irritation.

In the beginning they had gone everywhere together —for Kit tried as far as he was able, and no man can do more. But it is no easy thing, from the crest of a wave of popularity to be conscious always of the trough below, or to surrender the exhilaration of its peaks for the sake of those caught in the slough; and so (though she would never refuse when he did) Kit gradually gave up asking her to go out with him, and now—except to official or government functions where it was politic that wives should be present with their husbands—it was seldom that they went out together. Yet, inevitably, a certain amount of entertaining had to be undertaken at home, and though the servants were skilled and Kit an excellent host, still there was a part for her to play as hostess—a part difficult enough to play when the other actors belong to another world and almost speak another language, but for her, lacking both sophistication and the artifice that might have enabled her to conceal it, quite impossible.

Dinner parties, to Kit, were fun: he would come swinging home cheerfully after tennis, dash upstairs for a quick shower, come down glowing, delight the servants with a quip or a compliment on this dish or that, or an arrangement of flowers (they excelled themselves for him—many a memsahib would have been hard put to it to evoke an equal response) and, as eight o'clock came round, he would begin to sparkle. And Premala would

97

grow quieter, more rigid, more tense: and the graces which flowered so delicately when she was at ease among people she knew faded and stiffened into gaucherie.

"Here they come," Kit would say, and run down the steps to his friends, and they would come up in a cheerful, chattering group. And Premala would come out onto the veranda to meet them, smiling her diffident smile, and for a moment there would be a slight pause, then the conversation would begin again, flowing smoothly around and away from her, leaving her stranded on the rocks of her shyness.

Then there was dinner, and talk would revolve around parties that had been or were to be given, or the various sports tournaments at the club, or the doings of mutual friends, or sometimes (if someone had just come out) eager talk about London, the latest shows there, the score at Lord's, racing at Epsom, or about England generally. And Premala had little to say—and less and less as time went by—in any of these matters. She would sit silently, but without the peace of silence, flushing a little when a chance remark came her way, carrying out more or less automatically the actions that were required of her.

One night, she forgot. Dinner was over, the women were waiting for the signal to withdraw. It did not come. Somewhat desultorily the conversation, which had dropped, was revived; still Premala did not look up. To her left sat Mrs. Burdett—there were more women than men tonight—a junoesque woman who played tennis like a man and who usually partnered Kit. If she had wanted, she could have roused Premala from her preoccupation: a touch, a movement, were all that was needed. She did not so want; she sat languid, a little bored, on her face a look of extreme patience as if this sort of thing were, after all, only what she had always expected. Opposite, her husband, a short, not unkindly man, was stirring uneasily, trying vainly to catch his wife's eye: he looked as though, if his legs had been long enough, he might have kicked her, or even Premala, under the table. Conversation had begun to languish again: the pockets of silence were filled with awkwardness, embarrassment, sympathy for Kit, censure for Premala, a hint of pity too.

Kit, from his end of the table, gave up the attempt to

attract his wife's attention. He said, rather sharply, but with an attempt at jocularity, "Much as we like your company, Prem——"

At that, Premala looked up; her face went white, she rose jerkily, knocking over the saltcellar in her agitation. Clumsily, probably without thinking, she began to spoon it back, gave up the attempt, and at last we left the room.

By eleven—earlier than on other nights—the last guest had gone.

Usually Kit went straight upstairs to bed while Premala and I put away the silver and the drinks. Tonight he did not; he came into the drawing room, poured himself a drink, lit a cigarette and sat down, not looking at either of us, not saying anything.

After a little Premala stopped what she was doing. She said quietly, "I'm sorry, Kit . . . I don't know what made me forget. It was a stupid thing to do."

He looked up. "It doesn't matter," he said, a little wearily. Then, rousing, he added, "But really, Prem, it's such a small thing to remember."

If he had not been tired . . . a little ruffled as well . . . If the evening had been an easier one to sustain. . . . If, if. What matter now? The words were out—so reasonable, so full of hurt. And Premala had no armor either to deflect the blow, or to conceal the wound. She looked at him, stricken: her face went small; and then she went quickly from the room.

Kit sat for a moment irresolute, and then he followed her out.

I went on doing the little that remained to be done, slowly. Whisky in the cocktail cabinet—a garish thing all glitter and glass that lit up and showed its teeth when you opened it. Silver in the safe let into the dining-room wall. Then I remembered: Premala was wearing her ruby necklace . . . she would want to lock it away. Or would she? I hesitated a little, then I closed the safe door, pulled the heavy hasps to and locked it, sliding the panels over the keyholes. I was wondering what to do with the keys when I heard Kit come down again, heard him enter the drawing room and went after him.

"The safe keys," I said, holding them out.

He took them from me and laid them down on the table.

"You ought to put them away," I said, and obediently he picked them up and slipped them into his pocket. He did not seem to know what he was doing.

"I don't know what's wrong," he said. "I don't know what's wrong with her. Is it me? Do you know?"

Oh Kit, beloved. Staring at me like that, with my mother's eyes and my own too. So puzzled. So pained. Wanting to know, asking me. What shall I tell you? What is this devilish dispensation that gives clear vision to all save those most needing it?

Shall I say: She is a little upset, by tomorrow it will be forgotten? Or say: It is of no consequence, a storm that will pass with the night? Say: It is nothing; tomorrow I promise you, it will be as nothing. Say it, promise it. See that look go from his face.

I could not.

"It's late," I said, taking his arm, "you must get some sleep."

He did not seem to hear me. He was sitting, head bent, with his hands hanging loose and limp over his knees and his hair fallen over his forehead.

"It's very late," I said again, shaking him. "You must sleep, or you will be getting circles under your eyes."

He roused at that and smiled at me, a small tired smile. "Mirabai?"

"Yes, Kit?"

"You mustn't let me upset you," he said. "You mustn't let anyone do that."

He rose, pushing back the hair from his forehead. I still held his arm, I had intended seeing him to bed, but he disengaged himself.

"I'm all right now," he said gently. "Really, I'm all right," and he kissed me and I heard him go upstairs.

┤ CHAPTER SEVENTEEN ├

IT WAS AT Kit's suggestion that Premala first began going to the village.

"You might like it too," he said to her, "goodness knows why, but Mira goes often enough."

"I'm sent," I said.

"Not that often," he said.

Premala agreed: she would have agreed to anything. The docility natural to her had long fallen into listlessness.

We went once, and a second and a third time.

Richard had been right, it was amazing how quickly the villagers put down their roots. The scheme had begun late in November: by April the paddy was almost ready for reaping. "The first reaping," the villagers would say, and bring you a head of paddy and part the husk and show you, eagerly, the beginning of the white rice grain, and murmur, "The first harvest . . . the first of many, God willing." And we would echo, "God willing."

The village was not, as yet, as villages are: it still bore the look of its forced growth. But if you went early enough in the morning—before work began on the clinic, which was halfway towards completion, and the school, which was nearly finished, and the second well that was being bored, which was the noisiest work of all —if you went early enough you would see the blue smoke spiraling up from the clustering huts as the women baked the morning bread, and hear the wind in the paddy, and smell the earth, wet from the night's dew, and new thatching, which smells quite differently from thatch that has weathered, and then for a little you could almost believe that this village had always been here.

The fourth time we went—a day in June—the school had just been finished, and the man who had seen it through all its stages came out to summon us in. We were surprised: though we knew each other well enough by sight, we had never yet spoken, for we could see he was a missionary, and he could see we were caste Hindus, and between the two stretches the arid desert of un-understanding. Perhaps he felt he had to share his triumph with someone, though there was nothing in his manner to indicate he thought it so.

"I've so often seen you here," he said, "I thought you might like to look round."

No excitement, nothing to show that here was the culmination of many months' effort: the words were casual, chill, almost as if he were afraid of warmth. Yet there was something about him, an eagerness, well muffled in a cloak of restraint such as a man wraps about him who has known many rebuffs, but still struggling

101

into view, which made it a pleasure to say Yes, we would like to look round.

There were four classrooms inside—one large room, really, divided by wooden partitions—each provided with a blackboard mounted on an easel, a chair and a table, and three or four wooden forms in two of the rooms.

"The younger children will have to get used to sitting on the floor," he explained; and then, quickly (perhaps I had smiled—I had not meant to), "they are that, of course, but a stone floor is not quite the same as a mud one, is it?"

"Not at all the same," said Premala gently. "There is no kindness in it."

He looked at her, shadows of suspicion darkening his face as if he had not quite taken her meaning, as if he were used to the sly currents of mockery running beneath the smooth flow of men's words: but then he saw she was young and guileless and spoke as she was, and he relaxed—not entirely, perhaps he could never do that, but a little.

"I think you mean *comfort*," he said, "a floor can be *comfortable* or *uncomfortable*, it cannot be *kind* or *unkind*. Do you see what I mean?"

He spoke as if he were used to teaching, and Premala nodded, accepting his correction of her English. She might have been his first pupil in this as yet unused classroom.

"Yes, I do understand. . . . Only people can be kind, or unkind."

Now she was his star pupil: he gazed on her with delight. Nothing would do now but that we should see everything in that bare building.

We went upstairs: here there were two rooms, two long dormitories with double rows of string charpoys and one small cupboard at each end.

"We thought of individual lockers at first," he said, "then we realized the children would hardly have anything to lock up."

He began to smile sheepishly; we could not help smiling too.

"I thought this was to be a school," Premala said, "not a . . . a——"

"An orphanage," he finished for her. "Well, we thought it best to make provision from the first . . . in our experience orphans so often find their way to schools. They seem to know we won't turn them away. We wouldn't want to, either," he added hurriedly.

"And yet you cannot take in all who come?"

"We manage," he said simply. "We work, and pray, and our prayers never go unanswered."

Prayers are answered: buildings expand, money is found, children are fed. Almost he made us believe it, for somehow his faith stood firm: in the midst of poverty and starvation and human beings for whom there was patently no provider, his faith in providence remained unshaken.

As we were going Premala said, "It is indeed—indeed an achievement, all this . . ."

Once more he looked at her, uncertain despite everything. All this? All what? A building, none too large; a few sticks of furniture to sit on or sleep on, a blackboard or two.

"It must make you very proud," she said, quietly, so that even he could no longer doubt, and then you saw that indeed he was, his face came alight, the words "It does" were almost there; but even as they trembled on his lips he forced them back: the exulting fires that had reared so strongly dropped and died, suddenly, as if they had been deliberately trampled down.

"It makes me happy," was all he said.

Within a fortnight of the building being completed, the school began to function, and if you went there during the day you would see rows of children in the classroom, solemn, or surly, and most often curious, gazing at the missionary standing long and ungainly by the blackboard. Partly this was due to his efforts. Somehow within his yellowed bony body lay reserves of energy which sent him out day after day, coaxing reluctant children away from the sunlight into the classroom, and a tireless patience which kept them there long after lessons, from being a novelty, had become a serious nuisance. And, of course, he was helped by the fact that parents, busy in the fields, were not unwilling to be rid of their children for specified periods, especially with the added bait of one free meal.

Once the school began running, Premala's visits to the village became frequent and regular. Twice each week, she would leave home at eight in the morning, not returning until eight in the evening—even after the road had been surfaced, so that you could get there comfortably in an hour. And from each visit she came back glowing, revived, as if her parched spirit had at last found a spring at which to fresh itself.

Kit watched her, sometimes pleased, sometimes glowering, but without attempting to dissuade her from going. Once or twice he said irritably, "Really, Prem likes the oddest people," and again, "I can't think what she sees in that man, can you?" Which is a question no one can answer for another, and sometimes indeed not even for oneself.

After about a month of such visits, he said to her, with a sort of amazed curiosity, "I don't know how you can stomach it, Prem! All the proselytizing, I mean— after all, the chap's a missionary, he's bound to indulge —and really I don't know how you stick all that rubbish they put out!"

In point of fact Kit was no fervent disciple of Hinduism. If he went to a temple, it was because my mother had taken him; the last time he had seen a priest had been at his wedding; and if you questioned him about his religion, he would either treat it as a breach of good manners and ignore the question, or plead lightly to be spared and pass on to something else. Premala was different: her faith to her was a part of living, her feeling for her religion was deep and devout. And yet, somehow, at any slight to Hinduism, even the slight implicit in the preaching of another religion, it was Kit who came, bristling, to its defense: a loyalty, an aversion to interference, perhaps an inherited reverence for his own religion, made him impatient of, and hostile to, any who sought to convert its adherents. Perhaps Premala's faith was too deep-rooted to fear such pale winds as might play over it.

Now she said, serenely, "He means well, Kit. His views may not be ours, of course——"

"But they're so *narrow*," Kit protested. "I haven't met this particular chap of course—don't want to either— but I know the breed. I don't know how you stand for their impudent nonsense."

Premala looked at him. "He means well," she said

again, gently, "he is a good man . . . the children are already very fond of him."

To her, goodness of heart was almost the sum of perfection, and little else of consequence: for there are many keys that unlock the gates of men's liking, and each is differently fashioned. And so, with Kit, if you were light and bright and gay, and saw there was laughter in living, he was yours; and if you said to Govind, "I am of my country—it is my father and my mother," thenceforth he was your bond slave; and to Premala, if you were good, it was all in all, and she asked for no more.

One day Premala came back with a child—a small girl with eyes as bright as a blackbird's who still counted her age in months.

"She was found in the school," Premala said, looking a little guilty. "She doesn't seem to belong to anyone— the village crier is almost hoarse with asking . . . I said I'd look after her for the time being . . . the school's full, and besides she is rather a young child to be left there."

Kit said something noncommittal; he did not look any too pleased.

A week went by, and another. The child, with the happy adaptability of the very young, had already accepted this new home as hers. If she remembered whatever house it was she came from, or the mother who had abandoned her, she gave no sign. A brown chuckling baby, she crawled about the house with unflagging energy, clutching at whatever bright object she happened to spot, delighted if she was allowed to keep it, philosophic if it was taken from her. When she was hungry, she went to Premala and said so in her own unmistakable way; if she was very hungry, she whimpered, looking up trustfully at her new provider; and when she had been fed, she went to sleep and was not noisy again until the next morning or the next feed.

Kit liked the friendly child, but at the end of a fortnight he asked Premala what she intended doing about her.

Premala was sitting on the floor with a few fluffy toys playing with the little girl. Now she sat up on the settee, taking the child on her lap.

"I don't know, Kit," she said, "I thought—I hoped we might keep her."

"Keep her!" Kit echoed, aghast. "Are you crazy, Prem?"

Premala looked up: her face was white, there was a sort of wary desperation about her, the look of a mother cat whose kittens you are taking to drown.

"She has nowhere to go," she said in a low voice; and then suddenly, passionately, "Please, Kit. Please let me keep her."

Kit looked at her, startled: he had not seen her so vehement before. "Well, yes," he said, "if you feel so strongly about it. But really, you know, people will think I've slept with the serving maid and this is my bastard and you're just being nice about it."

"Does it matter," Premala said, "what people think? Besides, she doesn't look a bit like you."

"Children don't always show a likeness to their father," said Kit impatiently.

"Bastards always do," Premala answered, smiling.

Perhaps inevitably, there was talk. Though the town in which we lived was large enough, the circle Kit moved in was select and small; and where infidelity might have been looked on with a tolerant eye, what appeared a blatant acknowledgment of its existence pleased no one.

Premala did not mind. She had said, quite sincerely, that it did not matter to her what people said: and the important thing to her was that the child should have a home. Kit did mind; he chafed and grew irritable, and the child seldom, now, found favor with him; but still he allowed Premala her way, for gentleness was a part of him as I know. And Premala, seeing how it was with him, kept the child out of his way as much as she could, and her visits to the village, where both she and the child were accepted, where the situation did not appear as impossible as it did in the town, grew more frequent. Indeed, it was becoming her world, for she could find no place in the one her husband inhabited.

CHAPTER EIGHTEEN

I DON'T KNOW how, when you're in love, you manage to do anything except love, because all of you is taken up with this splendor. Yet I ate and I slept, and woke up and knew what went on about me, and I went to the office and worked—I suppose adequately, no one complained—and sometimes, though rarely, I split in two in the way one does, and the detached part surveyed the other and said, "You are happy, but it is a madness"; and the part that was absorbed knew it was happy without telling, and for the rest did not care, but went on its way exulting.

When the village was coming to life, Richard and I saw each other about once a week; then it began to breathe on its own and there was no longer any need for us to go, but still we saw each other once a week; then it was twice a week and sometimes oftener, and even this was not enough, and at last we were meeting each other wherever and whenever we could. The years between were, already, shifting and contracting: sometimes, walking through the bazaar lanes, I almost felt that I was back home, that Richard had never left, that he had always been like this beside me. I think he felt the same too, for one day he said, squeezing my arm, "I think this has been going on for a long time, don't you?"

"Yes," I said, "for me it has."

But those had been days of leisure: the long, slow hours had belonged to us, giving us full glorious measure of time in a way that was no longer possible. Now when we met, it was in the evening, after a good part had already been taken from the day; and though we made inroads into the night (sleep weighing but little in the balance) we seemed hardly to be together at all.

Yet I suppose it only seemed so, for we contrived to do a great many things. We lunched together nearly every day. We dined—not at the club, where we were known, and Richard was popular, and I could not keep him for myself alone; nor at the only hotel in the town— where there was one bar for officers and another for men, and people looked at you with speculative eyes whichever bar you went to—but in restaurants and tea-houses we found for ourselves in lanes no car could drive through, and where consequently we never saw anyone we knew. Wandering through these narrow streets and alleys was to tread again the paths of childhood, when many hours had been spent in just such happy anonymity with as little count of time: in childhood, before codes of conduct reared up and society hung out "not done" signs, and "residential" and "nonresidential" districts were as one in childhood's direct mind, and both equally capable of entry and occupation as they were compact of interest. And Richard? The conventions of his caste were no less rigid than mine: he came of a race which had acquired an empire, to which the people at home were largely indifferent, and of which the people on the spot were largely ignorant—and indeed, often confessed to this ignorance in accents of achievement, as if knowledge of an alien language or culture, or art or literature, or the understanding to which this might lead, were somehow shameful, disdaining those who now and then suggested it might not be a bad thing, after all.

At home, however, I had not known variety like this, for now we came upon quarters that were wholly Chinese, or Arabic, or Armenian, or Turkish—each with its distinctive flavors and foods and aromas, no less strange to me than to Richard.

Once, in a Chinese restaurant—well pleased with the place, and the food, and the green mild tea no less than the delicate cups with tiny lids in which it was served—I said to Richard, "I would never have come here but for you. And I would never have known how much I was missing."

He considered me with level eyes. "Why not? There was nothing to stop you."

"You don't understand . . ." I began, and I was going to launch into an exposition of conventions, but they had become unreal now, I felt I could never explain how those paper chains could hold me. I said instead, "It wouldn't have been much fun, coming alone," and he laughed and agreed with me.

We sat so long over our cups that the dregs of the green tea looked like the dregs of everyday tea; and at last the proprietor came to light the lamps, carrying oil to replenish the lanterns hung in niches in the walls, and tapers, and an earthenware dish with live coals in it from which came a thick, sweetish smell, and a pipe which he proffered to Richard.

"Benares opium," he said, kneading skillfully, pressing the pellet into the bowl, "it is the best."

I could not be sure whether he spoke the truth, or whether he said it to please me; but the smell was good. When at last we left, the proprietor came to see us go, parting the bead curtains for us, beaming, insisting that we come again, but we never did because we were never able to find that particular alley again.

One day we went to a Brahman restaurant, and Richard took off his shoes and sat on the floor like everyone else, as if he had been used to it all his life, and pleased the cook so much with his praise that the man kept popping in and out with fresh delicacies . . . and I thought, almost bursting with pride, there is no one like Richard, no one at all like my love.

If there was time—and you have to make sure you have plenty, in India a performance can last half the night—we went to a play, and sat in the very best seats, which were cane chairs put right up against the stage almost among the musicians, and the actors would sometimes introduce a few words of English into their dialogue, out of courtesy for Richard. . . . But Richard did not really need such help, he knew many of the stories from the Mahabharata, and he could follow what was said.

"I don't know another Englishman like you," I said to him one day, full of delight.

"You don't know any other Englishman," he said, which was true, I had only met others; but still I could not believe there could be any like him.

"You must come to England one day," he said. "It is a beautiful country."

"As beautiful as this?"

"It is my country," he replied gently; and after a pause he said, "it is a pleasing country . . . you would like it."

"I would be lost," I said.

"Why?" he asked, "Am I lost here?"

"You are with me," I said.

"You would be with me," he replied.

Inevitably, there were parties. There had been parties

before too, to which I went when there was no way out; grateful enough that, since leaving home, the feeling of having two left hands came less often, but otherwise without much enjoyment. Now I found myself liking them. Being with Richard was pleasure in itself, but besides, he knew what to do and say, and took you with him, so that you were free to enjoy yourself; and moreover, if you blundered, he did not mind: and when your companion does not mind, blunders lose their enormity and dwindle and shrink to nothing, for indeed in themselves they are nothing.

But Sunday was the best day of all, because the whole of it belonged to us. The office did not open, unless something very special was happening; and even aide-de-camps are not required to dance attendance every Sunday. And so we would motor out into the surrounding country, and eat when we were hungry in whichever village we were nearest to, and drive back at dark along the dazzling flarepath the headlights created in front while behind the midnight blackness folded and closed in about us.

"I wish this could go on forever," I said to him one night, half dreaming, leaning against him contentedly.

"Do you, darling?"

"Yes," I said, quite sure of myself.

"You would be bored," he said.

"Bored!" I said, amazed. "No, never! Not with you, it would not be possible."

When I said that, I felt him change: his body grew suddenly hard, his arms about me tightened. In a moment the peace, the tranquillity, were gone, scattered, ousted by this blinding trembling passion; but even as I was in flames, he let me go, and I cried, breathless, clinging to him, "You forget, I am no longer in my mother's house."

"I never forget," he said, kissing me with closed cool mouth, pushing back the tumbled hair from my forehead, "either that or anything else." And after a little he said, "We must go there soon, to your mother, your home."

"Why?" I said, unwilling, ungracious. "There is no need."

"It is the usual thing," he said, "before one marries."

"For you?"

110

"For you. For me there is no 'usual thing.' I have no roots here, I am alone."

"You have your chains of office," I said, "you told me so yourself once."

"I have learned to wear them lightly," he said, "as they should be worn."

"If we go," I said, "promise me you will not take No for an answer. Promise."

"I cannot," he said. "Dearest, how can I?"

"Well then," I said, disconsolate, "promise me only that you will make no promises, such as my mother may ask you to make."

"I shall not do anything rash," he said, with a glimmer of a smile, "or promise the impossible."

So we went home together as the year was ending—Richard had not been able to get leave earlier—and my mother said No. If she had said the times were unstable, the future uncertain, that we were of different races, that ours was infatuation not love—if she had said any of these things, we could have countered her arguments one by one. She did not: she merely said I was too young to marry.

"And yet," I said, stung, "I was not seventeen when negotiations for my marriage began!"

"They were begun by Dodamma," she said tranquilly, "do you not remember?"

Which was true.

"Wait until you are twenty-one, it is not long to wait," she said, smiling, "or do you think it will never come?"

"Certainly it will come," I cried, "but how do I know Richard will be here when it does? What if he isn't? What if he has to go? Do you think this is peacetime, to wait and wait and know we will wake to our tomorrows together?"

It was out: the uncertainty, one's helplessness, the fear, the despair, never allowed into the consciousness but always existing there; kept locked and barred and never allowed freedom but sometimes, as now, breaking out in a wild, black, savage flood.

"If he has to go," my mother said, "I will not stand in your way."

As we were leaving, she said to him, "Do you think I

am wrong? I may well be wrong. . . . Is it an unreasonable request?"

"No," he answered, "it is not an unreasonable request."

"One has to be careful in these things," she said.

"Yes."

"One must be very careful," she repeated, her eyes on him.

And he said gently, "Indeed, it is so . . . I would not wish—I would not be otherwise."

We went back; and the new year—that never-to-be-forgotten year of 1942—had hardly begun when the Governor began at short notice a lengthy tour of the troubled country, taking his aides-de-camp with him.

-◄| CHAPTER NINETEEN |►-

KIT WAS NOT alone in disliking Premala's frequent visits to the village and, incidentally, her meetings with Hickey, the missionary, there; Govind, so often at variance with him, for once fully shared his feeling. But Kit's dislike was to some extent superficial: it was more instinctive than reasoned out. To him missionaries were impossibly earnest people who belonged to a class one simply did not mix with, whose peculiar beliefs and habits were beyond comprehending. Govind's feelings were different, deeper, more dangerous. To him missionaries were not merely men who assaulted the religion which was his, though he might not cherish it, impugning its austere dignities in a hundred ways; they were also white men, who not only set up their alien and unwanted institutions in the land but who, for the preservation of these institutions, invariably sided with those other white men who ruled the country, with whom otherwise they had little in common.

I do not know if he said anything then to Premala, but one evening when Kit was at the club and Premala had not returned from the village, he said to me, suddenly, the words bursting out as if he had brooded over this for a long time, *"Why* does she go? I cannot stand the thought of her going."

"If she goes it is because . . ." I began, and stopped short.

"Because there is nothing for her here," he finished. "Why are you afraid of the truth? Why do you not say it?"

But how could I? Truth or no, there are some things which cannot be said. Had he not startled me into unthinking speech, the sentence he had completed would never have been begun.

There was a silence, and after a while Govind said, "Even so . . . I do not know what magic this man has . . . can she not see him for what he is?"

What was he? A man toiling among people not his own, in a country not his own, for the good as he saw it and for a reward which most men, so far from envying, looked at with pitying if not scornful eyes.

"I do not suppose she goes to see him alone," I said at last. "The village is—peaceful. There are other things in it besides a mission school and a missionary."

He stared at me somberly. "You know quite well," he said, "that when she goes, she is to be found only in the school, and not in the clinic, or the dairy, or anything else that our people run."

I know after this he spoke to Premala, for she said to me, a little hesitant, "Is it . . . do you think it is—wrong—for me to go to the village?"

"Why should it be?" I said warily. "What makes you think it might be?"

She did not reply for some time—I thought she was not going to; but at last she said in a low voice, "Govind does not seem to—to approve of my going. He does not think it . . . wise . . . that I should be away so often. But you know, I cannot see what harm there can be."

She sounded baffled and weary, with the tiredness that comes to people who no matter what they do, find they are erring and do not know why; and I said quickly, "You must not let it worry you . . . Govind has never been easy. Perhaps he misses you . . . he has come to see you many times, and you have not been here."

She looked up at me then, and she said quietly, "Perhaps it is as well."

Was it as well? If she had stayed away from the village because of him, given him her company, would the chain in the sequence of events have been broken and

113

all of us spared what followed? Or would it have meant merely another, more deadly, chain being forged? After so many years the question still remains: and if the choice had been placed before us then, perhaps it would have been beyond our strength to choose. But, of course, there was no such choice.

I did not see Govind for several weeks after this, and though I was used to his abrupt disappearances, I could not help worrying, for disquieting rumors were circulating about him. There had always been rumors, of course, almost since he had left our home: but now they were no longer vague and shadowy, you could not ignore them even if you wanted to. I would have gone to see him, but Govind was not like other men, he had no wife or possessions to curb and corral him in any one spot, he came and went as he wished, swiftly, and I did not know where to look. From various people, from newspaper reports (for he and the organization he represented had grown to the extent where they could no longer be overlooked), I heard he was in this town or that, that he had been seen in the villages, that he had been involved with the police. At this time there were, it is true, commotions and uprisings all over the country; and I knew of them and read of the people concerned and they were names; but Govind was my brother, and so it seemed to my uneasy mind that troubles followed thick and fast, especially in his wake.

When he was arrested for incitement to violence, there was little surprise, only speculation as to what the term of imprisonment would be; but somehow he cleared himself of the charge. After this he came back to town. I did not know of his return until the morning the editor told me the offices of the *Gazette* had been burned down.

"Blundell escaped," he continued, his voice expressionless; and I remembered now this was the man he had worked under for twenty years. "He was lucky, the crowd had got out of hand." He paused, and then with sudden exultation, "But he'll never recover from this, never! He's too old—he's broken, finished!"

I stared at him, I could not believe I had heard aright, or that so kindly a man could harbor such savagery. I turned away at last: everyone I knew was changing, as if a miasma were abroad in the air, evil, inescapable;

and those you had thought to understand moved to strange, hostile regions where you could not follow and looked upon the face of violence; and when they turned again, you no longer recognized them.

"Govind has gone too far." The voice was quiet once more, this was the voice I knew. "I hardly think he'll get away with it this time."

He won't get away with it. He'll be imprisoned. Prison, where you don't see the sun unless they let you. Stone floor, gray converging walls. That door without a handle. The jail superintendent: This is no place for young people. And Govind's imprisonment would not be like Roshan's: the crime was arson and violence, the punishment would be meet.

"Are you sure it was Govind?" I said, reaching for the last forlorn hope, the way one does.

"Pretty sure," he replied, with pity.

We waited, while the loaded, heavy weeks went by. Kit, bitter, quieter than I had known him to be for a long time, said he had no desire to discuss the matter; Premala had never been one to thwart his wishes in any way; and so the three of us, locked each in our cell of silence, behaved as if Govind were not and never had been one of us; behaved, indeed as if he did not exist; and this unnatural pretense, bearing mercilessly down upon us, squeezed out such peace as we might otherwise have had, so that at a time when we needed each other most, we found ourselves hard put to it to avoid quarreling and were left almost rigid with the effort.

It was a relief when at last the case came up for hearing—a relief that was soon swallowed up in the tension that mounted as each day went by. And yet living went on, as it has to, with that impersonality, both blessed and hateful, which possesses the power to prevent disintegration. We went to the office, we came back; we listened to the news, went to bed, read the papers in the morning, and we waited; waited while the law, unmindful of any considerations smaller than itself, took its slow, ponderous course.

It was Kit who told me of the result. He had been in court, and he telephoned me as soon as the verdict was announced.

"Govind's been acquitted," he said briefly. "He's a lucky man."

Everyone had been so sure of his conviction, my mind had dwelt so long on prison, on imprisonment, that for a moment I could not take it in; and Kit must have sensed my bewilderment.

"He had an excellent lawyer," he said. "Roshan paid." After a pause he added, "She testified for him too, at the last minute . . . swore he'd spent the night with her. It was cleverly done . . . the lawyer made great play of her being a married woman, her reluctance to come forward . . ."

"But it isn't true," I burst out, "there's nothing between them! Nothing at all, I know there isn't!"

There was no reply—I thought we must have been cut off, though I hadn't heard the click, and I jigged the rest up and down frantically; when Kit came on again, he sounded far away. "You'd better tell Roshan that," he said, "or Govind," and even over the wires I heard the bitterness in his voice.

The day after his acquittal Roshan asked me if I would stay with her for a few weeks. Govind was going to, and she needed a chaperon.

"I should hardly think it mattered—" I said, "not after standing up in court and swearing he spent the night with you."

"You don't suppose *I* care, do you?" Roshan said, laughing. "It's entirely Govind's idea: he's worried in case his stock with his party goes down—apparently morals enter into everything in this country. They know what I did was for the cause, but if Govind really stays with me, it'll provoke a scandal unless I can point to a chaperon. Govind's got to be somewhere reasonably comfortable," she added, "he's a bit shaky still after his experiences."

It was as near as I had ever seen her come to seriousness.

"He could always come to us," I began, and then I knew that of course he could not any more. Not to Kit's house—Kit who had been a district magistrate, who was a collector, a senior member of the civil service, a part of the machinery of government and who helped it to function and not, like Govind, one who was concerned only to wreck it.

With the threat of Govind's imprisonment lifted, and Govind himself lying passive in Roshan's house, I put away my cares gratefully, if cautiously, and told myself he had learned his lesson and would be careful in future.

"If you believe that, you'll believe anything," said Roshan equably, sitting on the table swinging her legs, smiling, unconcerned. "Govind is in everything up to his neck. He wouldn't want to be otherwise. I don't know why you keep wishing for him what he wouldn't wish for himself!"

"Because I don't want to see him in prison," I said.

"It's not that bad," she said, as she had once before. "You always did suffer from overimagination. It's frightfully uncomfortable of course, but it's not terrifying."

I could not bring myself to believe her, but I took comfort in her words, for I knew it was only a matter of time before she herself went once more to jail. She had been associated with Govind in many of his anti-government activities—to what extent I did not fully realize until I went to live with her—and moreover, her weekly article, from being imprudent, was now sometimes virulent, Govind, in point of fact, collaborating with her in writing several of them.

The editor, I think, was cautioned: he had already warned Roshan, to no effect; now he warned her again. Roshan went her way unperturbed, bright and fearless as she had always been. Under Govind's tutelage she began—and kept up, which was more than many people did—a boycott of British goods. She stopped smoking; she gave up, regretfully, using lipstick, until one joyous day she met an American officer who kept her supplied with American brands; there was the time she sorted out all her British-manufactured georgette and chiffon saris and repaired with them to the maidan where she threw them on the bonfire which other women of her convictions had kindled and were feeding with similar fuel—thereafter wearing, not without some distaste, the prescribed rough homespun. One thing alone she refused to give up, despite all that Govind could say: she still kept her English friends. She did not agree with their government of her country, they were, she proclaimed more than once, insufferable as overlords, but as individuals, she insisted, they were pleasing, humane, civilized, charming. Then she would turn to me, her eyes alight with laughter: Did I not think so? And I would feel my heart bumping in my breast, and the blood hot in my cheeks, and agree that I did, while Govind turned away, stern, disapproving. Curiously, the English accepted Roshan as she was, homespun, nationalism and all: when she chose to go among them, her popularity was no whit lessened. There was something in her, a flame, a vitality, which drew people to her despite themselves; and this quality, which she possessed so lightly as hardly to be aware of it, enabled her to surmount the barriers not only of race and creed, but also—perhaps even more formidable—that of politics.

Summer was beginning: save in the early morning, or after sunset, the winds blew hot and fitful, leaving people jaded and listless. The earth, where you could see it, was beginning to parch: already on its brick-brown surface lay the first faint tracery of lines which, later on, would split into wide gaping fissures. Above the pavements, from midday to midafternoon, hung the shimmering heat-haze, and until it dispersed and the slabs were cool once more, you would not see anyone walking on them save those who wore shoes or sandals.

In the residential area the smooth green lawns were mottled with brown, the flowers in the gardens were wilting for all that the malis, their bodies running with sweat, worked overtime watering the thirsty soil in which they grew. A fretful, ill-tempered time, like the beginning of a fever, when people find themselves querulous they do not know why, and others more unreasonable and aggravating than they have ever known them to be.

It was now that, suddenly, Roshan's paper was suspended.

There was nothing, of course, unexpected in this: we had all seen it coming, we had all told ourselves and each other it was only a matter of time; but the warnings had come so often, the rumblings had sounded so long, that when it happened there was still plenty of room for unpleasant surprise.

"I told you this would happen," the editor said to Roshan, on a note of outraged vindication. "Told you—how many times?"

"Oh, about a million," Roshan said impatiently. "The point is, what are we going to do?"

The editor made no reply; eyes lowered, he examined his fingernails; the others in the room were silent with him; and in the unquiet air were the anxieties, the fears for livelihood, family, and future which render men into cowards, and keeping these company, so many sharp invisible spurs to anger, accusation, reproach, and resentment.

"What are we going to do?" Roshan repeated her question.

The editor sat up in his chair, rousing himself with an effort which he made plainly visible; he did not reply directly at once.

"This is wartime," he said, "and in wartime there is little room for tolerance. Or even justice. The sooner one accepts that, the better."

"In other words?" Roshan's voice was calm with that excessive calmness which civilized people bring to cover their stresses.

"Do nothing," he said. "Send an apology and then keep quiet. Unless you want the suspension to be made permanent."

Roshan flushed; the color was bright in her cheeks. She knew, and we knew she knew, that feeling was running against her. At one time she had bowed to it, damping the sparks of her own fiery nature in reluctant obedience. Of late, however, more often than not she had elected to go her own way, although that was before matters came to a head. And now?

We waited, and the silence grew and towered above us, threatening any who should essay to speak. The hot color had gone from Roshan's face, even her hands were pale; small hands, long, pale fingers, oval nails, buffed and polished, looking curiously pink and naked without their customary coat of crimson enamel; but she was not looking down at her hands but at us, slowly, from one to the next; and at last she said, keeping her voice level, "Of course, if you are all prepared to accept this—if you don't want even to protest—there is nothing more to be said, is there?"

She looked round at us again; and indeed, there was nothing more to be said; and she went quickly out of the room, leaving us with the feeling, sour in our mouths, faint but unmistakable, that somehow we had been guilty of betrayal.

It was too much to expect, however, that, restrained in one direction, she would not erupt in another: the week following provided her with an opportunity after her own heart. For some reason or other—no one quite knew why, few could follow the tortuous workings of official minds in those days—certain areas were placed out of bounds to civilians: an order had already been in force for some time forbidding processions and meetings in public of more than five persons. Roshan, preaching freedom, loudly indignant, proceeded in defiance of both rulings. She called a public meeting, led the subsequent procession through the restricted areas, was arrested doing so, and in due course, but quite shortly, sent once more to prison.

-[CHAPTER TWENTY]-

IN JUNE RICHARD came back, ahead of the rest of the Governor's entourage. His bearer, a tall, impassive Northerner, was waiting for me with the note, and he turned away politely as I opened and read it. It was an impatient note, and only three lines to it:

> *Darling,*
> *Where on earth have you got to? I've been trying to reach you since this morning. Come when you get this—whatever the time.*
>
> *Richard*

It was now nearly seven. I had been out in the country all day—there was little inducement to stay in the restless, fermenting city, and with the office more or less closed, and only one of us required to go there each day, I had plenty of leisure to do as I pleased. Now I wished that I had not gone—there was not so much time that I could afford to waste any of it; I turned the note over and wrote "Coming" and handed it to the bearer, and then I raced upstairs to change.

Roshan, whom I was supposed to be chaperoning, was of course away; but when I was ready, I went down and told the servants I would not be in to dinner. Then, a little uncomfortable, I went in search of Govind.

"Richard's back," I said. "I'm going to see him—I may not be home until late."

He nodded. "Yes. I answered the telephone."

"I didn't know he was coming back today, or I'd have been here," I said, making uneasy conversation. Somehow Govind always made me feel a little guilty, for I knew he disapproved of Richard; and though I also knew this was not a personal dislike but one based on principle, and that the feeling he had for Richard he extended impartially to cover all who were British, it did not make matters any easier for me.

"I gathered that," he said dryly; and as I was about to go, he said suddenly, "You look lovely tonight."

I turned, surprised. Govind was not one to pay compliments; indeed, most of the time he hardly seemed to notice what you looked like, or if he did, never thought it worthy of remark. His face was serious, almost stern.

"You haven't looked like that for a long time," he said. "Is this so—important to you?"

"Yes," I said honestly.

"I know, I didn't have to ask," he said. "I used to hope it might pass . . . but there has never been anyone else, has there?"

It was not so much a question as a statement, but I repeated after him, "No. There has never been anyone else."

"And never will be," he said, speaking half to himself. "Isn't it funny how one gets tied up, and there's nothing at all one can do about it?" He stopped, and then, suddenly, violently, "I didn't believe that. I used to think it couldn't last, I used to pray it wouldn't. But it does, by God it does!"

He was sweating. I took his hands in mine and they were shaking. I began stroking them, and after a little felt him quieten.

"You must go, you are late already," he said, taking his hands away from mine; then, smiling, "You have an old woman's patience, dearest, to bear with me so long."

"It was not difficult," I said, and I meant it, for Govind's austere spirit seldom permitted anyone to approach, and moments such as these, drawing us close,

121

came so rarely now that none but a fool would have dismissed them when they did.

The clocks in the house were chiming the hour, as usual out of unison—Roshan liked to keep them that way, for some reason it delighted her that you could never tell the time by counting the strokes—as I went out to get the car. Roshan's car—a squat, ugly car which she had bought and painted and loved, and then, tiring of it, given me on indefinite loan. It was small and fast and furious, and had a disconcerting way sometimes of roaring like a tank, but I liked it because it was always so game. Like a peasant's donkey, it was sturdy and dependable, and however badly you treated it, it ran.

It was a dark, moonless night, with low cloud and most of the stars hidden. As I drove along, I kept wondering if Richard would be waiting for me—already he had waited all day, and then at seven I had said I was coming and it was now nine: would he still wait? More likely, I told myself, he would have gone out for a drink or dinner; and then I told myself, sensibly, if he was out, there was always tomorrow, but this thought made me a little frantic, and I had to reassure myself quickly that of course he would be waiting; as, indeed, he was.

He was sitting, as I had known all the time he would be, on the back veranda of the house, for it was here that the night wind blew when there was any. He was reading; the book lay open on his lap and he was leaning forward, elbows on knees and face propped in his hands in his favorite uncomfortable pose.

The glow from the small table lamp near by fell on his bent head, on his thick hair like bronze in this light, sleaved to a fine gold fuzz at the temples; on the milk-white nape of his neck, on the backs of his bare arms, tanned by the Indian sun.

He had not heard me come in; he went on reading, and for a moment I stood watching him. I had seen him, and not only like this, often and often. In the time he had been away, scarcely a waking hour passed when I had not thought of him and seen him in my thoughts, because that is how it is when you're in love. But to see him now, actually before me, was somehow overwhelmingly different; I felt my throat working and swallowed, and at that slight sound he turned and rose quickly from his chair and came to me.

"Mira. Darling, it's been so long."

I nodded, at peace and happy in his arms; but I could not speak, for the tears were coming; then they were there—splashing and spilling down my face—uncontrollable, unwanted, unbecoming tears which are one of women's plagues.

He held me closer, saying nothing; perhaps he knew happiness has a way, sometimes, of taking you by the throat, and then there is nothing at all you can do except wait.

"It's so nice seeing you," I said at last, "I'm so glad you're back."

"I wouldn't be, but for malaria."

Malaria. If you are born and live in India, you are, naturally, aware of it: but it is always something that happens to other people, peasants, or Englishmen. Now, impinging upon the consciousness, came from the darkness the small steady hum of mosquitoes, like the sound of an electric machine set at a low tempo, scarcely heard for its insistence. You could not see them except directly under the silk of the lampshade where they clung upside down, you could not feel them except once or twice when a less skilled mosquito burrowed too deeply for blood.

"You oughtn't to be sitting here," I said, "with your sleeves rolled up."

He smiled. "They don't come near, now. My blood's too bitter."

"Quinine?"

"Mepacrine. I'm almost yellow with the stuff."

"You ought to have a holiday," I said, "I'm surprised your doctor let you come back."

"He didn't. I just came. I wanted to see you before going away again."

I was silent. The happiness of a moment before seemed a mockery. Capped and belled, it jeered at me.

He said, "I wanted to come back before, when I heard about Roshan's paper, but it wasn't possible. I tried, I thought you would be upset."

Was I? Had I been? It had been a shock, of course. And later, when feeling flowed once more?

"I hadn't thought about it," I said at last. "I suppose

I was. One gets rather fond of the paper one works for
. . . and the silence is rather . . . unnerving."

The silence. That was it, that was the worst part. To
go to the office, and to find the clatter stilled, all of it,
typewriter and telephone and teacup; to go, and in place
of the usual noise and bustle to come upon this hushed,
unnatural silence; to wait, subconsciously, for something
to happen—for the operator to set the film in motion
again, for someone to slip the coin into the slot that
would start the machine up—and to know that nothing
would. I had thought to be with Richard, to exchange
these ringing silences for laughter, to flood the loneliness of those months with love. And now? And now.

"When are you going?" I asked.

"In a day or two."

"For long?"

"Six weeks."

"Where to?"

"I don't know," he said, "I haven't decided yet."

I said, surprised, "Can you go where you like?"

"Yes, of course. You don't suppose I'd go where they
sent me, do you?"

"Well, you do, don't you?"

"Not in a matter like this. Convalescent leave isn't like
a posting, or touring with His Excellency."

The night wind was stirring. I could hear it trailing
slight and frail across the darkness, a child's breath, no
more. My temples felt cool, where the drops of perspira-
tion were evaporating.

I was sitting on a cushion at Richard's feet, and I
leaned my head against his knees and I said, looking
beyond the circle of light into the darkness, "Take me
with you."

"Darling, I can't!"

"Why not?"

"I must think of you."

"I can think for myself."

"If you weren't so young——"

"Twenty isn't young. In wartime it's almost ancient."

"I love you so much," he said. "If you regretted it
later——"

"Why should I?"

"You've been brought up—differently. I've stayed

124

with you, I know your family. You're not like other women——"

"I'm exactly like other women," I said, striving to remain calm. "I have the same emotions, I feel the same things. Do you think the way you're brought up can stop any of that?"

"Are you sure," he said, "quite sure?"

I slewed round to face him then and I said, passionately, "Of course I'm sure, I've been sure for a long time. I've never looked at anyone else—there has never been anyone else from the day I met you. Even Govind knows that—he told me so!"

There was much more I wanted to say: thoughts came surging up out of the mind's deeps, and in their imperious jostling the bewildered brain was hard put to it to set words to them; and before I could speak again Richard bent and picked me up, was holding me in his arms; and he said, very gently, "All right, darling. We'll go anywhere you like, do anything you want."

"For peace's sake?"

"No," he said, and repeated again, "indeed, no."

Richard had one of those huge detailed maps the Army printed during the war. We spread it out on the floor between us, weighting the corners with books, and crouched down to study it, taking for our province the whole of India as if there were no part of that subcontinent inaccessible to us, as indeed in theory there was not.

"Kashmir," I suggested. "I've always wanted to go."

"Where would we stay?" Richard asked. "We'll never get a houseboat at such short notice, the hotels will be full."

"Any hill station, then," I said. "Naini Tal or Simla. They're both supposed to be rather nice." I was not keen on hill stations myself, but the climate would be good for Richard.

He pulled a face. "You know how awful they are in the season. We might go there afterwards."

"Afterwards?" I repeated, incredulous. "The monsoon will have started by then."

"So much the better," he said; and then, amused, "You've never seen a monsoon in the hills, have you? It's an experience."

I hadn't; we always left at the first gusty preludes. Now I found myself thinking perhaps it was something better seen than missed. So afterwards was settled. But first?

We pored over the map; we closed our eyes and stuck pins in it; Richard got out a guide book and we studied that; we could not decide.

"We'll leave it to chance, it often proves the best way," Richard said at last. "Plans are tiresome anyway. We'll go where the spirit wills and see what each day brings."

I stared at him: going anywhere without precise planning was alien to me—there was no member of my family who would not have regarded it as a lunatic, if not dangerous, proceeding. At home a holiday, or any kind of travel, necessitated vast prior organization: bookings were made, tickets bought, reservations checked and double-checked, and baggage packed and sent in advance to mitigate the first anguish of arrival; and it was only then, moving in the middle of a phalanx of servants, well cushioned against such blows as might fall, that we ventured forth.

Since living away from home, a lot of these frills had been cut; but, still, one did not in trustful simplicity go where the spirit willed; and indeed the spirit, from long disuse, would hardly have known how to will. The idea, however, was appealing—the longer I considered it, the more pleasing it grew: and it seemed to me now there was nothing I would like to do better than simply to drop the clutter and walk free. At the very thought I began to feel light somehow, as I imagined a soldier might who at the end of the day sheds his accouterments; and I nodded and said Yes, I thought that would be the best way.

Richard looked up, smiling. "Was that such an effort?"

"It was," I admitted.

"I thought so. But I don't think you'll be sorry. Which way shall we go—north or south?"

"We'll toss for it," I said.

And so, with delightful ease, we decided to go south.

There was little difficulty in getting the necessary leave. The editor had already said now was the best time if anyone wanted to get away, he expected we would be busier than usual after resumption of publication. Actually, I was the only one to ask for leave: we were all on half pay, and I suppose the men at least thought it best to go carefully.

Roshan of course left most of these matters in the hands of the editor: she acknowledged him to be abler, and anyhow she was fair in all her dealings with people; but nevertheless I went to see her, subduing, if not conquering, my usual dread of prison. To my relief—I say relief, though I did not really expect anything else—I found her as cheerful as ever.

"Of course you must go," she said, "it'll do you good. Where are you going?"

"Where the spirit wills," I said smugly.

"Really?"

"Yes, really."

She got up from the wooden bench on which we were sitting and moved to the small window set high in the wall. If you stood on tiptoe you could look out, but there was not much to see: a covered, paved courtyard, circular, with a patch of earth left bare in pity for a date palm, stunted and twisted and with half its roots exposed, that had somehow struggled into existence there. For a moment she stood looking out, her back to me. She was wearing her usual homespun—political prisoners were often allowed to wear what they liked; the coarse, lumpy material clothed her clumsily, giving illusory bulk, yet I could see how thin she had grown, even as I knew it was not prison that was to blame, for she was one of those people who live for the spirit and by it. Even in the past, for all her grooming and elegance, it had been so: the spirit was nurtured and cared for first, and it was only then, carelessly, as an afterthought, if there was time, that the body was thrown its scrap of attention.

She said, not turning, "I wonder if you realize you've changed. And how much."

"I think I do," I replied, "but it isn't only me."

"No." Then, looking round: "Still, I'd never have thought, when I first met you, that you'd travel quite so far."

"We've all come a long way," I said, "beyond going back."

"You're not sorry?"

"No. Are you?"

127

She said, laughing, "What do you think? Of course I'm not sorry! I'd rather go to the devil my own way than be led to heaven by anyone else. And I wouldn't give up being free like that for anything . . . it hasn't always been that way—no, not even for me!"

I understood quite well what she meant, although nowhere else could she have been as securely fettered as she was here, behind a locked door in a cell behind the high walls of a prison; and yet, of course, here she kept her freedom. It was more an instinctive understanding then a reasoned one: if anyone had asked me for an explanation, I should have been hard put to it to supply a coherent one. But then none who belonged to my generation would have needed to do so, and to those who did not belong, the sense and the spirit would alike have been incommunicable. It is this shared understanding, this common awareness, diffuse in the atmosphere, yet not absorbed by all, which makes the ground split, the crevasse to appear, between one generation and the next.

CHAPTER TWENTY-ONE

SOUTHERN INDIA, IN June, is extremely hot: by any standards, and even if you are born there, it is hot. The sun seems very close; it climbs swiftly, and when it is vertically overhead, it glares at you in a white-hot fury out of a pitiless sky. People take shelter then, in shadowy thatched huts or under a palm; behind water-sprayed khuskhus blinds in their bungalows; under the fans and high ceilings of cool club rooms; beneath the gaudy sun-umbrellas that open like exotic flowers beside swimming pools. They drink the clear cold milk of tender coconut, or suck the moist, dewy flesh of the red watermelon, or sip gin and lime out of glasses frosty with ice. Most of all, they stay as far as possible indoors: it is the sensible thing to do.

But one cannot always be sensible; and it is hardly possible to traverse a thousand miles of country under cover.

We were motoring slowly south, keeping mostly to the banyan- and tamarind-lined trunk roads which connect the main towns, but sometimes branching off onto lesser roads or even cart tracks to come to the interior. When these petered out, as they often did, we walked, leaving the car in a ditch, or perched angularly upon a bank, immobilized, somehow incongruous in a country of open fields and oxcarts and cross-barred plowshares. Except for the car, we were traveling light: no thermoses, no rugs, only one change of clothes and one case. After the cumbrances of a lifetime, I found this pared simplicity singularly pleasing. I could hardly rid myself of the conceit that, like a hermit, I had peeled off the superfluities to come at last to the core.

"I could live like this forever!" I said one day, in an excess of enthusiasm. "I know I'd be perfectly happy."

We were sitting on a charpoy in the shadow of a hut, eating roasted Indian corn. The kernels were tender and milky, and arranged in even pearly rows along the spike. Our host, first suspicious, then curious, then courteous, had picked them for us himself, choosing from amongst the best in the still unharvested portion of his rustling field. His wife had roasted them over a wood fire—the tang of smoke, a rough pleasant burr, lay faint and tantalizing under the taste of the corn.

Richard said, "I feel I could too; at this moment I'm certain I could. But you know, I don't think one can keep the world at bay for a lifetime?"

"People do," I said.

"Not people like us," he said, "and not in times like these."

In front of us the land stretched away endlessly in the hot colors of summer. Bleached yellow of maize and millet stubble; the brownish-red of turned earth; the scrub, withered and whitened; the fields of golden sugar cane, thriving in the heat, stiff and bristling like sabers, the liquid sugar rising in them like sap. Soon the colors would change: the stubble would be lifted, the cane cut, the earth sown, the fields would be green once more, the gold mohur shed its flaming petals. This was the permanent pattern, changing only within its set frame; this was the world, this was living, not the other of parties and factions and prison and rioting, of panoply beyond need and complexity beyond understanding, where you walked with care and looked for the meaning in the unspoken halves of speech, where the only changes you saw were in the natures of men, unforeseen, unforseeable, coming by dark, secret ways and altering them in the twinkling of an eye. And yet it was our life, by our own choice, by being born when we were, even, if one were so minded, by destiny. We created it, as much as it created us; belonged to it as much. This other living, so briefly ours, was an escape, an interlude, set in a definite limited span of time: when it was over, and the last grain of sand had run through, there could be no glib turning of the hourglass. To keep our peace, we would have to go back then to the world from which we came, to which we would always return because it was a part of us even as the earth was of these others who stayed. We could no more renounce it than a bird, the air; or fish, the sea; or any other creature, its element; even though it might be one we had evolved into, rather than one into which we had been born.

Richard said, "You look so serious. Too serious."

"I was thinking."

"You mustn't do that," he said, "not while we're on holiday. There'll be plenty of time for that later."

"I didn't want to," I said. "You started me."

"That's soon remedied," he said, pulling me up. "Come on, we haven't seen anything of this delectable place."

With Richard, one always had to do a lot of walking: it was only determination on my part, and often sheer mulishness, which kept it within reasonable limits.

On the tenth day we came to the ridge of jungle country which begins on the borders of Mysore and extends well into the interior of that state; and here, for easier progress, we decided to leave the car. There are, in fact, good motoring roads for those driving through: but if you are meandering for pleasure and without stern purpose, it is best to travel as the people of the region do—on foot, or by bullock or pony cart. And here, for the first time in my life, and in Richard's, which was not so strange, we saw, struggling through a tangle of jungle grass and creeper, and quite near the dâk bungalow where we were camping, a half-grown tiger. It was lame, otherwise it would have got away long before we were anywhere near; but some sportsman had shot it, and before it could stumble away into the undergrowth, we had a close view of massive shoulder and smoldering eye and snarling hatred.

The bearer in charge of the dâk bungalow, an old man with a brown, lined face who reminded me of Das, almost wrung his hands in his concern for us: in all his time he had never known of a tiger approaching so near the travelers' bungalow; in the morning, before sunrise, he would have the beaters out; and even thereafter we must not venture out alone—he would himself see to it that we were safely escorted. To think—he shuddered —of what might have befallen us!

"It bolted as soon as it saw us," Richard said gently. "I don't think we were in any danger."

But the man would not be comforted: we were in his trust, and he would discharge it honorably. True to his word he provided a guard—two stout men, armed with staves, who came crashing through the undergrowth after us wherever we went. This made the bearer happy —you could see his face visibly relaxing—but on the second day we decided to move on. The old man came to see us off, smiling, and, I could not help surmising, pleased to see us go: perhaps it was a relief to him to have us leave his domain still, as it were, in one piece.

And from there, still traveling by easy stages, we came, at the end of the second week, to the southernmost tip of India, beyond which there is no further land progress except up along the east or western coasts. Before the British came it used to be called Kanya Kumari; afterwards it became Cape Comorin and remained so until they left. The locals themselves have never known it save by its old name, and whether you call it by the one or the other depends on which school you went to, and when.

If you look at Cape Comorin on the map, you will see that here the V of India comes sharply to a point, and be aware, as you walk on the sands, that under your feet a continent ends. Nor does it need much imagination to enlarge the map and see, as though in actuality, the two coastlines converging and meeting and shelving down to the sea—the sea which one side is the Bay of Bengal and on the other, the Arabian Sea, and you can beguile yourself with the fairy thought that you can bathe in the waters of either.

Built on the sands, overlooking the sea, stands, sumptuously, a hotel: quite empty at this time of year, but still with its retinue of servants. There being no other building in sight, we booked in here, myself with an acute awareness of our lone suitcase, our lack of presentable clothes, Richard complaining that the place was hollow and rang. And so, after only a half-day, watched by the amazed servants—who could not imagine where else we could stay in this sandy desert—we moved.

This time we were lucky, for when we had walked a couple of miles—away from the hotel, from its swimming pool, its reserved beach, its patch of sea, tamed by breakwater and wired against sharks—we came across a row of catamarans and fishing boats drawn high up on the beach and bone dry, as if they had not been used for some time; and, turning inland at this point, soon came to a small fishing settlement.

The head of this community, a tall man with a lean body burned almost black by the sun, treated us at first with some caution, which was not altogether surprising: there is after all no place on earth where deviation from the usual is not also taken as a deviation from the normal; but complex societies, without either the time, the will, or even the ability to distinguish between the one and the other, have a way of forcefully urging you towards conformity, whereas less sophisticated ones still possess the quality of simple acceptance.

Once he was assured of our harmlessness, the headman insisted on placing his own hut at our disposal. I suppose he was glad of what we would pay—a fisherman's living is meager enough when the catches are coming in, it must often be austere when the boats are laid up—but withal it was a kindly gesture, for any lesser one would have done. As things turned out, we hardly used it at all, for the nights were warm enough to sleep out, and as far as Richard was concerned, the whole day could be spent in the sun, or in the sea.

"Remember what happened to you and Kit last time," I said warningly. "You'll be sorry for all this nakedness."

"Why," he said, "don't you like it?"

I looked at him, wet and sparkling from the sea, and I could not deny it. Already, though this was only the third day here, he was beginning to tan, the color lay evenly upon him, no longer ending abruptly where his clothes began. A creature of gold he seemed, lying there in the sun, with the water dripping from his hair and glimmering on his forehead, his body turned to a pale gold, the hairs glinting golden against the skin, the skin as tight and firm as a silken sheath. A body that might have been sculptured, though not from marble, hard and smooth, lean-flanked, its lines and surfaces clear-cut, unflawed, and a warmth to it—such a warmth, that could wrap you about gently or make you melt, or set you on fire and burn with an incandescent heat itself. And yet seeing him as he was now, quiet, serene, passive, the passion was not to be suspected. But I knew, although each time it came as a surprise, an incredulous ecstatic surprise as if it had never happened before; and I hugged the knowledge to myself, the knowledge, one of the other, that lies—rich and full and splendid, their supreme secret—between a man and a woman.

Richard said, raising himself on an elbow, "What are you thinking about?"

"About you."

"What about me?"

"How passionate you are."

"Does that surprise you? It shouldn't, I've waited for you for a long time."

"Too long," I said, "I used to wonder——"

"If I had any blood in my veins?"

"Oh not, not that," I said emphatically, "never that. Only I used to wonder at your—your restraint."

He said, gently, "A man doesn't take a girl the moment he feels attracted to her, if she means anything at all to him."

"But later," I said, "when it wasn't just attraction, when you said you loved me."

"Don't you know why?"

"Because you weren't sure of yourself?"

"Because for you there has never been anyone else. You told me that yourself, but you didn't have to."

The atmosphere between us was moving, changing, alternating between light and dark as swiftly as might the surface of the sunlit sands we lay on under scudding cloud. His eyes were on me, I saw them darken.

Even in the clarity of that midsummer day they were more black than blue.

"A man doesn't lightly lie with a woman," he said, "when it's the first time for her. Especially if he loves her. It is better to wait for her to come to him."

As I sat silent, he reached up, pulling me down beside him.

"I fevered for you so long," he said, "it became a permanent ache. Can you understand that?"

"Yes," I said.

"I'm still in a fever for you," he said, kissing me; and his lips on mine were without gentleness, and his body against me was no longer passive. Obeying some obscure instinct, I struggled away, moving away from him, his urgency, striving to sit up.

"Not here," I said, "not——"

"Yes, here. Now."

"No," I said, breathless, "it's——"

"We're alone," he said, holding me still. "Quite alone." And the skies were empty, the sands were bare; I listened and there was only the sound of the sea.

"You see," he said softly, "there is nothing and no one. No one but us."

Slowly my senses awoke and responded, the buds of feeling swelled and opened one by one. In the trembling silence I heard the blood begin its clamor, felt its frantic irregular beat; then the world fell away, forgotten in this wild abandoned rhythm, lost in the sweep and surge of love.

When I awoke the sun was setting; its brilliant orange disc hung low over the horizon, suffusing land and sea and air alike with an intense amber glow. The effulgent light came streaming down upon us, without warmth, but touching our bodies to a fiery copper.

Richard was still asleep, one arm flung heavily across me, his hair tousled and tumbled across his forehead, his face flushed in sleep. I lay very still, not to disturb him—so still, perhaps, that he roused, calling me softly.

"Mira?"

"Yes?"

"I wondered if you were awake, that was all," he said, turning on his side to look at me.

"I've only just woken up," I said, moving back against him, half drowsy still, warm and contented.

He said, with the tenderness that comes to a man afterwards, "I'm so happy with you, darling. You're wonderful to be with—not just now, all the time."

"I wish we could be together all the time."

"We shall be, soon."

"But you may have to go away."

"I'll come back. I'll always come back to you."

I believed him, believed he was right—as if love were a talisman that would somehow keep us together, protecting us against war, the world, everything; as if a million others, believing this, had not already been undeceived.

"I never want to leave you," I said. "I never will."

I believed that too. I locked my arms about him, holding him fast. Flesh of my flesh. Beloved.

"I never want you to," he said.

Slowly he began stroking my hair, I felt the tips of his fingers on my face, on the nape of my neck, delicately following the line of the throat, tracing the curve of the shoulder. I lay quiet under that gentle caress, full of my pleasure but not sharply, for now its edges shelved softly away into peace; full of my happiness, aware of it, but not starkly as people are who have glimpsed the abyss and ending.

At last I said, sitting up reluctantly, "I suppose we ought to move."

"Yes."

"It's getting late, we ought to go."

But still we sat on, while the twilight faded and darkness came striding over the seas toward us. When at last we rose to go, there were emerald lights in the waves, and walking along the wet foreshore we left in the sands a glimmering track of our footprints, outlined each in a purple phosphorescence.

CHAPTER TWENTY-TWO

THE HOT WEATHER was ending: you could tell that by the way the sunlight was yellow once more, instead of white, though the heat was still the same. The monsoon had begun: you could tell that too from the rate at which people were streaming down the hills, though in the plains no rain had as yet fallen. The compartments in all four coaches of the Mountain Express were full—bulging. For nine months in the year probably not even the railway authorities remembered this little rack-railway line; for the remaining three the train, making up for lost time, was as full of passengers and importance as an express, although without the speed of its namesake. Now it fussed into the station, the faces at its windows noticeably wan, with that expression of incredulity which comes of a sudden encounter with a heat whose strength has been blessedly forgotten during the green, cool months in the hills.

"When we come back from the hills," Richard said, casting a critical eye on the passengers who were alighting, "you'll look just like that."

"I shan't," I said, "I shall have the sense not to wear any make-up, I shall sweat with complete dignity, like a pig."

We sniggered together like schoolchildren, and Richard whispered, "The men look awful too, darling. Just look!"

White skins had turned to a mottled red; dusky ones, to a curious purple. Women who had powdered and painted in a reasonable clime, 7000 feet up, now had faces of varying textures and surfaces, like a wall whose plaster is beginning to peel. Irritable, burdened with cranky children and inefficient servants without whom, however, they never traveled, they piled on to the platform, which, as all platforms in India always are, was already full. With them the impedimenta regarded as indispensable to India travel: hold-all with blankets, bedding, and mosquito nets; large crate of bottles of soda water, drinking water, and milk; smaller crate, containing smelly breakables—ammonia, lemongrass oil, Flit, Phenyle, Keating's powder, and the like to combat insects; rugs against the cold, topis for the sun, glasses against the glare; thermoses clinking with ice and (a nagging suspicion throughout the journey) perhaps broken glass. Then the incorrigible servants with their shapeless bundles of unnamable things tied in dirty towels; their water goglets, their battered tin trunks; their noisy ministrations and fulminations.

The train that would bear this human cargo away—away to its various stations in the plains—had come clanking in, but now it was engineless: in the distance you could see the locomotive cautiously backing onto a turntable—tiresomely slow. People got into the carriages, dusty, fretful, ill-humored because they could not be borne away swiftly, more swiftly, from this arid, hot, enervating halfway house in the foothills.

"I wouldn't go away at all," Richard said, "if coming back made me feel as harassed as that."

"When we come back," I said, "we shall feel just as jaded. And look it."

"But darling, can you tell me *why* people should get jaded?"

"Because of the heat," I said.

"No," he said, "it's because they have to worry about their hundred-and-one possessions. They don't know how to travel light."

"Whereas we do," I said hotly, for this was now something of a sore subject with me. "We're going to the hills, where it's fifty degrees minus, and here and now it's a hundred degrees plus, and we've exactly one suitcase between us and the monsoon's started."

He said, "I've bought you a coat, haven't I?"

I was silent. He had, though he must have scoured the countryside to do so; a coat in the plains in summer is rarer than diamonds in a desert.

"Most women would be delighted," he said, "to have a new coat. Especially——"

"I've dozens at home," I said, "just lying there, being eaten by moths."

"I couldn't bear to see you," he said, "in a moth-eaten coat. Any other way, but not like that."

The Mountain Express, on the opposite platform, was showing signs of starting, otherwise the argument might have continued.

We got in with our suitcase. We were the only two in the compartment. The other train, which was nudging forward along the narrow straight track, was crammed with people.

Richard said, "Are you sure we're going the right way?"

"I'm sure we're not," I said, giggling. I was feeling a trifle light-headed, perhaps because of the heat.

"Let's get out then," he said, and he got out.

"Richard!" I shrieked, looking down at him from my window. "Don't be ridiculous! You'll be left behind! The train's about to start!"

The train was moving, gliding slowly out of the platform. "Richard!" I cried again, frantically. "Get in! We're——" Then I realized it was the other train that was moving, and I became calmer.

Richard said, laughing at me, "I've thought of another way of traveling."

"Oh yes?"

"Yes. I'll tell you if you'll get out. You'd better. The guard's waving his flag."

So I got out too, indignantly, flourishing the two rail tickets. "What did we buy these for? What shall we do with them?"

"Do you collect tickets?"

"No!"

"Then throw 'em away."

I did that too, I was so furious. The pasteboard pieces fluttered down on the tracks of the departing Mountain Express.

Richard said, "We'll go in one of those open buses. I've never been in a bus in this country. Have you?"

"Why didn't you say so?" I said. I was even getting past indignation. "Rail and bus tickets are interchangeable." And so they were, for some odd reason.

"Darling," he said, "don't be so mean. I don't know where you get these traits from."

But for this I would have rescued those tickets. Or at least I would have pointed out that if we were going by bus, we might as well go in our car, which was merely accumulating garage charges.

Unlike the up train, the bus, when we got on, was almost full, for it is only social life that closes down in the hills when summer is over; and those people who still go there, having no notion of social seasons, usually travel by open bus, which is cheaper than rack railway.

The bus had a roof, but no sides. Benches were screwed into the floorboard, and the individual who sat at each end saved himself and those next to him from sliding off by clinging to iron rods stapled to the footboard below and the roof above. Courteously room was made for us on the bench immediately behind the driver, people pressing hard on the unfortunate stops at either end in their efforts to see we were not cramped.

Overhead a scrabbling was going on as the driver clambered about lashing our suitcase to the roof. Everyone's possessions were piled on top, there was no room anywhere else: trunks and bundles, sacks of potatoes, vegetables in string bags, poultry in wicker baskets, bunches of bananas, even bundles of firewood.

"I hope it'll be safe there," I said nervously. "It's the only one——"

Before I could finish, a dozen voices reassured me. Quite safe, quite safe. The driver, stopping his labors to peer down, repeated, Quite safe, quite safe. These statements, however, proved to be founded on optimism, for at the first corkscrew bend we came to (taken at speed by the driver, who seemed to scorn all road signs) a large tin box flew from the roof and, bouncing off the road, burst open, scattering its contents. We stopped then for the wailing owner to trudge back and collect his belongings, helped by his grinning fellow passengers. We stopped again, just as we were gaining height, for one of the women passengers to be sick. We stopped twice more as it began to be cold and men and women disappeared down the hill slope on opposite sides of the road. There was a further halt for a meal, and another when it began to rain and the driver had to unroll the canvas blinds down the sides of the bus.

After the previous almost alarming openness, I began to feel a little sick traveling boxed in like this—there was no way of looking out, except through the small section kept clear for driving, or through the narrow slits of yellow mica let in to the flapping canvas, which only jaundiced the green, lovely landscape—and the colder air seemed to have exhilarated the driver, who was now hurtling round the sharp hill curves at maniacal speed. I would have nudged the driver—this was the accepted way of stopping the bus—but I knew Richard would sneer. I held myself in, watched by my sympathetic but anxious neighbor, until to my relief the rain stopped, as suddenly as it had begun, and the blinds were lifted; and looking out once more, I saw the mists were swirling about the peaks of the hill range, but where we were the air was like crystal, and faintly sweet with the smell of the pines on the higher slopes of the hills.

It is not difficult, once the season is over, to find somewhere to stay in a hill station. The hotels are empty, there are houses to let; and so we dawdled through the late afternoon sunshine, rejecting house after house because one was too large, and another too new, and one had no garden, and the next had no view . . . until at last we came to one that we both liked, set in a fold of the hills, with an unkempt garden in which magnolias grew and a sweep of pines beyond, and this we took, while servants hurried to prepare a meal and light a fire before nightfall.

"This is perfect," I said, stretching my hands to the blazing fire, enjoying the delicious sensation of warmth (though a scant five hours since it had been anything but enjoyable). Outside it was raining heavily, and the sigh of the wind, the sound of rain, enhanced the feeling of shelter.

"We'll go out later," Richard said, "when it's eased a bit. It won't be too dark."

"We shall get drenched," I said. "We haven't brought a thing. Not even umbrellas."

"Umbrellas would be worse than useless," he said, "in this weather. But we can borrow from the servants. They're bound to have a mac or two between them, living here the whole year round."

I couldn't help smiling. "That was one of the first things you did, after arriving in this country."

"What was?"

"Borrowing servants' clothes. My mother was shocked."

We laughed, the memory a bond between us, and I thought, he has not changed, since that day; and I loved him the more, because he had not changed.

But we did not go out that night after all, for the rain did not ease, the winds became violent, and sitting before the fire, listening to the trees creaking like the timbers of a rocking ship, we grew drowsier and drowsier.

"I'll ask them in the morning," I heard myself saying, and to my surprise I found it was morning, the words must have woken me up. A bright sunny morning, and the tall slim trunks of the eucalyptus trees were still once more and their scent strong in the room, and the light coming in through the double window shutters lay like golden combs on the floor.

CHAPTER TWENTY-THREE

HOLIDAYS END ON a Sunday, work begins on a Monday —it is the same anywhere. Reluctantly we packed, had our last meal, sniffed the mingling scents of fallen petals in the storm-swept garden, and settled our bills for the milk we had had, the curds, the eggs and butter and home-made beer, for the logs we had burned, and the clothes we had borrowed and kept. Then we went off to smell the pine woods once more and look at the camellias, and gazing on the hill slopes, tawny and glowing in the monsoon light, we said, We must come again.

The road down the hills descends in a sharp corkscrew: in a matter of hours you have lost your 7000-foot elevation and are once more at sea level. Gone in a few hundred feet are the pines, the eucalyptus trees, the belt of dark evergreens that crowns the peaks; drop another hundred feet and you will not even see their tops for mist. Descending, still descending sharply, and now you have left behind the clumps of rhododendron, the thick, matted bushes of wild raspberry, the waterfalls seem fewer, the air is warmer, you shed your scarf and coat.

Posted along the twisting road, like dwarf sepulchers, are small white stones to show your elevation, and each time you come to one of these—twice for a thousand feet—the scenery is different, the air has changed. Until at last you are among palms and bamboo thickets and banana groves, and the road is straight once more, and the heat of the plains comes fuming up to meet you.

Here we collected our car and by midday on Sunday we had reached the outskirts of the town, having left the morning before. We had been together so long—sleeping and waking, day and night—it came as a shock to realize that soon, now, we would each be going a different way, that from now on the whole weary day would go by before we even saw each other.

I tried not to think about it. We were now in the main bazaar, and I gazed out of my window at the area we were driving through. Everything seemed very quiet. With a sort of half awareness I noted it was quiet, even for a Sunday, but this fact did not more than register itself on my consciousness; it did not dispel the gray misery that grew and grew inside me. On forlorn impulse, in an effort to postpone the actual moment of parting, I said, "Let's walk . . . we've done enough driving for one day."

There was the question of where to leave the car—of someone having to come back for it. Richard only said, "All right," and turned into a narrow blind alley where he parked, switching off the ignition. When the engine stopped, you became aware of the silence. It stood round you like a wall, it was a weight upon the eardrums, and yet being incomplete, it was not a silence. In the next street a bullock cart went by, creaking and rumbling; I heard the clip-clop-jingle of a pony trap, the crack of a whip, the clang of a bicycle bell, the swish as the man cycled by; but still found myself listening, uneasily, for something more, without knowing what it was. Then suddenly it came to me: the sound, as of a gigantic humming-top, that rises endlessly from a market street, had stopped: the top had ceased to spin.

For a few moments we sat irresolute, then Richard began winding up the windows while I combed my hair, brown and streaked with dust, and wiped the smudges of sweat and dust from my face.

Park a car in a bazaar lane and from nowhere, seemingly materialized out of thin air, beggars appear; and they are but the nucleus of a crowd of idlers and children, eager to see if anything is to be had, which soon forms. Now no one came. Not a soul. We got out of the car. Richard took my arm and we began walking. Up that blind alley and into a lane, down the lane and into a street. All along doors were shut, casements were closed. Against what? Against the sun. The shutters of the shops were down. Why not? It is a Sunday. But the lean-to stalls which never close were curtained off with gunny sacks—flies were buzzing angrily against these brown, unexpected barriers.

Richard said, "What's happened? Do you know?"

"No. I'll ask."

On the opposite side of the street, in the half-open doorway of a tenement building, I saw the figure of a man silhouetted against the light from within, and leaving Richard, went across to him.

The man eyed me with a faint neutral suspicion. He was chewing betel nut, his lips were stained with the juice.

He said, "You want to know?" looking me up and down.

"Why else should I ask?"

He said with contempt, "Why, where do you come from?"

"I've been away six weeks."

He seemed to relent; he bent forward and whispered a few words, which I did not catch. He was about to repeat them when Richard came up, and he stopped short, spat into the open gutter in front, and turning, went in. The door closed with a thud.

"What did he say?"

"Nothing."

"He was talking to you."

"I didn't hear what he said."

We went on. The streets had not been cleared—there were a few people about; and it was broad daylight; but otherwise it was like being out during a curfew. There was the same creeping hostility, that came after you like a living thing, lost among shadows when you looked, dissolving into nothing when challenged; the same brooding watchfulness of people whose presence you felt but never saw, whose eyes you sensed behind each shuttered window, each blind unseeing door. Involuntarily I found myself turning round sharply, as if to surprise whoever it was that watched; but there was no one. I had not expected to see anyone. There was nothing. The unremitting scrutiny went on, street by street. In growing uneasiness I looked at the hoardings, the bills flyposted on walls, for some clue, an inkling, a meaning. There was none.

Richard said, "Can you read that?" He was pointing to a banner that straddled the narrow street, an insignificant tattered strip of material I had not noticed. A number of words had been crudely painted on the cloth, the dye had run from one line of characters to the next, and I had difficulty in deciphering them; but there was no mistaking the sense of that message which began and ended with obscene abuse, and which had been written with a hate such as only an occupied country can generate.

"Let's go," I said, taking Richard's arm.

"What does it say?"

"Nothing I can translate."

He said, "I can understand some of it, not all."

"Let's go," I said again.

I walked on, hoping he would follow. He did not; he was standing under that flapping banner, puzzling out those black smeared words. The street curved sharply here; a few more steps and I had lost sight of him, though I did not notice it. Please come, I begged him wordlessly. Please come away. Please . . .

There was a splintering crash, heavy, with glass in it. The sound seemed to zigzag down the street to me, swelling as it came. It seemed so loud it almost stupefied me. For a moment I stood where I was, staring at the sky which was suddenly full of beating wings and flying black shapes; and in that moment became aware of another sound, a low soft hiss like escaping gas. Then I found myself running, frenziedly running before that lurching tower of fear could topple down and crush me.

Richard had not moved; he was still standing where I had left him. He caught me as I almost fell, supporting me against him. I did not hear what he said at first, there was a roaring in my ears. I clung to him. Tightly, hold fast, never let go. Let go and you will be swept away. You will go and he will be left, or he will be swept away and you will be lost.

Speech returned slowly.

"What was it? Are you hurt?"

"I'm all right," he said. "Come on, we'll go."

"What was it?" I said again.

He stubbed at a jagged triangular piece of amber glass with his foot. "I'm not sure . . . something not very pleasant."

Whatever it was had been carefully aimed and thrown with force, and, missing him by a few inches, had broken against the stone-lined edge of the gutter; most of it had sunk in the sluggish, viscid stream below. The contents had sprayed out over the street, a curious pungent odor hung in the air.

Near by was a small alcove formed by the crazy walls of two semiderelict houses. It looked as if it might have been used as a shrine at one time: there were the remnants of a thatched roof, and a rusty spear, spade-shaped head uppermost, had been dug into the ground in front of a narrow altar stone. Richard drew me back into this recess; I sat down on the stone—I had not realized till then how much strength had ebbed from my limbs. Overhead crows and kites were still circling, black against the sun.

Richard said, "Wait here. I'll get the car."

I stood up. "No. I'll come with you."

"You look a bit shaky. Let me get——"

"No. Please—I would rather come with you."

"Why? Is it safer that way?"

"I merely want——"

"Is it?"

"Please, Richard," I said desperately, "please don't ask. I want to be with you, I would rather we were together, that's all. Is that so unnatural?"

He did not ask again. We walked back along those selfsame streets, and the unadmitted truth fastened upon us like a vampire, sucking from us the life blood of love which is the communication of one with another, the union and surrender of each to the other.

And now there was a change—so subtle, so secret, I could not tell how it had come about, I was only aware that it had—and though I questioned the awareness, it kept its mystery, and hardened into knowledge with denial. For I knew now that the silence of these streets enfolded me, too. I was a part of it, it no longer repudiated me, and from within its invisible envelope, do what one could, there was no easy reaching out to those who stood outside.

A little to my surprise the car was where we had left it. It had not been touched. Richard reversed and began backing out of that narrow alley. The quiet of the street picked up the sound of the engine, amplifying it, radiating it in raucous waves; the noise was a vulgarity—a tasteless offense against the closed-in quiet.

Richard said, "We'll go back the other way—skirting the bazaar."

"Yes."

"It's much longer . . . lucky we filled the tank."

"Yes."

Casual talk, as if we were acquaintances; small talk to mend those rifts which might become chasms into which we might fall and be lost.

An hour's driving through its jigsaw streets brought us to the fringes of the main bazaar, and here, already, you could feel the atmosphere beginning to lighten. Imperceptibly, grain by grain, the weight of oppression lifted, the climate grew milder. Slowly, gradually, the need to keep talking declined and died; silence was possible now, and a slow uncertain peace came wavering up between us.

Then we were in the residential area, and from here, among bland detached houses and smiling, pleasant gardens, it was difficult to believe that what had gone before was anything but a nightmare. I prayed that it might be, as one often does in the first headlong flight from reality; I was willing, if it were a nightmare, to endure it to the limits of endurance, and so to come at last to a release and an awakening; but all the time I knew there could be no such facile escape, that already one-way doors were opening through which we must pass and that it would then be beyond our power to return.

Richard said something; he had to repeat the words.

"Where to? Kit's?"

"Roshan's. My things are still there."

Roshan's house, which so seldom sheltered her, which she forsook at whim with not even a backward glance at its comforts. An early colonial house, its lines disciplined but without severity, and relieved by the graceful arched portico and entrances, and by its two delicately wrought outdoor staircases that curled up decoratively to the roof.

We were getting close now. And what had still to be said came with us like a wraith that there is no way of exorcising save one. I will speak now, I said to myself; and a mile of road went by. *Now*. And we covered another mile. Then we were off the main tarred road and on the unmade one leading to the house; from here you could see the bougainvillaea in full bloom, heavy trusses of orange and purple vividly hung against the white-washed walls.

"Richard," I said at last, "you mustn't think——"

Nearly there, nearly at the entrance to the stone-flagged carriageway. Swollen thoughts, refusing to fit into words, words shying away from their obstinate turbulencies.

We were slowing down, stopping. Words had not come. The engine died. You could hear the papery rustle of the wind moving among the waferlike petals of the bougainvillaea.

Wordless, Richard put his arm about me. I leaned against him with eyes tight shut, and love like a pain in my breast. For a few moments only, then the wraith was there, unquiet, insistent; and I said—moving away, trying to look at him, "Richard—this feeling isn't for you. Or—or for people like you. You must believe me," I added desperately. "I would not lie to you."

He looked at me with level eyes. He said, "It is a terrible thing, to feel unwanted. To be hated."

"Listen to me," I cried, "I've told you—this feeling isn't for you. Do you think I don't know?"

He said gently, "Do you really think people can be singled out like that? One by one, each as an individual? At a time like this? After today?"

No, of course not. There is not the patience, the courage, the time. You belong to one side—if you don't, you belong to the other. It is as simple as that; even children understand it. And in between? There is no in between. You have shown your badge, you have taken your stance, you on the left, you on the right, there is no middle standing. You hadn't a badge? But it was there in your face, the color of your skin, the accents of your speech, in the clothes on your back. You didn't ask to be there? Ah, but you had no option; whatever you thought, there was no option, for you there was no other place. But one can make another—one can . . .

"You're trembling," Richard said, holding me to him. "What is it, darling? What are you afraid of? It's all over now."

But it was not; it was just beginning, though exactly what, I could not tell.

There is a time in one's life, they say, when one opens the door and lets the future in: I had the feeling I had done so, but had neither the power nor the courage to recognize the shape of things to come; and therefore I could not speak.

CHAPTER TWENTY-FOUR

A LITTLE TO my surprise, Roshan was at home. She had been released, she explained, to make room for others.

"I wasn't sorry to get out," she said. "I was feeling a little cramped in that cell. But when I got out, there were queues waiting to get in—if I'd known I wouldn't have gone like a lamb!"

You could never tell, with Roshan, whether she was serious or not.

I said, "Has there been so much trouble?"

She shrugged. "Not as much as some people expected."

"Govind, for instance?"

She said, carefully, "Govind for one . . . but he demands more than people can give."

"We came through the bazaar today," I said, "for part of the way."

"And then?"

"Then we drove round it."

She nodded. "Yes. There has been rather more feeling there."

I had told her nothing she did not know.

We were both silent, both thinking of Govind, our thoughts almost gave him palpable presence; and the sense of communication was so strong that when I said, barely murmuring the words, "I hope he is not . . ." Roshan knew I spoke of him, and what I wanted to say.

"He is in no trouble," she said, "but he has of course been very active . . . especially in the bazaar districts."

I nodded: this had occurred to me, and more as truth than guesswork.

"He ought to have rested a little longer," I said at last, wearily. "He looked worn out."

"You know him as well as I do," she said. "Do you think he can?"

I went to my room to pack, and Roshan came with me, though not to help. She curled up on the divan, her clothes drab against the crimson silk cushions, watching while I stuffed my things in the hold-all, and when I was ready, she said, "Going back to Kit?"

"Yes."

"I wish you weren't."

"Any special reason?"

She looked as if she were about to say something; changed her mind; said, lightly, "Well, it certainly isn't because I shall miss you—with all this shuttling about, I don't think we've been in the house more than one at a time."

It was true; I could not help laughing, a little helplessly; and the question remained unanswered. After a while she said, cheerfully, "We may soon be working together again . . . my forbearance seems to have worked miracles."

She said it calmly, as if even from prison several other courses had been open to her.

I said, "Has there been anything definite?"

"No, but Mohun thinks so, and he never allows himself to think unless he's pretty certain."

I could not help wondering how he could be certain with a person like Roshan about, but I kept this doubt to myself. It was, anyhow, cheering news, and it was with lifting spirits that I went home to Kit.

Premala, in a soft sprigged cotton, the child at her hip, came smiling to meet me; and there was a tranquillity about her which made me feel even better.

She had been sitting in the garden, in the shade of a laburnum; and as we walked back she said affectionately, "Darling, it's lovely to see you again after so long. And the holiday's done you a world of good—you look so full of sun and fresh air . . . you mustn't let it wear off too soon."

"You're looking rather well, too," I said, smiling at her, "sleeker somehow, and not quite so pale."

She said happily, "I'm glad you said that. I must tell Kit—he wanted to send me to the hills, you know, he said the heat wasn't good for me. But of course I couldn't go."

The child, now that I was a novelty no longer, had begun wriggling impatiently, flopping over Premala's arm in alarming attitudes to get down. Stooping, Premala put her in her play pen, where the little girl sat for only a moment before scrambling up. She did it carefully, with concentration: hands spread-eagled firmly on the floor, bottom uppermost, knees slowly straightening, then a breathless defiant movement as she lifted her hands from the ground and lurched upright, staggering a little, but maintaining her balance.

Premala was laughing; her eyes rested gently on the child, who was chuckling over this feat. She said, "She's a bonny baby . . . I've never had a moment's trouble with her, not even in the height of summer. I did think of taking her to the hills, when Kit wanted me to, you know. But, really, there's been so much to do."

"In the village?"

She nodded; then eagerly, "You must come and see it soon. . . . You'll hardly recognize it, it's grown so much. I wouldn't have believed it possible, but you know, Hickey was right."

"Right? In what way?"

"Well, he always said the money would be found . . . and he didn't worry, he just went ahead, and the money *was* found. Fourteen more children have been taken in now, there's a whole new wing being added, and then we hope——"

Of what had been done she spoke with loving precision, of what was yet to be done with equal precision, and with a calm assurance, as if the ropes were already being twisted which would anchor these castles in the air to the ground. Excitement had sent the color to her cheeks; and there was something else, less evanescent, about her too—a glow, a serenity, which had not been there since she had come to live in this city. Yet it was a serenity of a different order—finer, more tempered, as if the dross had been taken from its virgin gold in some unknown fiery crucible—a serenity that does not come save on the far side of suffering.

She said, "You'd never have dreamed, in the beginning, we could possibly look after so many . . . we have had a lot of help, of course, people are wonderful, once you get them to listen. . . ."

"And do you?"

She said, "It is the difficult part."

A gusty wind was blowing, sending the petals of the laburnum down in quick, light showers. The child, in her pen, stood entranced with small face uplifted, hands reaching out for the eddying golden petals, too swift for her wondering grasp.

Premala said, "The rains are late this year . . . I hope they won't be too late."

"Too late," I repeated, "for what?"

"The crops," she answered.

I don't know why her reply should have dismayed me so—I had known for some time the village had become her home, and she a part of its life. Perhaps it was because I had been away, and had forgotten this a little, and Premala noticed my expression. She said gently, "Mira, you mustn't think I'm never at home . . . I only go when there's nothing on. And Kit doesn't mind."

So it had even come to this, that they agreed to go their separate ways, tacitly acknowledging thus the imperfect articulation of their marriage. And why not? Many marriages worked, if haltingly, on this basis, which would otherwise not have worked at all, sometimes enduring to the end without breaking down; and if my heart cried out for them, it was, I told myself, because I stood too close, and for those we love nothing short of perfection will do.

Premala had reverted to the village—her plans, Hickey's, the children in the school, the new wing nearing completion.

"Hickey wanted to open it this Saturday," she said, "but he decided to wait when he knew I wouldn't be able to go . . . he's very—considerate—in many ways."

"But why won't you be able to go?"

"There's this party," she said, a little flatly, "I promised Kit——"

"Party," I repeated after her, "what party?"

"The usual Government House one," she said, looking at me in surprise. "Why, didn't you know?"

Of course I knew: it was held this time every year. Yet it was with a sense of unbelief that I accepted that it would be held again this year, at this time, and that the routine was not to be varied.

At any rate there were six days to Saturday, and perhaps by then it would not matter.

CHAPTER TWENTY-FIVE

IN THOSE SIX days the silence spread from the center of the bazaar to its outermost circumference, thence rapidly outwards until almost the whole city was held in its toils. It was as if some huge spring were uncoiling, but somehow without surrendering in the process any of its tension. The residential area alone had ignored those tentacles; life went on here as usual. And yet by curious inversion it was the usual, now, that had acquired unreality; and to move from the menacing, lowering atmosphere without to this ordinary, unmoved air was to exchange living for fantasy.

I spent the whole of that Saturday morning in the office with Roshan, for we were now preparing for resumption of publication. In the afternoon I went to see Richard, who was in bed with a slight attack of malaria, and did not get back until teatime.

A little to my surprise Premala was not at home; when I asked the bearer where she was, the man answered that he did not know, only that she had ordered a taxi and left "in a hurry," taking the child with her. There was a note for Kit, however; it had been written in haste, the writing had smudged with careless blotting, and Premala's usually neat small hand had become a scrawl. Kit came in soon after I did, and I gave him the note which the servant had mistakenly handed me. It could not have contained more than a line or two, for Kit hardly glanced at it before he said sharply, looking up at me, "Did you know?"

"Know what?" I asked, startled: there was something almost like accusation in his voice.

"That she was going to the village tonight?"

"No," I said. "In fact she specifically told me she was staying for the party."

"Well, she's not," he said shortly. "She says she's had to go—she doesn't say why—and she hopes to be back in time . . . but of course she won't be able to make it—it's nearly six now. I shall have to go without her," he added, frowning. "It's so—awkward."

I was silent; and he said, his voice suddenly gentle,

'Did I nearly bite your head off just now? I'm sorry . . . I didn't mean to."

"I know," I said, and then impulsively, half breathless, "Kit! I wish you wouldn't go—to the party, I mean. Just this once."

"Not go?" he said, staring at me. "Why ever not?"

"I'm not sure," I said again, "but there may be trouble. . . ."

"Trouble? What kind?"

"I'm not sure," I said again. "I think there may be a demonstration of some sort . . . a disturbance . . . it may not come to anything, of course——"

He said, "How do you know?"

How did I know? Everyone knew; everyone who in any way belonged to the country, though they formed no more than a drop in its stream of consciousness. But those who merely floated on the surface—how could they feel the pull of its currents, how visualize its deeps? How could they know? And yet, how explain this? What could I say?

Kit did not press for an answer: it often happens that one can sense the difficulty of another, without struggling through to its root. He said, instead, "Aren't you coming? Richard'll be there."

"Richard's in bed," I said, "but I'll be coming."

He said, half smiling. "To take care of me, darling? Or what?"

But again I could not say: certainly it was not with any idea of taking care of him—the very thought was preposterous. What then? I can only suppose it was a feeling of kinship asserting itself, the sort of instinct that draws straying members back to the herd in time of trouble; and the feeling was too strong to be resisted.

Seven o'clock came. Premala had not returned. Kit said, frowning, looking at his watch, "We'll give her another quarter of an hour."

We waited in the quiet drawing room, Kit in his evening clothes, his black hair brushed and gleaming, I in the shimmering sari of green and gold he had once given me.

Outside, someone was playing a flute; the low, thin notes drifted in of the melody that is not to be heard save on evenings when the monsoon is near.

A quarter of an hour by the loud ticking clock—and how much by any other reckoning? Half past seven struck, destroying that fragile song from the darkness.

Kit rose. "We'd better go."

"Yes."

I went up to collect my bag and wrap. When I came down, Kit said abruptly, "I wish I knew what took her there so suddenly. Haven't you any idea?"

"If I knew, wouldn't I tell you?"

He said, surveying me, "Would you?"

"Why, Kit," I said, troubled, "of course I would. Why shouldn't I?"

"No reason at all," he said, turning away; then, briskly, "let's go."

On semi-official occasions like this, the chauffeur was usually retained. Now Kit dismissed him, taking the wheel himself; the man seemed relieved to go.

Outside it was pitch-black; when you stepped into the night, the darkness closed over you like water. It is often this way before the rains come, when the laden clouds sink closer and closer to the earth, and even the rims of starlight are hidden. Kit had to switch on all headlights; and that stark white brilliance, the glow from the dashboard panel, instantly created a cell in which we moved in isolation, while darkness closed round like a wall. Until, nearing Government House, the boundaries fell back, the walls dissolved, for here light was everywhere and darkness the intruder.

Whoever had been responsible for the lighting, this year, had made a good job of it. At short intervals along the approach to Government House standards had been erected from which swung ornamental lanterns; colored lights were festooned about the railings and strung among the trees. Government House itself was floodlit; and under arc lights the lawns were a jewel green, the cannas glowing carpets of color.

On either side of this bright avenue people had gathered. They came each year when the lights were lit, to watch the cars stream past, to marvel at the clothes of the women, to cheer as the bandsmen swung by. Now they simply stood, dark, quiet throngs of waiting people.

Lining the route in front of them, to keep them in order, stood the police constables in khaki uniforms and puttees and scarlet turbans; a handful, no more; no more

154

than in any other year. In charge of them, as usual, one lone European sergeant, also in khaki, but wearing a peaked cap and with a Sam Browne belt clipped about his waist.

Cars were now bumper to bumper. We crawled at walking pace between those double ranks, past the rows of watching faces, purplish in the mingled light from red and blue bulbs. The air was heavy and close and pressed down upon us; it seemed full of an expectancy, crouched and waiting like an animal about to spring.

And yet, was it really so? Could it be that this oppression was as nothing to others—the people who gave this party, the people who went to it? I looked about me, down the smaller roads branching off the main one, past the glare of the illuminations to the shadows beyond, seeking the extra policeman, a guard, a barrier, a soldier, that might point to awareness. There was nothing beyond what you might see each year—a few policemen to control the crowds, a sergeant as usual in command.

We moved slowly on, stopping and starting, painted erratic moths along a beam of light.

As we drove past, I glanced at the sergeant on duty; a stocky middle-aged man, his face flushed and sweating a little; assured, untroubled.

At the gates we were stopped, perfunctorily, by the sentries—two young soldiers in wartime khaki, fresh-skinned from England, with clear eyes and calm faces.

In the grounds, standing on the lawns, were other men like them; some as young as they, as untouched; others older, with skins the color of teak; all of them with those same clear faces, the same casual air.

Was it blindness? Or the knowledge that where a wind is sown, a whirlwind is reaped?

Or was it vision—so whole, so rounded, it could look beyond immediate urgencies; a vision that had long since perceived the signs of danger, interpreted them, accepted the danger itself, and seen in this impregnable calm the best way of emasculating it?

After all these years I still do not know. Each nation shapes its own unique character, distills its own esoteric awareness; the fences around both are high. But this I do know: I looked upon the faces of men bred in another country, another tradition, and they were fearless;

and if this fearlessness was begotten of insensitivity in some, it was not so brutishly sired in others, for one of these men I knew well, and loved.

We were waved on, drew up in the portico, alighted. A policeman came forward to park the car, taking over from Kit. We went in. A number of people had already arrived, perhaps half the total, and were standing about as if uprooted in the curious unsettled state that bedevils the first stages of parties. Indians and Europeans, men and women. Benares silks, satin gowns. Bare arms and shoulders, bare feet; bare midriffs; half-bared bosoms. Enameled nails and tinted palms and eyes like brilliants, blue, green, and brown. Jewels, lustrous alike on white skins and dark ones, flashing and sparkling in the chandeliers' light.

For nonstop dancing, two bands in attendance: the one a community group, made up of small, quiet men in seedy evening clothes; the other the Governor's band, splendid in scarlet and gold, gold braid, fringed epaulettes, and leopard skins about their drums. One of these had started playing. We began moving towards the ballroom—Kit already the center of a small knot of people, sparkling, animated, handsome in any company, assured, at ease.

Outside the wind was rising; it filtered through even here, to this gay, crowded room, setting the drops of the chandeliers tinkling. Soon the oppression would lift, dispelled by the winds, clamping down again when they died. Unless the winds meant rain—there was no way of telling yet.

Someone asked me to dance, I do not remember who. I remember it was a waltz. We circled round the room. On the walls, in heavy gilt frames, portraits of governors and viceroys, paintings of battles and surrenders, Clive and Hastings, Plassey and Seringapatam—British faces, Indian history—circling and circling around us.

The dance was over, the band stopped playing, we sat down. Kit brought me a drink, cool and fiery. The second band struck up, the floor began to fill.

The wind was stronger now: a sudden gust swept down the ballroom, rocking the heavy chandeliers. A peon went to close the windows, the ornate double doors; I saw him lift the catches that held them ajar. Then he drew back, flattening himself against the wall; the doors, eleased, began to swing violently, tugging at their hinges. He made no effort to hold them. I stared at the man, or I could see nothing; at the doors that swung crazily, emptily. Fear began to stir, I felt its prickling preliminaries; but before it could advance, occupy, overwhelm, while amazement was still uppermost, I saw, in the corridors beyond, a ragged column of men moving with disciplined determination towards the ballroom. Then they were at the door, spilling through the doorway, filling the room, the air was full of a cry, though of what I could not say, and there was no time left for thought.

For a few grotesque moments the band went on playing, the dancing kept on as in some runaway time without bearing, then the music began to falter, it died in a final jangling discord. The dancing was over.

From where I sat, I had a confused picture of the ballroom, of the crowded floor, the swaying chandeliers, the startled dancers still in each other's arms, stock-still, tight-locked as if in some unbreakable embrace; of the men with close, tight faces who ringed them about; of the policemen interspersed among them, booted and uniformed, their bobbing red turbans like warning hostile symbols. Then the lights went out. Only the glittering image remained, retained on the reluctant retina.

I did not move, I sat in the silent heaving darkness, and then the quiet broke, like a spell, and I felt the floor shudder under the feet of hurrying men. Through the darkness, the noise, Kit's voice came to me steadily.

"Mira? Are you there? Are you all right?"

"Yes," I answered, "I'm all right."

"Another of these anti-British demonstrations," he said, his voice hardening. "Let's hope it stays nonviolent."

I felt him reaching for me, groping in the darkness, his hand closed over mine. In that instant I felt someone else take hold of me, roughly, gripping my shoulder so fiercely I almost cried out, was about to when I heard my name being called, and the voice was strained and harsh, imperative, but familiar.

"Mirabai! Mira, answer me!"

"Yes," I said, obeying, holding back that cry. "Yes, Govind. What is it? What——"

"Where is she?" His voice was shaking. "Where is Premala?"

Kit replied before I could. He said harshly, coldly "It is none of your concern. She is my wife."

"You fool! You blind fool!" Govind's voice was almost a sob. "Tell me where she is! She's your wife, she ought to be with you, but she isn't, she never is. Where is she? Do you know? Do you care?"

I had to interrupt him then, I could not let him go on.

"She isn't here," I said, and heard my voice rising, "but it's nothing to do with Kit. She's in the village— she said she had to go. We didn't even know she was going, we waited for her, but she didn't come back."

There was a silence. Silence! As if such a thing could be in that room ringing and resounding with medley of sound. Yet it seemed so—as if our emotions had created around us a moat whose black, still waters no outer conflict could cross, behind which we might watch events but without involvement, aloof and withdrawn.

The darkness was yielding now, no longer a pall but a screen against which the silhouettes of men and women were thrown in a deeper, darker confusion—a moving, shifting pattern, as if formed in some quick-turning kaleidoscope in which the pieces of glass were jet-black.

Moving along the corridors, you could see pale yellow circles of light as the servants hurried in, carrying swinging hurricane lanterns.

All this, then—the demonstration, its denial, the darkness, the three of us caught in it, Govind and Kit and I —all this had lasted no more than a few seconds, the few seconds it takes to light a lantern. The bewildered brain jibed at the truth, refusing to accept its artificiality.

Govind said, "We'd better go to her."

There was no questioning his authority, the validity of his words, the need to go to her, the need to leave now. I rose, Kit's hand still held mine. I felt the impress of Govind's fingers on my arm, but it could not have been, for he was leading the way in front.

We followed, passing those men standing against the walls, their faces half lit by the dim lantern light, half eroded by savage shadow. They looked at us I thought with contempt as we went by, but they let us go, they did not stop us. To the end, even this unforeseen abortive end, their discipline did not falter.

Someone had fastened both upper and lower catches on the doors; they stood wide open, no longer swinging but the bolts rattling in their sockets in the high wind. We passed through, into the corridors, into the grounds.

Outside the lightning was flickering. In its darting light I saw, sprawled across the road, a tamarind tree uprooted by the wind. It was one that had immediately lined the roadway; wires and bulbs, deadened and black, were still entangled in its branches. Its roots thrust starkly into the air; you could smell the earth still clotted about them. I remember I had to step over the tree, and I could not in my finery, and Kit lifted me over. I remember him saying we ought to go carefully, because of the live cables . . . but it would not have been possible in that fitful light, we did not even try. I remember wondering how long it would take the electricians to mend them and restore the illuminations, and thinking it would not be before dawn and by then it would not matter.

I suppose we must have walked down the row of cars until we came to ours. I suppose we must have driven along the road that led to the village, but I have no recollection of it; neither how we got there, nor of anyone we passed, nor how we were grouped in the car, nor even who drove. I remember only the wind buffeting the car, rocketing past it, sometimes a force against which the engine noisily labored, at other times impelling us forward until the wheels seemed to spin independently of the motor.

And I remember what was said, and that they were the only sentences spoken: Govind's tortured, "Why did she lie to me? I asked her a dozen times, she said she would be at home tonight," and the sudden squall that hit the car then and in the short lull that followed Kit's voice, hard and even, cold as stone, "After whatever it was that you told her, did you really believe what she said?"

Then the rain began, I heard it drumming on the roof, and we were in the village. I saw the thatching of the huts, sodden and dripping. I saw the land, now continuously lit by sheet lightning; and I saw, between the straining trees, the leap and glow of flames and embedded in that fiery heart the unfleshed skeleton, still standing, of what had once been the school.

We were out of the car, running—wildly, senselessly, for who could do anything now—towards that burning building, until the air grew hot and acrid, full of fiery flying cinders that stung the skin and scorched our throats and fell smarting on the eyeballs, and we stopped, gasping and half blinded. Near by men were standing in groups, in the rain, brightly, lividly outlined. Two groups. One of townsmen, the other of villagers huddled together, huddled close together, and in their midst, his clothes blackened and soaked and clinging to his bony body, a coarse cloak of coconut fiber slipping from his shoulders which someone had thrown about him in compassion, was Hickey.

He was kneeling on the wet earth, praying; I had not seen him pray like this before. His hands were clasped, so tightly that the fingernails bit deep into the flesh. His eyes were wide open, fixed upon the fire, held there almost unwinking as if by a powerful and pitiless will which would spare him nothing; as if to turn aside now, to cover the shrinking eye, to seek even a moment's respite from pain, would be the final dereliction of the duties of the spirit.

I do not think he saw us, he went on praying. I heard him calling the name of his God, his voice rising above the roar of the flames, the howling wind; then it sank, the words became meaningless, until once more came that clear cry.

The villagers were standing around him mutely, in a kind of protectiveness. One or two had laid hands on him, as if expecting some wildness, in a restraint which had not been needed. They made way as we came up; parted, closed their ranks, waited. Even Govind waited for a moment before interrupting him; then he thrust forward to confront the kneeling man, and of those two faces I cannot say which was the more anguished.

"Where is she"—his voice was hoarse and cracked—"where is Premala?"

Hickey looked at him with dull eyes; for a moment he did not seem to understand, then he said, thickly, "She is with God," and turned his gaze once more upon the flames.

I think Govind must have gone out of his mind then. I saw him step forward. His face was working, his hands were groping forward; but even as he did so, Kit gripped him, dragging him back so that he almost fell.

"Let him alone," he said, and he spoke jerkily; his

voice was ragged and uneven. "Are you out of your senses too? Can't you see he's crazed?"

Hickey turned at that; he seemed to rouse a little. He looked up at Kit, his eyes half dazed, and he said, muttering the words, "I'm not very well . . . I'll be all right in a moment . . . but thank you, I——" He stopped as his gaze came to rest on Govind; he slid slowly onto his haunches in the oozing mud, and then, looking up at that tormented face above him, he began to laugh.

I wanted to run, to shut my eyes and cover my ears and run, blindly, anywhere, so that I could see and hear no more, but I could not. I wanted to shriek, but that cry reached my lips as a laugh, and I choked it back. I looked at the faces of the men about me and some were twitching, but no one moved, no one. We stood there rigid, as if held by some implacable power, as if our punishment for some hideous crime was to be forced to listen to this sound out of hell.

Hickey had begun to speak now, the words came between spasms of laughter, slurred and shrill, meant only for Govind, though we all heard them.

"You're Govind, aren't you? I know, I've seen you. You loved her—I know that too, she told me! Well, see what your love has done—your love! Ask your men—there they are!" He raised himself to his feet and pointed; his arm, his whole body were shaking. "They know—why don't you ask them, what are you afraid of? Ask them! Ask——"

I found myself running, and the sound that pursued me was a howl, but whether it was the wind or his voice I cannot say. Kit was ahead of me; I saw him running towards the men who were grouped near a hut, I saw him thrust past them. I was only a few paces behind; I would have gone with him, but they would not let me through. I struggled, I threw myself against them wildly, but they hardened their bodies against me, they would not let me pass. Then Govind was with me, in front of me, breaking, bursting through that tight formation even before it could yield to his fury, and I followed, followed so close it had not time to re-form against me; and so together—in the space left clear by those watching men, under the meager shelter of the projecting eave of a hut—we came upon them.

Kit was kneeling, he had taken Premala in his arms,

161

was holding her against him. His head was bent, his hair had fallen forward, I could not see his face. Premala I saw quite clearly, and I wondered why they had tried to keep me from her, for there was nothing about her that was frightening, unless it were death itself. But I could not believe she was dead. The feeling would not come, then. I looked at her, and she had always been beautiful and she was beautiful now. Her forehead was pale and unmarred. Her hair had worked loose and fell about her shoulders, thick and shining black and lovely. How could life have slipped from her so easily? How, from the miraculous fusion of the two, could the soul have freed itself and gone from the body, prying up with infinite labor, infinite pain, each clip, each pincer that grappled them together more close and fast than any surgeon's row of stitches, without leaving some track of that labor and pain? But there was none that I could see upon her serene face.

Then Kit laid her down, the light of the flames flowed full upon her; I saw the flaring nostrils, and the tiny veins had swelled and burst under the delicate skin; and what I had taken for shadows about her face was a stain, a faint purple discoloration as though from bruising; and I knew she had fought for breath, for her life. And then the feeling of her death came to me.

Kit stood up, but he spoke no word—I know, I was standing there beside him. Next to me was Govind; it was he who spoke first, and his voice dispelled the numbness gathering about me, it was so raw.

"She loved you," he said. "You never loved her—you do not even know the meaning of love. You gave her nothing—not even a home. You drove her to the village —you drove her to her death."

His eyes were on Kit, he seemed unconscious of anyone else. His face was bloated and distorted—but oh Kit! not only with passion, not only with hate, can you not see the grief there? How much plainer must it be, this anguish on a man's face, before forebearance comes?

But Kit did not hear me, he did not see; his own hurt was too deep, the blood flowed too freely, for him to perceive the wounds of another.

"She helped to build this school," he said. "You knew what it meant to her. You and your henchmen destroyed it, and you destroyed her with it. You are as guilty of her death as if you had strangled her with your own hands." He paused and, turning, confronted those waiting hostile men; his gaze passed from one angry, threatening face to another; came to rest finally upon Govind; and, deliberately, he called them the most terrible name by which men can be called.

He said that, and he was not afraid: he turned his back on them, and walked out alone into the night.

I do not know what blind instinct led me—what cry, what warning sounded that I did not hear, yet acted upon; but in that moment I flung both arms around Govind, pinioning him, holding him tightly, tightly against my breast. I could feel the red-black frenzy of his maddened heart.

Then it was all over. There was a slight sound from the darkness, swamping wind and rain and the hissing flames; the beginning of a cry, its torn end. The crowd surged forward, and I was with it, I was in front, I came to him first.

He was lying in the mud a few yards away. Kit, my brother, lying in the rain, in the mud, in darkness but for the lightning. I knelt beside him, and he was not conscious. I took his head in my lap, leaning over to shield him from the rain, and he roused a little. I saw his eyes open and they were bright; even pain, this mighty pain of impending death, could not blur them. He looked at me, wondering and a little puzzled, then recognition came and I think he tried to touch my face, but he could not; the slight movement of his arm was never completed.

He said, "You must not worry," and he smiled at me; he could not move, but he smiled at me.

I said, "It will be difficult not to."

I think he laughed then, I cannot be sure. He said, "You never could lie."

He lay still after that, while time unwound and moved to its end, and just before he was borne over that edge, he spoke once more. Only I knew whom he meant, and in that moment I saw her again, the silken-haired girl my brother had known, whose face I had almost forgotten.

I continued kneeling there with my body bent over Kit and his head resting in my lap. Somebody touched me once, then again; I heard my name being called. I did not move or answer, I could not; I could not do anything except keep on doing what I was doing.

Then I heard a whimper; it grew louder. I raised my head. Propped against the wall of a hut, quite near me, was Premala's child. She had not been there before.

I laid Kit's body on the earth. It was Kit's body now, no longer Kit. I went to her.

She was crying, the tears too bitter for so young a child. I picked her up and she clung to me, full of her fright and bewilderment.

"We must go home," I said to her, foolishly: we neither of us had a home. The sound of my own voice startled me, it sounded so unchanged. It seemed to soothe her—who knows what wildness she had heard that night?—the convulsive sobbing died away into hiccups, she raised her tear-stained face from my shoulder.

"You're a bonny baby," I said to her, "no trouble, no trouble at all." She chuckled. I felt her straining away from me, arms outstretched towards the fire, and the tears not yet dry on her face.

"Pretty fire," I said. I did not want to look at it, I looked at her, but her eyes were full of it, her skin reflected it, all about her were those dancing, glittering spears and points of light; and in the end I had to turn and look.

The school was still standing. I found myself trembling. Dear God, how long had I been here then? So short a time?—so short a time that that frame still stood —could still endure, still stand as I had first seen it, its bones unconsumed and holding together in that raging inferno?

I leaned against the wall, and the giddiness came in waves. I would have fallen, but I was afraid for the child. I held myself upright, staring at the fire, and then, slowly, I saw the change begin, and the faintness went. The framework began to buckle. The iron girders, melting and supple, were swaying back and forth, in and out, tirelessly, until the last rivets gave. For a moment the girders hung motionless; then, slowly gathering force, they fell, twisting, writhing, white-hot limbs that lashed and coiled and clung to each other, and so in this last furious shapeless embrace dipped closer and closer to that violet bed of fire.

I closed my eyes. I could not watch the final consummation. I felt the ground quake, felt the heavy blasts of air flung back in waves from the crash, heard the roar that followed and as it subsided, a deep, long-drawn sigh like a sucked-in breath. When I opened my eyes again, the school was a mangled burning heap above which rose sparks and streaks and streamers of fire, red and white and orange and purple, like flowers in the night, and the wondering eyes of the child in my arms were full of their brilliant beauty.

-=[**CHAPTER TWENTY-SIX**]=-

MY MOTHER CAME for the funeral. She had sworn never to travel by air, but she did all the same. I think my father was with her, but I cannot remember. I think Premala's parents came too, but again I cannot remember. I remember only my mother, who had grown old in a night, and I could not comfort her.

I tried, but I could not touch her. It was not so much that I approached and she retreated: it was as if no channels of communication between us had ever been. Frightened, full of my inadequacy, I went to her, and she—somehow drawing the meaning from my fumbling inarticulacy—said quietly, "You must not worry if I am alone . . . people are always alone." She paused and added, "You will understand, when you are older."

Older? How much older? Were not the years already like ashes in my mouth, what difference how many more came?

I did not reply, and I heard her say softly, half to herself, "Kitsamy was not so old either . . . I have forgotten how old he was . . . but young, quite young."

I stood there, helpless. She could speak of Kit, while my mind still trembled and fled before thoughts of him.

She said, "He was too young to die. Do you not think so? Truly, he was beloved of the gods . . . I have always known it."

I could run no more. I gathered myself, and I said, "He was. Indeed he was."

Until then she had seemed hardly aware of me; now

she said, gently, "You have told me so little . . . would you rather not?"

"There is little to tell," I said. "He died quickly."

"Without speaking? So quickly?"

"He told me not to worry," I said, "and he called——"

"For Premala?"

"No," I said; and I mustered all my strength, and I met her eyes and I said, "no. He called your name."

I do not know whether she believed me. I hope she did, and I think she did.

Immediately after the funeral she left, taking the child with her. There was nothing to keep her here. I would have gone too, but I could not, for I had been subpoenaed to appear at the inquest. I would have disregarded the subpoena—it meant nothing to me, a piece of paper adjuring me to appear somewhere, at some time, and to take warning if I did not—as if anything could frighten me now!—but Richard would not let me.

I do not know what he said. I heard my voice saying "No," and "No," and crying, "Why can't they leave me alone?" and "What more is there to tell?" and his voice closed in around me, a rampart I could not push down or get past, and at last I was so tired I leaned against it and it was no longer a restraint but a support; I had no more desire to escape.

In the calm he asked again, and I said "Yes," and he said, "It is the beginning. There is a long way to go yet," and I wanted to tell him I knew, but then, suddenly, I dropped into sleep.

When I woke I was in Richard's bed, and the luminous clock said three. Dawn had not yet begun, the air was dark and cold, it fell limp like a dew on my limbs.

Richard was lying beside me, on his back; I could see his profile against the night, and that his eyes were open. I must have shivered, for he half turned, drawing me to him; his arm was about me, our bodies were touching, and I felt the abundant flow of his love for me and there was no passion, only this outpouring of an overwhelming tenderness. I lay quietly against him and let it enfold me, this tenderness not of the kind a man brings to his first loving, nor yet the kind that comes after; but of a third order, coming gently to enlarge the meaning of love.

I must have gone to sleep again then. When I woke it was dawn, and I was still in his arms. He had not moved, I do not think he had slept. He felt me stir, and he called, softly, "Mira? Are you awake?"

Slowly, slowly, it came to me; and the tears I had not shed for Premala, or for Kit, or for my mother, which I thought had dried within me forever, began to flow now at this echo of another day, another awakening.

CHAPTER TWENTY-SEVEN

I WENT TO the inquest and the courtroom was crowded, and the canvas was unspotted and new. New and clean, as if nothing had happened at all, as if no one knew anything at all had happened and as if nothing could have been, save what would now appear under our hands. And we stepped forward and the picture grew, the picture I never wanted to see again was set up once more, and now the blanks were painted in, all but a few.

Kit had died of a stab wound. That I knew. Premala had died of asphyxiation.

They were the only two—"casualties," said the coroner, then he amended the words to "fatalities."

So others had been hurt, I thought. I had not noticed.

There had been several people present that night, said the coroner, people who did not ordinarily reside in the village; he would invite them to tell him why they were there. His gaze passed from the line of Govind's men to Govind, from him to me.

Govind gave his evidence first. He had gone to the village, in company with Kitsamy and his sister, because of a rumor he had heard that an attack on the school was planned.

"No other reason?"

"No other reason."

"Could you say why Kitsamy's wife, Premala, had gone to the village?"

Govind said, "She must have gone to warn Hickey."

"Hickey?"

"The superintendent of the school."

"Then she knew of the attack planned against the school?"

"She—must have done."

"She had learned of it from you?"

"I did not *know*. I had merely heard the rumor."

"But you repeated this rumor to her?"

Govind said, "I did not—I did not tell her anything. She must have guessed from—from something I said, I don't know what. I only asked her where she would be. I wanted to be sure she wouldn't be in the village. She said she would be at home—she promised——" He stopped, his voice had begun to jerk.

There was a flutter of papers, a rustle in the crowded room.

The coroner said carefully, "You understand, this is not a cross-examination. There is no compulsion on you to give any explanation which you might consider incriminating."

Govind pulled himself together. He said, "Everybody knew it would be a—disturbed night. It was natural for me to want to reassure myself of her safety."

"Did you——"

The voice was a river, flowing steadily on. I tried, but I could not concentrate; sound came to me clearly as a bell, but sense was a tardy echo. Sometimes it did not come at all. I kept my gaze fixed on the coroner, and it hardened into a stare. I glanced away from him, and gazed round the court, and a row of men at the far end of the room caught my eye, they looked so different. Then it came to me these were villagers. There were six of them—I wondered how they had been picked from so many who had been present. They sat pressed close together on one bench, uneasily, as if awed by the array of authority—all except the headman, who made some show of composure. At either end of the bench stood a police constable, as if to prevent anyone from slipping out—perhaps it had not been easy to get them to come, despite the witness summonses.

One by one they shuffled forward, took the oath, made their statements.

Yes, they lived in the village and they had been present that night.

Yes, they knew the young man had been killed, they saw him afterwards, they saw the knife in his body . . .

The coroner said sharply, "Did you see who threw it?"

They shook their heads. No, they had not seen. And one spoke of the flames, and another of the storm, and another of the darkness, and the headman said, sadly, for all of them, "It was a wild night."

The questioning went on. The coroner said, "You were standing in the open?"

"Yes."

"Watching the fire?"

"Yes."

"Your huts were close, were they not, to the burning buildings?"

"They were."

"They might easily have caught fire?"

"They might."

"But you stood watching."

The headman looked up, distressed. He said gently, spreading his hands, "What could we do? There was nothing anyone could do."

"In fact you did nothing?"

There was a pause. The headman was old, much older than the coroner, his thoughts were not to be marshaled as quickly.

"There was no need," he said at last. "God sent the rain . . . we were saved by God's grace."

"Did you not fear any other danger?"

"What other danger?"

"For instance, that the huts might be set on fire? That you or your people might suffer some violence?"

The old man looked up; he seemed at a loss to understand why such a question should have been put. Then at last he said, simply, "How could there have been such a danger? Are we not Indians?"

A sharp movement in the room, it went round like quicksilver; another stir and rustle; he was asked to stand down. A verbal tussle began which I could not follow. It ended. I heard my name being called, and I got up and walked to the witness box. It was exactly like seeing someone else get up and walk to the witness box.

The coroner was kind. I must find these proceedings most distressing, he said. He had a duty to perform, he went on, but he would try and be as brief as possible:

169

there were only a few questions he wished to put. I said I understood. I answered his questions.

Yes, I had gone to the village that night.

Yes, I had gone with Kitsamy, my brother, and Govind, my adoptive brother.

Could I say why I had suddenly decided to go there at that late hour?

I looked at him helplessly. How could I explain to him the events of that night—how, in this unimpassioned courtroom, convey its fears and our feelings? How tease from their entanglement the threads of information and instinct and proffer only the one in this court where fact had to be trimmed and boxed before it was even presented for acceptance?

"My brothers were going," I said at last. "Naturally I went with them."

"Because of something you may have heard or overheard?"

"Yes."

"Can you tell us what transpired after you reached the village?"

I had to take hold of myself then, I could feel my mind beginning to edge away, but before I could begin the coroner said, "Would you say the statement you have made to the police describing the events that followed is substantially correct?"

"Yes," I said, "it is correct."

"According to your statement, shortly before his death your brother had broken away from the group in which you were standing to walk to his car?"

I said, "I do not know where——"

"In the direction of his car."

"Yes."

"Shortly afterwards, within a few seconds in fact, you heard a cry, and in company with others you came upon his body?"

"He was not dead then," I said.

"But he died shortly afterwards."

"Yes."

"And you did not see who threw the knife that killed him."

"No," I said, "I did not."

That was all. I was conducted back to my seat. Someone brought me a glass of water, and I drank it all. It

170

was hot in that room, with so many people. The fans were full on, but the blinds were down because of the glare, and the air came in sparsely.

Someone was reading the statements made by other people. I had not heard the beginning, but I recognized my mother's: the way she spoke came through even that official voice, the dry report. Then I heard the voice I had listened to that night and never since except at night, for it only came to me in my sleep. But it was not slurred and shrill now, but pale and cold, almost desiccated, and quite steady. I looked up at Hickey at last. I nearly cried out when I saw him.

It was not that he was pale and thin beyond most men: physical poverty had long been his, I was prepared for its exaggeration and emphasis. It was not that he had aged, for I had seen my mother. It was because he seemed to be a man already dead, who contrives by some superhuman effort of the will to continue to live; as if the body went on living after heart and soul had been scooped out, though what took their place it was impossible to tell.

Questioning went on.

Yes, he was superintendent of the school that had been burned down. Yes, he had been there that night.

Actually on the premises?

Hickey said, "I live—used to live—on the premises, but when the fire started, I was in the clinic with one of the children."

"What did you do when you heard of the fire?"

Hickey said, "In a village there is nothing—no telephones, no——"

The coroner interrupted him, not unsympathetically, but he knew all this.

"What did you do?"

"I ran to the school. Most of the building was already on fire. I went in, I wanted to save what I could. You understand, it had not been easy—it had taken a long time, a very long time, to—to——"

The coroner said sharply, "Naturally you first roused the children, who would have been asleep at this hour?"

Hickey stared at him; he said, stonily, "There was no need. They had all been warned and taken out of the building."

"And then?"

171

"I kept on as long as I could; I went in—five or six times, I cannot remember clearly. The last time was when I saw—saw Premala."

He was speaking with difficulty; you could hear the laboring breath. He had to stop before continuing.

"I did not know she had come to the village, I did not know she was in the building . . . she must have gone in after the children came out; no one knew she was there."

"She was looking for you, possibly?"

"I think she was. But I was not looking for her. When I saw her I thought I was—was imagining it. She had fallen behind a—a door. It was jammed, I had to force it. Otherwise I might have—might have——"

He was stammering, his voice so low you could hardly hear.

The coroner said gently, "What did you do next?"

"I picked her up"—Hickey's voice suddenly rose to a thin scream—"I carried her out, and I gave her body to her murderers."

There was a loud buzz; people stood up, there were cries for silence; the various legal advisers were on their feet, trying to make themselves heard; then the noise and commotion settled.

Outside someone was saying "Tr . . . a . . . a . . . ap, tr . . . a . . . a . . . ap," slowly, at intervals. I could feel my mind revolving round the word, circling it like a cautious cat; then the motion stopped and I realized it was only the croaking of a bullfrog. Bullfrogs come out after the rains, and the rains had come—when was it? Three days ago? Or four? But it was not a human voice.

"You say you were a short distance away when you saw him turn and walk towards the car?"

That was the coroner's voice.

"Yes."

Sound and sense were keeping together now; I began to listen.

"Can you say what that distance was, approximately?"

"Approximately ten yards."

"Quite close, in fact."

"Yes."

"You heard him cry out?"

"Yes."

"But you did not see who threw the knife that killed him?"

Hickey took hold of the witness box, his bloodless hands curved round the edge, gripping it tightly until flesh and skin fell away from the cruel jutting bones, and he said, stiffly, "I did. It was Govind."

Govind? *Govind?* How could he? Had I not held him, felt him against me, heard the frenzy of his heart? Had I imagined all this, even to those heartbeats? How could I? How . . .

I stood up where I was, then, and I said, "It was not Govind. He could not have done, because I had my arms round him."

Hickey turned slightly in the witness box to face me, his eyes met mine. Across the crowded room we looked at each other, and we were alone. The coroner, the court, the people in it, the whole ordinary world to which they belonged, had swung away sharply, and we had moved to this icy other planet, this region remote and lonely where none could follow.

Then Hickey looked away, his eyes left mine, and he said, distinctly, "You are mistaken."

CHAPTER TWENTY-EIGHT

THREE DAYS AFTER the inquest Govind was arrested and charged with Kit's murder. Subsequently he was brought before a magistrate and the case was adjourned. There were two further adjournments. On the final hearing he was committed for trial and remanded in custody.

I went to see him in prison. Richard would have come with me, but I would not let him.

It was the same prison Roshan had been in, but a different block. Almost automatically I was about to turn into the corridor to the left of the superintendent's office, but one of the warders (there were two) stopped me, indicating a similar one which ran at right angles to it. He said, mildly surprised, "You have been here before?"

"Yes." (But that had been in another age.)

He said, "Are you . . . ?" But the second warder was frowning and he did not finish the question.

We walked on, the warders escorting me slightly in front and one on either side. My sandals flapped against the stone paving of the corridor, but they walked softly in their bare feet, the footfalls almost soundless.

The corridor ended in a flight of three steps, beyond was an open stretch of ground. The second warder motioned me to descend. "The remand block is farther on," he said briefly.

We crossed the open ground and came to a building standing on its own, squat and low like a barracks, but with an outer veranda. We entered.

The room we were in was long and narrow, cut in half by a partition with a door in it, and bare except for a few chairs.

The warder said, "If you will wait here." I sat down, drawing a chair up to the partition. It was of wood to a height of three feet, above that was an iron grille that extended to the ceiling. The warder was unlocking the door; he entered the room that lay beyond the grille. There was a further door here; I saw him unlock it and go through. I waited. The warder left with me was about to say something, he began clearing his throat, but then his companion came back and he was silent.

Govind was with him. He did not look any different, the suffering was the same. I rose quickly as he came up, but there was the grille; I could not touch him.

He said, "It is—so good to see you. But you should not have come."

"Why not? I wanted to see you."

"Prison is no place for wom—for a woman like you."

"Prison is nothing," I said. (Nothing now. It used to be.)

The warder said, in English, "You must speak English. Sahib's orders."

We had been speaking in our own language; we seldom spoke English unless Kit was there. (But Kit would never be there any more.)

Govind said, "You look tired. Tired and pale."

"It is natural."

"You ought to go away," he said. "There is nothing to stop——"

"There is the trial."

"Not for a month. You could go——"

(Where? Where could I go and find peace? Nowhere, unless I left my mind behind. The mind, in which alone were manufactured my peace and un-peace, and reality

174

and dreams and awakenings. Without it there would be nothing. But that was death.)

He said gently, "You must not fear for me. It is one man's testimony against many . . . my associates have testified for me, there were many there that night . . . they will testify again."

(But what is their testimony worth—the testimony of these men who are your associates? The guilt is there, and the knowledge of it, somewhere in that interlocked group—how could it not be—but there is only denial.)

I was silent, and Govind said quietly, "Even if there is no—reliance—on their evidence, there is still yours."

I said, "There is also Hickey's."

His word, and mine.

He nodded, and we were both silent, and I leaned forward, but there was the grille, I could not reach him, and behind each of us was a warder.

Govind said, abruptly, "What is the feeling?"

I was about to say I did not know, but then he said, "It is believed, this Englishman's word?" —and it came to me that I did know, that it was not for nothing I went among people, and read what they wrote, and listened when they spoke and watched their faces; and all this, in imperceptible coalition, had grown, grain by grain, into a knowledge which until that moment I had not known I possessed.

At last I said, "It is—divided," and he nodded, not asking if it were equal or unequal, but as if he knew where the division lay.

Our time was at an end. The warder with the keys had the bunch in his hand, he was selecting one from it. Once more he would unlock that door, he and Govind would pass through, he would come back alone. . . .

But I could not go yet. There was still something.

I said, "Hickey says I am mistaken. He thinks he saw you—saw you throw the knife. He says it, he swears it. But how could you? Did I not hold you?"

And Govind answered gently, "Do you not know? Did you not put your arms around me?"

I came away. Richard was waiting for me at the gates, in his car, his arms crossed and resting on the steering wheel. The roof was open, the sun came streaming down upon him, upon his arms, upon his hair, like beaten metal in this light, each plane and surface a variant of gold, each strand moving to its dark gold root and rich like silk between the fingers. But the tan was going; I looked at his hands and they were only faintly brown, the glow beneath the skin was already gone.

I said, "You have let it fade too soon."

And he said, glancing at me, "So have you. But there is nothing one can do about it."

"Your hands were much paler," I said, "when you first came out. They'll never be———"

Never, not ever. It is a potent word. You have only to say it to feel its power. Say it of small things and the feeling is born. Say it of love, or life, and your heart can be rent in two.

He said, "They'll never be . . . ?"

I roused. "Never be that color again," I finished.

"I'm not sure I want them to," he said.

We both fell silent then. There was only the sound of the car, and the tires slushing through puddles of rain-water. It had rained again the night before, the air was washed and sparkling. The sunlight came through it a bright pure silver, the shining pools along the road rose in rainbow sprays on either side as we drove. I could feel the warmth of the sun upon my shoulders, feel the wind soft in my hair; those flying droplets of water left a cool wake.

"It is a beautiful day," I said.

"Too beautiful," he replied, and I knew his thought even as he had known mine. Too beautiful to be in prison. Too beautiful to have the sunlight tarnished with such thoughts.

Then we were home—Richard's home, which was mine too. Living had become as simple as that. We went inside, and the rooms were cool and sweet-smelling, full of the fragrance of the khuskhus blinds that hung at the windows, and of wet earth from the flower beds outside.

I sat down and Richard was beside me.

"When all this is over," he said, "we will have a holi-day. Would you like that?"

"But we have just had one."

"We will have another," he said, taking my face in his hands, "to chase these shadows from your face. It is a pity, to spoil it with such dark shadows."

"They will go soon enough," I said, "when all this is over."

When all this is over, and the truth has been established. The truth, which I possess, which must yet be set up and paraded like some pathetic effigy in court after court, there to be set upon and battered by whosoever has a mind to; and beside me is this other man, who would overthrow this truth that is mine and substitute the truth that is his—which he says is his, which he has sworn is his alone. Is the truth, then, divisible? So that Hickey and I each clasping a fragment could believe it to be the whole? That we could both look upon it and see each a different aspect? But it could not be, it could not.

"I do not understand Hickey," I said at last, "I do not know what possesses him."

Richard said quietly, "It was a confused night . . . few people knew what others did, still less what they did themselves."

"But he says he does know," I said. "How can he?"

Richard said, "The school was his life."

But still I was troubled. "I held him," I said, "I do not know why, but I did. Do you believe me? Do you think I would lie?"

"No," he said, "darling, no. I do not think you would lie."

Outside, it had begun to rain again—not as it does when the monsoon breaks and the very skies seem to swing open like sluice gates, but steadily, mildly, dispelling the oppression that gathers after each rainfall in the pattern of the monsoon.

I said, breaking the silence, "Do you believe Hickey?" And before he could reply, I said again—and the words were Govind's, they were not mine, even my voice had changed, "Do you believe it—do you believe this Englishman's word against mine?"

I said it, and it was as if I had inflicted some wound on myself. I stared at him, frightened, I saw the blood slowly ebbing from his face, and then release came, I went to him, blindly, groping, crying, "I did not mean ——" and "It was not me——" and "Beloved, you must not think——" and he held me, murmuring wordlessly as one does to a child, until all passion was spent. Then we were quiet once more, listening to the soft purling of raindrops on the roof; and before long the gutters began to run like swollen streams, gurgling and impatient.

CHAPTER TWENTY-NINE

ONCE MORE THE streets were full. The lull that had followed Kit's murder, and the inquest, and Govind's arrest, when people were too bewildered to know what to think—this stunned lull was over. Now people knew what to think, and if they did not, they were told; after which they were certain they had never had any doubts in their own minds. If you walked in the streets, now, you would see gathered small groups of not more than five; and if you were one of them, their voices would rise as you went by, and if not, the voices would drop, and you would not even know they were discussing the trial, though you might guess.

All day the city was full of a whispering. There were rumors, murmurs, and mutterings . . . of little faith in courts; of conspiracies; of men who were jailed for their beliefs, and jails that were full to bursting. And the wind of this content would pass from end to end, from quarter to quarter, and every little alley and side street would be alive to its message. This is the price you pay if once you have sought to circumscribe freedom, for you may censor reports, proscribe newspapers, muzzle the air, proclaim a curfew—you may do all these things, only to come in the end to the truth that has always been there, that you cannot stop men from thinking: and having traveled this weary road, arrive at last at its bitter end, the knowledge that you have forged a new and terrible weapon—this whispering wildfire that sweeps through a city and is more deadly than the truth, loudly shouted from the highest hilltop, would ever have been.

And having once done these things, there is no going back. No use to say: This time it is different, this is the truth, this is what happened in the village, this is what happened in the courts, this is the evidence on which a man has been arrested, this is why he is to be tried, these reports that are printed in your papers are the truth, the whole truth. No one believes any more. Men have long memories; they judge from the past, and the past that lies within them is both conscious and unconscious, so that sometimes even they do not know how or why they have arrived at a judgment.

Along the walls, on hoardings, on crazy parapets in the bazaar district, now, messages began to appear, sometimes scored in white chalk or ocher, sometimes hand-blocked on poster paper and pasted on, and in any one of half a dozen languages. You would not see these except at night, for in the morning the police would be round with mops and ladders, industrious, scrubbing and tearing down. But at night they would not go there. After sunset no one went there, except those who belonged. As darkness advanced, the district would draw in on itself; then you would see the police go by in their trucks, and soldiers who had been standing by march past in pairs, and occasionally Indian men in European clothes would pass who had been deputed by the government to get the feel of the country, but to whom the writing on the wall meant nothing unless it was written in English. And as darkness fell, the district would close in on itself tightly, as tightly as a clenched fist, and you would not see an alien face there any more, or a uniform, or an Englishman. Then the lampions along the shop-window ledges would begin to glow, the gas lamps to flare, the air would be full of the smell of burning oil, of kerosene and naphtha, and once more there would be groups and gatherings, though there was no longer anyone there to restrict their size, and the banners would go up, the posters, the placards: and out of this bitter cauldron Hickey would take shape—not as a liar, or a madman, an avenger, a man driven by hatred or by the lash of his own heart's despair, not any of these terrible things that my frenzied brain, moving from one to the next, thought he might be—but, simply, as a tool in British hands, which they would use without ruth to destroy a man who was dangerous to them.

And Govind would appear—not as a man who had suffered, who was still suffering, who was on trial for his life accused of a murder which I swore he could not have committed—but, also quite simply, as a man who had fought for freedom, for which crime, and for none other (whatever the courts might say), the British would soon make him pay with his life.

179

And if Govind was innocent, who then was guilty? Who cared?

But the British did things differently. They started a fund for Hickey. No poster, no placard; nothing to show where their belief and their sympathies lay except this fund into which the money came pouring (though few had heard his name, and still fewer knew Hickey the man, apart from those junior civil servants who perforce had to tour in up-country villages); and you would not even know of this fund unless you went to the club. And at the club you might hear a mild opinion or two, for here the British were free as they were nowhere else, the walls of the building were their bastions of freedom behind which they could be as they were, beyond which no Indian could intrude except those who had passed through the fine sieve of selection, and whose intrusive powers were therefore minimal; and so at the club you might hear a man ask, reasonably, "Why should he lie?" or even hear him say, unforcefully, "I do not think the man is lying"; and violence and evil and hatred would be stared out of existence by a pair of calm eyes that had never seen blood flow save in some passionless war or mortars and shells with an unknown and unseen foe.

But why should I lie? No one asked; except, later on, the man who was paid to ask such questions.

The days went by and the dust rose thicker and the streets were alert and teeming; and the feeling swelled and mounted and came to a passionate peak and poised there, quivering, unbearable, and then, abruptly, there was silence. The streets began to empty; the shutters came down on shops, the maidan was almost deserted. The police, kept busy so long, stood idly swinging their lathis, the troops had already been withdrawn. Quiet clamped down on the city, holding it rigid and still.

The day before the trial Roshan's solicitor came to see me. He was also acting for Govind, for whose defense he had briefed counsel.

There was nothing, he said, for me to be afraid of; I had only to speak the truth. I had never done anything else, I said, I had no intention of doing anything else. I must not allow myself to be flustered, he went on, it was easily done . . . and, especially, I must not be upset by fine distinctions: his client, he said, had asked him to stress this point. His client was Roshan; Govind was his client-the-defendant. I would try not to be, I promised him. As a parting injunction he said I was not, under any circumstances, to make any demonstration of any kind. I wondered what he thought I might do; I think he was mixing me up with Roshan.

I did not sleep well that night, for the oppression was building up once more; the air was heavy and still—it was like trying to breathe under a blanket. In the morning it was no better, though now you could see, in the far distance, the first faint outline of storm clouds.

Richard came with me to the court. We sat closely together, quite silent. About a furlong from the court the crowds began; they too were quite silent.

The police constable at the gates saluted, waved us on; the car moved in, drew up at the entrance; we entered the building together. There were a number of people there too, both Indians and Europeans. I caught a glimpse of Roshan—she always stood out in any crowd. Then an attendant came up. "This way," he said to me, politely. For a moment of panic I clung more tightly; but then he said again, his voice a little louder, his eyes curious, "This way, please," and I let go Richard's arm and followed the man.

The lobby into which he directed me was lofty and spacious; there were one or two people in it, whom I took for court officials. Beyond lay an anteroom, in which more people were waiting; I could hear them shuffling about, but I could not see them clearly because the doors had frosted glass panes.

I sat down in one of the leather-upholstered armchairs. The lobby was rather like the reading room of a library, except that there were no books or newspapers; it was paneled in wood to within a few feet of the ceiling. On one side was inset a row of glass windows, but there was nothing to be seen except the corridor along which I had come. Opposite, a door gave access to a narrow passage which led, I presumed, to the courtroom. The ventilators, one on each wall above the paneling, were open. Three of them mirrored the quiet, empty lobby; in the fourth you could see the throngs outside reflected in each of the quarter-sections of glass. I sat watching, though there was little to see. Several people, I noticed, had covered their heads; the sun must have gained in strength then—it had been bright, though not powerful, when I set out. But that was an hour ago. I found myself shifting restlessly; but when I looked away from my watch, the feeling went, the sense of timelessness came back. Above in the ventilator I could see a gentle rise and fall in the ranks of people outside —the slight jostling movement inevitable in a crowd. It must be tiring, I thought, standing so long in the sun, and felt a transitory ache in my own limbs. Then I saw a sudden surge forward, heard the crowd roar. That must be Hickey, I thought. There had been anger in the sound. It was followed after a long interval by a deep-throated shout which could only have been meant for Govind. I looked at my watch: it was a quarter to ten. The trial began at ten.

After that nothing much seemed to happen. I heard footsteps in the anteroom, heard people whom I could not see walking up and down the corridor. The footsteps were usually in pairs: prisoner and escort perhaps —but Govind would be in the dock, he would not be walking up and down the corridor. Witnesses, probably; but were witnesses escorted? I thought not; then it came to me they would have to be conducted in, they would hardly know where to go otherwise. Now and then I heard, faintly, a name being called, and repeated and repeated again, like a litany. I counted about twenty, and then gave up. Could these all be witnesses? I had not realized there would be so many. Hickey would be one, I knew, and I would be another: the conflict, I imagined, would be resolved between us. Nor had it even occurred to me that other evidence would be called— police and medical, for instance. Then it was lunch-time. I did not want any food; I felt I could not eat until all this was over. But it might not be over for three days, or a week. Well then, I would not eat, for three days or a week. It came as a surprise that in the middle of a trial there should be an adjournment for lunch.

Afternoon. I wondered vaguely what was going on in the courtroom, but not with any lively sense of curiosity —I was too numb for that. I was glad in a way that feeling was blunted; I hoped it would last. Somewhere, distantly, I heard Hickey's name being called: and once more I could feel my brain picking and pondering, selecting and rejecting . . . not in a frenzy now but delicately, like a child pulling petals from a flower: Liar—madman—avenger—cheat. Liar—madman . . .

My name, my turn. It was midafternoon now. I went into the court, into the witness box; I took the oath. I seemed to have done all this many times before.

To my right, facing the judge, I saw Govind in the dock. He looked tired, but no more so than many others there.

My eyes wandered from him to Roshan. She was wearing her usual sari of grayish-white homespun; I noticed the yellow jessamine flowers in her hair. Mohun was there too, in the press box. And Richard. He was sitting immediately behind the group of legal advisers and counsel; between us lay the whole width of the room. I could not see Hickey; I wondered whether he was still in the building, or whether he had gone back—but where would he go to? Were there homes that would take him, as he had taken homeless children?

The questioning voice grew sharper; perhaps my answers had not come promptly. But there were no traps in this examination; they would come later, I had been warned, under cross-examination.

"You have known Mr. Hickey, the superintendent of the school, for some time?"

"Yes."

"You have said that you saw Mr. Hickey at the scene of the fire, and that he appeared to be praying."

"Yes. He was praying."

"Did he see you?"

"I cannot say."

"Can you tell the court why you are unable to say?"

I said, "He looked—as if he were out of his mind. He could see me quite clearly, but he did not seem to recognize me, although he knew me quite well."

There was a murmur, quickly stilled. Counsel switched his interrogation to a different track.

"Were you very fond of your brother?"

"Yes."

"Would you shield his murderer?"

"I would not."

"Whoever he was?"

"I would not shield him whoever he was."

"Casting your mind back to those few seconds when

183

your brother turned and walked from you, can you tell the court what your next action was?"

The anesthesia was going now, the pain was coming back; but there was nothing to be done about it.

I said, "I put my arms round Govind, and I held him tightly."

"Did you have some particular reason for doing so?"

"I wanted to prevent him from doing anything he might regret later."

"You therefore held him?"

"Yes."

"Holding the accused as you say you did, would it have been possible for him to move without your knowledge?"

"It was impossible for him to move without my knowledge."

"Are you positive——"

I said, "He did not move. Whatever Hickey has said, whatever he saw, Govind did not move."

Counsel said, "You must allow me to finish——" But he was not allowed to finish then either. Some sort of legal wrangle began, the judge became involved.

I sipped my water, which was warm and unpleasant, noticing as I did so that everyone had been provided with water, there were glasses and carafes placed even among the general public. It was a necessary precaution—the courtroom was stifling, over-full of people. About half of them were Indian, the rest were European. They were not grouped rigidly: you might see a brown face in a row of pink ones, or bleached heads among the black; but mostly they sat together. There were even one or two Englishwomen; usually they did not come out when the heat was like this. Not so much heat either as a heaviness of the atmosphere, a dank humidity which you felt like shaking off, but could not.

On all four sides the ventilators just below the domed ceiling were open, the cords holding them open hung down the walls and ended in neat loops. The triangular vanes, lower down, were tilted against the sun but kept half open for air; seen from here their aluminum surfaces were as nothing, but from outside they had been a row of shining fins. It was only now that I recalled what they looked like: I had not consciously noticed them at the time.

The examination began again. I found myself answering almost mechanically—to most of the questions I merely had to say Yes, or No. I felt grateful that not much more was required of me, though I realized this was probably in Govind's interests, and not out of consideration for me. I wondered why I could not simply set out the whole sequence of events, instead of having it dragged out piecemeal like this: but of course counsel would know what he was about.

Then it was over; the cross-examination would begin now. I must keep calm, think, answer with care; there was nothing to be afraid of. But I was. I was afraid of this man who was rising now to question me, who would strive through me to show that Govind was guilty of murder. I was afraid in the way people are who do not believe black can be made to look white, but who have been assured it has been done by those who have witnessed the happening.

Yet there was nothing frightening in his manner; to these questions, too, I merely had to say Yes, or No. Moreover, most of them had been put before. Then, gradually, they were no longer quite the same, no longer quite so simple.

"You have stated you were fond of your brother."

"Yes."

"The accused is also your brother?"

"My adopted brother."

"But you regard him as a brother?"

"Yes."

"Naturally, therefore, you are very fond of him?"

"Naturally."

"So that you would be grieved if any harm should befall him?"

I stood there, trembling; and the court was silent.

I said, "If he were guilty I could not——"

"Please answer the question."

"Yes."

My senses were no longer blurred now: in this new acuity every detail stood out sharply, as sharply as if the whole scene before me had been engraved on a plate and the edges eaten away by acid until the design emerged clear-cut and vivid.

"On what terms would you say your brother was with the accused?"

I said, "They were brothers."

The prosecutor said, "Would you say the relationship between them was that usually obtaining between brothers?"

I stared at him wildly: What was he trying to make me say? What could I say? Govind, my dearest, what lay between you—long, long before Premala? Am I now to answer, and place that noose round your neck? There are so many of them, dangling on those walls, all round you, all . . .

I pulled myself together. They were only loops of some light cord, holding the ventilators open. I looked up, and reflected in the glass were the people outside. They surrounded the building, they seemed to press upon it, I could almost feel that massed weight, that crush of sheer numbers.

The prosecutor said, "You have not answered my question."

"I do not know," I said, "what the usual relationship is between brothers. Govind was adopted, and Kit was away many years in England."

"I put it to you"—the voice sounded a little impatient—"I put it to you that relations between them were strained. I put it to you further that your brother's career had been markedly promising, whereas the accused has had no known employment, which might account for the strained relations which existed between them."

I said, and I could not keep the scorn I felt out of my voice, "My brother was brilliant. He put everyone in the shade, not only Govind. Their relations were not strained because of that."

"There was some other reason, for their estrangement?"

"No," I cried, "there was no other reason!"

"But you have just said their relations were strained?"

"I did not! I did not mean that!"

"Will you explain what you did mean?"

Hold fast now, hold fast. Let go, and your bowels turn to water in which your very life can dissolve, and the surgeons stand round you, helpless: "He would not fight. He lost the will to live." But it was not my life to lose.

I said, "I meant there was disagreement between them
186

because Govind belonged to his country, and Kitsamy did not."

The prosecutor said, "I put it to you that the cause for the 'disagreement' may have been even more fundamental: that in fact the feeling the accused entertained for his sister-in-law was one of love, and that——"

How could he know? Only four of us knew, two, living, and two dead. I gazed at him, dazed: then it came to me. Premala had told Hickey, and he had shrieked of it that night to us, to the villagers. But the villagers knew no English, it was only through Hickey that he could have learned of it.

I said, "Everybody in our family loved Premala, not only Govind. She was a lovable woman."

"I suggest to you there was a difference between the love her relations bore her, and the love the accused had for his sister-in-law."

"If you mean they were lovers," I said, "you are wrong. Premala would never have permitted such a relationship."

There was a brief respite after that. I wished he would finish with me soon, because I could feel the sense of reality beginning to slide from me. The vividness was still there, each detail still possessed an almost abnormal clarity, but every now and then the whole scene before me would waver, as if it were no more than a skillfully painted backdrop in a theater, swaying slightly with each careless movement behind it.

It must be late afternoon now, the crowds were getting restless. The courtroom doors were closed, the windows set too high to look out, but in the ventilators you could see reflected that impatient eddying of the throngs outside; even if you did not look up the flickering ceaseless movement caught your eye.

"Are you feeling all right?"

I heard the voice, I did not know whose it was. "Yes," I said, "I'm all right."

The voice said, "Reverting to——"

So it had been the prosecutor. I wondered why he should have troubled about me: his questions seemed charged with a deliberate cruelty.

"Yes," I said, "what I have stated is correct. I flung my arms around Govind."

"With the idea of preventing any—rashness?"

"With some such idea—it was not very definite."

"Witnesses have testified it was a wild and confused night."

"It was."

"I put it to you that you may be mistaken in thinking you held the accused before your brother fell."

"I am not mistaken."

"I suggest it to you that while the intention to hold the accused was there, you were too late to put it into execution."

"That is not so."

He said, "Evidence has been given that the accused was seen to draw, and throw, the knife that killed your brother."

I said, "That is a lie."

"I put it to you that the evidence of this eyewitness is true, and that the evidence you have given the court is false."

I said, "I would not lie."

But I had lied. I had lied to my own mother, and she had believed me. I began to shake. Why should this thought come to me now, this torment, this malignant doubt, now when I needed most strength? But I was not lying, I was not; it was the power of this man before me, the terrible power of the English, whom this man represented, and of which I had been warned, that could even make me think that I was. In that moment, suddenly, I hated him. I had known love, and fear, and now I knew what it was to hate. The wave surged over me, black, blinding; I felt myself borne on those dark lashing waters, helpless, but not weak, full of a fury, and I wanted to turn on him and shout with all my fury, all my strength, "Govind is innocent! I have told you, but what do you care for the truth? You do not believe me, you do not want to believe me. You want to destroy him, you will destroy him, whatever I say." But in that moment Richard moved, very slightly, and I turned to him, and his eyes were quietly upon me, watchful, calm; and sanity came back and hatred died, and with it went the fear and the fury.

I said again, firmly, loudly, "I am not lying. Govind did not move, he is——"

Before I could finish there was an interruption. From somewhere came an inarticulate cry, and a man at the far end of the courtroom stood up. It was Hickey. Before anyone could restrain him, or even realize what was happening, he had slipped past the row of surprised onlookers, and dodging the attendants who automatically tried to intercept him, came running up the aisle of the courtroom. As he did so, two police constables, recovering themselves, rushed from their station at the main doors to stop him, but Hickey, tearing himself free, ran forward until stopped by the barrier before the dock. For a moment he stood panting, breathless, disheveled; then he cried, hoarsely, "Govind is guilty," and as his breath came back, he began to scream as he had that night, over and over again, torturing the nerves of all who heard, "Guilty! Guilty! Guilty!"

And from outside, like a monstrous perverted echo, its frenzy matching the madness in Hickey's voice, came the deep, loud shout of "Innocent!"

It rolled into the courtroom, this sound, and there were a thousand voices in it, the strength of a thousand convictions; there was no withstanding it. And yet someone tried; someone said, and made himself heard, "Clear the court."

But there was no way of clearing the court. The people were round it, they surrounded the building, they were advancing upon it. You could not see them yet, but you felt them, felt that weight, the power, felt the pressure of air moving before them like a wall and bearing down on the court from all four sides. Up the steps they came, bare feet scuff-scuffing on the stone, chanting as they came, "In-no-cent—In-no-cent—In-no-cent"; the simple syllables were a savage drumming in the air.

In the court people were standing up, waiting. There was nothing else they could do. There was nothing anyone could do, now. Outside were the police armed with their steel-tipped lathis, and before long they would be ordered to charge and would use their lathis and a few men here and there would fall, but those huge seas outside would still come pounding in. Later the troops, urgently summoned, would arrive at the double, armed with rifles and so many rounds of ammunition per man and orders not to fire except to restore order. But now there would be no order, and law would have gone with it; there would only be this thing called martial law. And justice would be dragged from its pinnacle, no longer

189

mighty, no longer above any considerations other than itself, and both sides would claim it with the inflamed passion two curs might bring to the division of a bone, tearing at it until it was no more than a bloodied travesty of itself. By then it would even have two names, and mean two different things, and each name would be the shield for further excess and outrage.

But there were no troops yet to fling back that wave. At the entrance it checked, a moment only, then the heavy teak doors began to bulge, they fell, the people came swarming in over each of the nine fallen doors, and met and massed in the courtroom. But these were not people any more—this was a mob, to which each human being within it had surrendered his personality to create a new giant identity, the blind, unreasoning, powerful, exultant, inhuman identity of a mob. Within the court it paused, this mob, for as yet it had thrown up no leader, its movements were those of a robot, functioning only through this one vast force within it; then it swung round on Hickey.

The missionary had retreated to the judge's dais. Whatever madness had assailed him, it was gone now. He stood quietly, his face pale, but no paler than it usually was, and around him the English had formed themselves tightly, protectively, and those faces were fearless still, but grim, with that dawning of cruelty which comes to Englishmen who see the codes of decent conduct broken, the rules of fair play flung aside, but who do not understand the forces behind these happenings, believing them only the emotional excesses of an excitable race, though not for that reason forgivable.

The black surging mass closed in about that determined handful of Englishmen in the middle of which stood Hickey, his missionary's robes flapping, proclaiming, uselessly, that he was not one of them, that he did not want to be one of them; but you had only to look at his face to see that he was.

I turned away; I did not want to watch as that tight little island began to break. It was brave, it was honorable, its principles were lofty and it would die for them; it would defend Hickey to the end because it believed in his word, even as it would defy a mob that justice might be done; but it was only a matter of time before those

190

fierce dark seas submerged it, because it had no understanding.

While a few seconds still remained, Roshan acted. I saw her mounting the dock in which Govind still stood, I heard her shout; and then I saw the crowd change direction, swiveling round towards her. The barrier in front of the dock splintered like matchwood before that advance; the sides of the dock caved in like an empty matchbox under a heel. Govind was free. The crowd milled round him, gloating, howling, exultant: they had freed Govind, they had freed an innocent man, they would bear him away with them, the country to which he belonged would shelter him, would never give him up until one day it belonged to him, as one day it would! It would! It would! The crowd was singing the words, it was happy, drunk with its power, its viciousness draining from it with this fleeting, facile victory. It formed itself into a triumphal procession, and Govind was at its head. He went with it, he could not help himself; but there was nothing but ashes in his face. He could have gone, as he was going now, in the days before his arrest, and few would have known where he went, and none would have told. He had chosen to stay, to stand trial in a court of law believing in its justice, knowing that whatever truth he carried in his heart, he must still prove it before men and women. Now he would never return to stand by his innocence; never, after the evils which this day would unloose, would he be free to appear in court as he did now. And though the doors of our home would never shut against him, he would never feel free to knock on them. Life had orphaned him not once but twice. Link by link, he had forged his own chains. Whatever the crowd might sing, he would never be free. He knew it, and I knew it, and he went with them.

Soon, I would go too. When the tail of that procession went through the door, I would join it, and Richard would stay behind. This was not a time for decision, for he knew he could not come with me, and I knew I could not stay: it was simply the time for parting. What had been given us had been gifted freely, abundantly, lit with a splendor which had colored and enriched our whole living, it could never be taken from us. We had known love together; whatever happened, the sweetness of that knowledge would always remain. We had drunk deeply of the chalice of happiness, which is not given to many even to hold. Now it was time to set it down, and go.

Go? Leave the man I loved to go with these people? What did they mean to me, what could they mean, more than the man I loved? They were my people—those others were his. Did it mean something then—all this "your people" and "my people"? Or did it have its being and gain its strength from ceaseless repetition? They are nothing to you, cried my heart. Nothing, nothing. If you go now, there will be no meaning in anything, evermore. But that stark illuminated moment—of madness? of sanity?—went, and I knew I would follow these people even as I knew Richard must stay. For us there was no other way, the forces that pulled us apart were too strong.

It is all one, I said to myself. In a hundred years it is all one; and still my heart wept, tearless, desolate, silently to itself. But what matter to the universe, I said to myself, if now and then a world is born or a star should die; or what matter to the world, if here and there a man should fall, or a head or a heart should break?

Outside, a wind was stirring: the reddish dust of earth, loosened by many feet, came swirling in, and at last I turned to go.